Dana nodded, then ripped his shirt open, exposing his rippling chest. As she ran her palm over his muscles, Chris grabbed her hand, brought it to his lips and gently kissed it before pulling her tee shirt over her head. Dana attempted to cover her upper body with her arms because she didn't want Chris to see the extra flesh hanging over the waistband of her shorts. But he pulled her arms away.

"Baby, you're beautiful," he said. "Just like I imagined."

*To Patricia*
*Thank you for your*
*support. Enjoy!*

# A LOVE OF
# HER OWN

## CHERIS F. HODGES

*Cheris F. Hodges*

Genesis Press Inc.

# Indigo Love Stories

An imprint of Genesis Press Publishing

Genesis Press, Inc.
P.O. Box 101
Columbus, MS 39703

ISBN: 1-58571-136-5
Manufactured in the United States of America

First Edition

Visit us at www.genesis-press.com
or call at 1-888-Indigo-1

# ACKNOWLEDGEMENTS

To Adrienne Dease, Jonique Platts, my wonderful and supportive parents Doris and Freddie Hodges, my agent, Sha-Shana Crichton, and my editor on this project Sidney Rickman, thank you.

To the readers who have inspired me to push through writers block and have encouraged me with e-mails, thank you for your support and allowing me to take up some of free time with my novels.

To everyone who as ever tried to please everyone but themselves, this book is for you.

CFH

# CHAPTER ONE

Dana Ellison tapped her black Nine West boots against the tile floor as she sat at her desk peering over the top of her reading glasses at her student. It wasn't what he was saying that annoyed her; it was the fact that she was sitting in the classroom. If Dana had her druthers, she'd be in her kitchen, elbow deep in flour, kneading dough and mixing batter for a cake or some rum brownies. She wanted to smell the aroma of sweets floating through the air. The only sound she wanted to hear was the ping of the oven timer telling her dessert was ready. The last thing she wanted was to sit there and listen to endless excuses from this student. Dana didn't want to teach. It wasn't her dream or her passion. She didn't care that she came from a line of educators. This was not for her.

She decided to put an end to this discussion and put the responsibility for Martin's education on someone else.

"Martin, I'm calling your parents," she said. "This is totally unacceptable. You haven't turned in any assignments in the last week."

The 12-year-old boy tugged at the bottom of his Washington Redskins sweatshirt. He'd run out of excuses. Dana looked at his oval-shaped face and his blank eyes. During the first half of the school year, Martin had been one of her best students. Now he wasn't doing anything. She wondered if it was because he could sense that she didn't want to be in the E.L. Wright Middle School classroom anymore.

"Ms. Ellison, I'm sorry, but I forgot it."

"You forgot your science fair project? You had two months to put it together. No one else forgot their projects. You had two months to do it. Are you trying to repeat the sixth grade?"

He dropped his head and Dana regretted her harsh words. "Listen," she said. "I'm going to talk to your parents and we'll work something out so that you can do some extra credit. I don't want to see you fail."

"Yes, ma'am," he said softly.

"Now, go before you miss your bus," she said as she glanced up at the black and white clock hanging on the wall.

He ran out of the classroom, happy to get away from her tongue-lashing.

Now in the classroom alone, Dana pulled out her red ink pen and started marking the day's spelling tests. She felt like a robot as she circled misspelled words. She sighed and ran her hand though her silky, relaxed tresses. *Why am I still doing this?* she thought. *I'm so sick of teaching.*

Dana had been teaching for three years. The only reason she became a teacher was that her father, Frank Ellison, had pushed her into it. Frank was a champion of education and he wanted his only child to follow in his big footsteps. He was the first black man to lead the Richland County District Two schools as superintendent. His trademark was his booming voice and dedication to making the school system better. Under his leadership, the struggling school system, where 30 percent of the students couldn't pass the standardized tests, became a model for the state of South Carolina. After he retired, he wanted Dana to continue his legacy. So he began grooming her before she graduated from high school. He wanted to shape her in his image, despite what she wanted to do.

When she was applying to college, he told her that her major would be education and she would work with middle school students. "Middle school," he would say during their endless education chats, "is the place where students start to slip away." He'd always quote a statistic about peer pressure, drugs and teen pregnancy and STDs in youth.

Dana wanted to major in marketing and go to Atlanta to work for Coca Cola. She wanted to get away from Columbia, South Carolina. She dreamed of a fresh start, but she couldn't say no to her family, no matter how hard she tried. That was how she'd ended up at E. L. Wright, hoping the teaching bug would bite her. Never happened.

In Columbia, the members of the Ellison family were the Rockefellers of education. Denise Ellison, Dana's mother, was one of the co-chairs of the African Studies Department at the University of South Carolina. She and three other professors had lobbied to bring African studies to the university in the late '70s. It was Denise's moment to shine and step out of her husband's shadow. Like the steel magnolia she was, Denise took on the administration and wealthy alumni to get the program off the ground and running. She could turn on the charm when it worked for her, but most of the time she was cold and hard. Especially when it came to Dana's life. She wanted her daughter to follow in her footsteps, have a suitable husband and a career in education. Anything else was out of the question.

Dana was tired of living her life for her parents. She felt like a computer program; her parents hit the keys and she reacted. Dana shoved her papers into her black Coach briefcase. She had to meet her fiancé, Andre Harrington. Most women would think Andre was a perfect catch. He had a pair of piercing hazel eyes, a dry wit and stunning good looks. He was ambitious and would do anything to get ahead at the University of South Carolina, where he was a first year African American history professor. Dana suspected that's why he was with her. What better way to butter up the department head than to wed her daughter?

As for Denise, she quickly fell into the role of matchmaker. She felt Andre would be a good influence on her nearly 30-year-

old child. Which explained why, all of a sudden, he began showing up at the family barbeques and holiday dinners. It took him
two months to ask Dana out. She went because she knew her parents approved of him and she was tired of dodging her mother's
questions about dating. Though she dated infrequently, she rarely
brought a man home to meet her parents because of the hoops he
would have to jump through. Moreover, she was content in her
single status. Yet and still, Dana started dating Andre because she
was expected to do so. And Dana always did what was expected
of her, even when she didn't want to.

After she started seeing Andre, her mother began talking
about engagement rings and wedding dates. She pointed out all
of Dana's friends who had gotten married and even brought
bridal magazines to Dana's house. Dana wanted to tell her mother there was never going to be a wedding because there was no
chemistry, no passion, nothing. Not only that, but marriage was
the last thing on Dana's mind. She was still trying to figure out a
way to get out of teaching.

Then Andre proposed. The Ellisons had gathered in front of
Frank's 52-inch TV to watch the Clemson and South Carolina
football teams fight for bragging rights. Everyone settled on the
black leather sofa with bowls of popcorn, potato chips and soda
pop on the table. Dana didn't really want to be there, but her parents had asked her to help cook dinner and that was rare, so she
came.

The family had decided not to make the trip to Clemson
because Denise had some important meetings to prepare for, at
least that's what Dana had been told. At halftime, Andre pulled a
black velvet box from his pocket. He dropped to one knee and
quickly proposed during a Budweiser commercial. Dana was sure
her mother had a hand in it. But she accepted because that was
what she was expected to do. That was a year ago. Dana still had-
n't set a wedding date. How could she? She liked Andre, but she

didn't love him. He wasn't her ideal man. Sure, he was smart and attractive, but Andre was dull. All they ever talked about was work. And the sex. It was like taking out the trash, something that had to be done at least once a week. If it weren't for a silver bullet vibrator and an active imagination, Dana would never have an orgasm.

Sighing, Dana slung her bag over her shoulder, shut the lights off and headed out the door. The smell of chalk was making her head hurt. Neither teaching nor Andre was in her future.

The kitchen was calling her. All of the teachers loved it when she brought her moist seven layer cakes to the potluck meals. German chocolate was everyone's favorite. Dana got more joy from cooking pies, cookies and cakes than she did from being with Andre. She found ecstasy as she kneaded dough and smelled the aroma of her creations wafting through the house. But she wouldn't have time to bake tonight. Andre wanted them to have a romantic evening at his place. *Ha, like he can even spell romance,* she thought as she unlocked her silver Honda Accord and threw her bag inside. Dana plopped behind the driver's seat and started the car. She half wished it wouldn't start and AAA would take all night to get to her. But that wouldn't happen because she kept up with scheduled maintenance.

She turned down Gervais Street heading for Andre's. *Maybe I should tell him this marriage thing is a mistake,* she thought. As she slowed down for a red light, Dana looked up at the sky. Clouds were rolling in, indicating rain was on the way. Already the wind was picking up, whipping dry brown leaves around the sidewalk. When Dana pulled into Andre's driveway, she saw his black Chevrolet Impala was parked outside the garage of the two-story house. Dana looked up at the yellow shutters and frowned. She didn't want to be there but she threw the gear in park and took her keys out of the ignition. The front door was open. "Dre," Dana called out as she walked in.

"I'm in the kitchen," he replied. "I got a steak on the grill."

She kicked her boots off and headed for the kitchen. "You know I don't eat red meat."

"I know. I'm making you a salad."

Dana sighed. She wanted more than a salad for dinner. She'd skipped lunch because she'd had to monitor lunch detention. "You don't have anything other than steak? And isn't it getting too cool to cook on the grill?"

"You're complaining?" he asked, with annoyance in his voice. "How often do you get to go home and not have to cook?"

Dana frowned. If Andre knew anything at all about her, he would know she didn't mind cooking.

He looked at the scowl on Dana's face and rubbed her arm, attempting to comfort her. "We need to celebrate tonight. I don't want to fight." His hazel eyes were glowing like stars against a clear sky. Dana wondered what he was so excited about.

"What's the occasion?"

"Our wedding date," he said as he took her into his arms and spun her around. "I was talking with Dr. Ellison today and she said March 14th would be the perfect day for us to get married."

Dana pushed him away. "What else have you and my mother decided about my life?"

"D, we've been engaged for a year. It's time for us to become husband and wife."

She looked into his hazel eyes and faked a smile. Dana didn't ever want to be Andre's wife. Why couldn't he take the hint? She didn't want to have to spell it out. She'd hoped Andre would get tired of waiting for her to set a wedding date and move on. Her mother would accept Andre ending the relationship without question. Dana sighed and turned her back to Andre. "This isn't my mother's wedding."

He reached out and stroked her back. "I know. But she

thought—"

Dana violently jerked away. "I don't care what she thought," she snapped. "Who do you want to marry, me or her?"

"You're making a mountain out of a mole hill." Andre waved his hands as if he were swatting away annoying gnats.

Dana rolled her eyes. She was tempted to grab her shoes and leave. How in the world did he think he could plan a wedding with her mother and expect her to go along with it?

"Anyway, babe, after dinner, I have something special planned for us."

Dana could care less what Andre had planned. She just wanted to get through dinner and go home. She simply nodded and toyed with a loose thread on her jacket.

Andre continued laying out his plans. "Your mother and father are coming for dessert. They're bringing a wedding planner."

She looked up at him with her brows furrowed and a hand on her hip. "That's the surprise?" *How exciting.*

"That and a hot bubble bath." A mischievous gleam danced in his light eyes.

Dana looked at the soot stain on the bottom of his gray USC tee shirt and said, "I can't spend the night. I have papers to grade."

"Put it off."

"I wish I could, but these book reports aren't going to grade themselves."

"I'm sure they can wait."

"Just as much as your grading can wait." Dana hated it when he made light of her responsibilities. Andre never thought her work was important. But when he had something to do for the university, he couldn't and wouldn't be bothered. He didn't give Dana the same respect about her work, though. He thought teaching at a public school was just basic, not as important as shaping the minds of college students.

"Touché."

Dana sighed. She couldn't see herself making love to him tonight. Not tonight or any other night. If she didn't get out of this relationship, she was going to be trapped.

When Andre headed outside to check on his dinner, Dana followed him out onto the patio. Glancing to her left, she saw a tall chocolate brother, holding a shovel and standing by the empty pool. The setting sun made his skin glow. Despite the fall air, he had on a thin white tee shirt that clung to his rippling muscles. His Fubu jeans hugged his hips. He had a pair of dark Ray Bans on his head and brown gloves on his hands. Dana's breath caught in her chest. He looked like a chocolate Adonis. She didn't know who he was, but she wanted to find out.

"What is he doing out here?" she asked as she turned away from the man and toward Andre. Her voice wavered, but Andre didn't notice. He focused on his overcooked NY strip that he dropped on a plate. When Dana looked at the coal-colored meat, she was happy she had given up red meat three years earlier.

"Getting some work done on the pool. Maybe we can have our reception back here."

*Not likely,* she thought.

Andre turned to the worker Dana had been stealing glances at. "How's everything coming, Chris?"

"It's coming along," he said. His voice was melodic, like a quiet storm DJ's. It turned her on, made her feel as if an electric current sizzled through her veins. Dana had never felt such an instant attraction for someone. Lust attacked her senses, nearly rendering her powerless to take her eyes off Chris. She'd never before seen in person a man like him. He should have been on the cover of a magazine or parading down a runway. He walked with the confidence and grace of a panther. When he passed Andre and Dana, he smiled at her, revealing pearly white teeth.

Dana returned his smile.

"When will you guys be finished?" Andre asked.

"One more day, if I can keep the crew together."

"All right. Tell Charles I'm happy with the work so far," he replied, shutting down the grill.

Chris nodded and looked at Dana. "How are you, ma'am?"

"Fine," she sputtered.

He smiled again and Dana's heart did somersaults. This total stranger was stirring something in her. She couldn't put it into words or explain it. When she walked inside the house to catch her breath, she got a better look at Chris as he walked to his truck parked across the street. He and two other men hopped in a white Ford F-150 that had Jones's Pool and Landscaping written on the passenger side door. Dana wished she had the nerve to call his job. But what would she say? "Hi, I saw you at my fiancé's place and the only thing I can think about is how you would move your hips underneath my sheets."

Dana turned away from the window, but his image was burned on her brain. *Zariah would do it,* she thought as she listened to the truck engine roar. At the thought of her best friend, Dana walked into the living room, picked up the cordless phone and then dialed her number.

"Yeah?"

"Zariah?"

"Dana, girl, what's up? I thought it must be Andre calling, looking for you again."

Dana snorted. "Please, I'm at his place now for the wedding ambush."

"Huh?"

"My mother set my wedding date," Dana said bitterly.

"Oh my God. Your mother set your wedding date without your input? She's really determined to make you Mrs. Andre Harrington."

"I know. How am I supposed to tell them that this is not what I want?"

"Easy, open your mouth."

"I wish."

"You're 29 years old. Last time I checked that means you're a grown-ass woman. You need to start acting like it."

"Z, I know this."

"You know that you don't love Andre and a marriage would be doomed from the start. He has to know that you don't want to marry him. Hell, if our professors had been as dense as he is, I might have graduated magna cum laude."

Dana stifled her laugh. "I just don't want to hurt him. I honestly believe in his own twisted way, Andre loves me. Maybe one day I'll come to love him too."

"And maybe one day the sun will stop shining and maybe one day—"

"I get it."

"Then tell them you aren't going to marry the nutty professor. By the way, have you looked into the opening at the bakery?"

"Not yet."

"Dana."

"Zariah, my contract with the school is up in May. I can't just up and quit."

"Yes, you can. What is the school going to do? Sue you? How many nights do you call me and complain about that school? If you aren't going to make a change, I don't want to hear about it anymore."

"The school system might sue. I don't know. Besides, Zariah, if I can't vent to my friends, who can I vent too?"

"Well, everyone is still talking about that red velvet cake you made for my sister's baby shower," Zariah said. "You need to go into the bakery business because it's what you want to do and you're good at it."

"You think so?"

"Uh-huh. And I want you to bake me a cake this weekend. That seven layer German chocolate one."

"All right, I'll do that," she said. "I wanted to do some baking this weekend anyway," Dana said.

Andre walked in, carrying his plate and grilling utensils. "Babe, can you get the door?"

"Z, I'll call you back later." She hung up the phone and closed the patio door.

Andre set his plate and the forks on the marble top counter. "Playing Betty Crocker again?" he asked.

Dana sucked her teeth and forced her venom-filled reply down her throat.

Andre glanced over at her. "You're not going to bake our wedding cake. I don't want you looking tired at the altar."

"There's something I need to tell you about the wedding," she began.

Andre pulled a wooden bowl from underneath the counter. "What is it, darling?"

"I don't think—"

"Hello, hello," Denise called out. She and Frank walked into the kitchen. "I know we're early. But I was so excited, I had to get here. My baby's getting married, *finally*." Denise kissed Dana on the forehead, leaving a pink lipstick stain. Dana wiped her forehead with the back of her hand and sighed. She didn't need this right now. She wanted to tell Andre that she wasn't going to marry him without having Frank and Denise standing there staring at her.

"Hey honey," Frank said as he kissed Dana on the cheek.

"Hi Daddy," she replied flatly. Dana looked at her father. He was dressed in his signature red suspenders, white dress shirt and perfectly pressed black slacks with razor-sharp creases. He still looked like a school administrator.

"Dana, why don't you have on slippers?" Denise asked when she looked down at her daughter's stocking feet.

"Mother, what are you two doing here?"

"Well," she said as she took off her silver fox fur jacket and handed it to Frank. "We have a wedding to plan. You two have wasted so much time. I just don't want this to be one of those tacky affairs. Julia is the best. Her weddings are classic and unforgettable. I can't wait to see what she does with this one."

*Last time I checked, you and Daddy were already married,* she thought bitterly. *There isn't going to be a wedding to plan.*

"Dana was just about to tell me something about the wedding. I don't think she's happy about the date, Dr. Ellison." Dana shook her head as she looked at Andre. He was acting like a little tattletale.

"Andre, we're not on campus, call me Denise. What's wrong with the date, Dana?" Denise sat at the head of the dining table, crossing her legs and placing her hands on the table as if she were a queen sitting on her throne.

Dana pulled one of the bar stools out and sat down. "Mother, this is my wedding and I want to set the date. It isn't your place to do that."

Denise laughed and pulled her leather event planner out of her purse. "Well, you've had a year to set the date and there still isn't one. The wedding planner said she would be here in 45 minutes. That should give us enough time to pick a date and set out the coconut pie."

Dana stared at her mother in disbelief and rolled her eyes. *You're early and you want to come in here and take over. Damn!*

Frank looked at his daughter with sympathy. He knew how Denise was when she wanted something and her mission these days was to get Dana married. Frank cleared his throat. "Andre, where can I put this coat?"

"In my bedroom. It's down the hall."

Frank scurried off and Dana turned to her mother. Anger flickered in her eyes, then quickly disappeared.

"Mother," Dana began. "March isn't a good month for me to get married. The state tests are in March. We can't take days off and there is no way I get everything done that I need to get done and prepare my students for the test."

"I didn't think about that. What about April? I hope it isn't a rainy April. Rain on your wedding day would be horrible luck."

Probably for the first time ever, Dana stood up to her mother. "If I'm going to get married, then I'm going to be the one to set the date."

"If?" Andre questioned, a look of confusion on his face.

"I said *when*," Dana replied, desperately trying to cover her tracks.

"You said *if*," Denise corrected. "What's this all about?"

"Look, I don't need this stress. Why don't the three of you enjoy the pie? I'm going home to grade papers," Dana snapped.

She bolted out of the kitchen, nearly knocking her father over as she dashed down the hall. She stuffed her feet into her boots and stormed out of house. Dana couldn't get into the car or out of that damned driveway fast enough. She didn't look behind her, just pressed the gas pedal and started backwards. A horn blared as Dana was about to slam into an oncoming truck, and she slammed on her brakes. She wanted to curse the driver and tell him get the hell out of her way, until she noticed the sign on the side. Jones's Pool and Landscaping.

"Damn, lady," Chris said when he hopped out of the truck.

Dana got out of the car. "I'm sorry," she said. "I wasn't paying attention."

As Chris looked at her, a smile tugged at his lips. "I'm forgiving you because you're pretty."

Dana smiled back and unconsciously fingered her blouse. "Thanks."

"Is your old man inside?"

"Huh?"

"Andre," he said with a bad British accent.

Dana laughed. "Yeah, he's inside."

"He's a lucky man."

Dana rolled her eyes. "Whatever," she mumbled under her breath.

Chris turned to walk to the front door. "Hey you," he called out before he rang the doorbell. "Since you almost ran me over, you owe me a drink."

"Excuse me? How did you come up with that one?"

"I'm shaking over here at the thought of your car backing into me. In order to get my nerves right, I need a drink. Tonight would be nice."

Dana smiled. "I have papers to grade."

Chris walked over to her. He stood so close to Dana she could feel his breath on her top lip.

"You know you want to."

"You're a cocky son of a—I'll do it. Give me your number and I'll call you."

"Yeah, right. Give me your number. I know the brush-off trick."

Dana reached into her pants pocket and pulled out a scrap of paper. Chris handed her the pencil from behind his ear. She wrote her number on the back of the Winn-Dixie receipt and handed it to him.

"When I call, be ready."

"Do you make a habit of picking up women who nearly run you over?"

Chris folded the paper and stuffed it in his pocket. "Nope. I'll see you later. Don't hit the truck on the way out. It's not mine."

Dana smiled and waved as she walked to her car. *Oh my God,* she thought nervously, *I can't believe what I just did.*

# CHAPTER TWO

When Dana got home, she rushed upstairs to her bedroom, kicked her boots off and flung the closet door open. How was she supposed to dress for a date with a man she only knew by his first name? What if Andre found out? She could hear Zariah telling her to slow down. "It's just a drink," she said aloud as she pulled a pair of skintight red leather pants out of the back of the closet. She hadn't worn those pants since she was in college. They were a reminder of her wilder side. For a while, she'd partied with Zariah every Thursday and every weekend. They would hit the clubs just to see how many free drinks they could rack up from men pretending to be big shots and trying to impress them. Dana felt as if she owned the world when she wore those pants. She didn't mind the catcalls she got when she walked in the club dressed to kill. She liked walking by a group of men and hearing them say, "Lawd, have mercy." Now she prayed they still fit. Tasting her cakes had added a few more pounds to her thighs and hips. Dana unzipped her black slacks and tossed them on the floor. Then she squeezed into the pants. They fit, barely. If she ate another slice of cake or even a pinch of her rum brownies, her ample thighs would be too much for them. Dana grabbed a tan Parasuco tee shirt with three quarter sleeves. She laid the shirt on the bed, then walked into the bathroom and looked at herself in the mirror.

*Why did he think I was pretty?* she wondered. She stared at her chocolate brown skin, coal black eyes and mid-length light brown hair. She wanted to cut her hair, but her mother thought she looked better with longer hair. Dana unbuttoned her blouse and dropped it on the floor. Her breasts were about the size of navel oranges. Andre didn't know how to handle them. Sometimes his awkward squeezing and biting made her feel as if she were nothing but produce.

Something in the way Chris had looked at her, the way he'd licked his lips, led her to believe he knew how to handle her breasts as well as the rest of her body. She closed her eyes and imagined his big hands roaming her body, his thumb tweaking her nipple. Shocked by her thoughts, Dana shook her head frantically. She didn't even know this Chris person and she certainly wasn't the kind of woman to give in to lust.

Dana splashed water on her face, hoping it would clear her head. Then she dried it and walked back into the bedroom and put the tee shirt on. *What if he doesn't call?* she thought. *I'm making a fool of myself.*

Before she could talk herself out of going anywhere with Chris, the phone rang.

"Hello," she said after she picked it up on the second ring.

"Hey you."

"Chris?"

"Yeah. I hope you haven't changed your mind."

"No, I haven't. I was finishing up my work," she lied.

"Toss those papers aside and meet me at the Rib House on Augusta Road."

"That's a long way from where I live."

"I'll make it worth the drive," he said.

"And how will you do that?"

"Come over here and find out." His tone was seductively playful and Dana couldn't help smiling.

"I'll see you in about 30 minutes," Dana said. She was giddy with excitement.

"All right, Ms. Lady."

"What? My name is Dana or do you always talk like a player?"

Chris laughed. "Talk like a player? I just think you're a class act. You don't meet a lot of ladies these days."

"Thanks," she replied shyly. Dana hung up, then stole one last glance at herself in the mirror. She grabbed her tube of M-A-C peach lip-gloss and thinly glossed her full lips. Then she ran her fingers though her hair. She was going to do this. It was only a drink. Dana scooped up her keys and headed out the door. For a change, she was doing something that she wanted to do. She liked the feeling.

When Dana got to the Rib House, Chris was sitting at the bar. He had a cigarette between his fingers, but it wasn't lit.

"You smoke?" she asked. Major turn off.

Chris peeled the paper off the cigarette, revealing the candy inside. "I found a pack on the way here."

"I haven't seen these in years."

"Want one?" he asked as he held the red and white box out for her.

Dana took a piece of the candy and held it between her fingers. "I used to love these things."

Chris smiled. "So, Ms. Lady, what are you drinking?"

"I'm not a big drinker." Dana was feeling nervous as she sat there looking at Chris.

"So, I have to drink alone?" He waved for the bartender.

Chris mesmerized Dana. His body language screamed confidence. Dana wished she could have an ounce of that.

"I guess I'll have a Shirley Temple or something," she said, shrugging her shoulders.

"You really don't drink, do you?" He laughed, causing his eyes to twinkle.

"That's right. But I'm hungry. So you drink and I'll eat," she said as she picked up a menu.

"You mean you didn't have dinner with the professor?"

Dana rolled her eyes and clicked her teeth. Chris looked down at the three-karat princess cut diamond ring on Dana's finger.

"He must really love you," he continued to probe.

Dana rolled her eyes. "Whatever. Look, I don't want to talk about him."

He threw his hands up. "Sorry about that, Ms. Lady. I'm just the hired help."

"Why are we having this particular conversation? You said I almost hit you and I owe you a drink. Let's just have a friendly conversation. What do you think the Gamecocks are going to do this year?"

"I'm sitting here with another man's fiancée. I want to know what kinds of games are being played. And I don't care about the Gamecocks."

Dana rolled her eyes and stuck the candy cigarette in her mouth. "There were just too many people in that house tonight."

Chris nodded. "His parents horned in on the romance?"

"Those were my parents."

"Really? You would think he was already in the family."

Dana nodded in agreement as she bit into the candy.

"So, you needed to get away. I guess I'm an escape hatch?"

Dana rolled her eyes. "I don't want to talk about my parents either."

"All right. Let's talk about you."

"You must want to be bored to death." She rolled her eyes.

"I can't believe that. Everybody has a story. And those eyes have a story behind them."

Dana looked at Chris. His face was vibrant and his eyes were warm and serious. His skin looked as smooth as satin. She wanted to stroke his cheek, but she fought the urge. "I'd rather hear your story," she said.

"I'm a landscaper."

"I know that. Are you married, in a relationship?"

"Single as the day is long. I just do what I feel like doing when I feel like doing it."

"Living by the seat of your pants?"

Chris shrugged. "You could say that. You know what the problem with most people is? They live their lives following other people's rules. How can someone else tell me how to live my life? That's like telling the snake how to crawl or telling a bee how to buzz."

Dana nodded. The bartender walked over to take their orders. Chris requested a Bud Light and Dana ordered a club soda with a twist of lime.

"Be right back," the bartender said.

Chris turned to Dana and looked at her, fixating on her thick thighs. He was a leg man and the way she filled out those pants, she definitely had legs. When he inadvertently licked his lips, Dana's face flushed with embarrassment.

"What would your man say about you being here with me tonight?" Chris asked.

"I don't know," Dana replied. "Why? Are you going to tell him?"

"Nope. But what if I want to see you again?"

She raised her eyebrows. What kind of game was he playing? He knew she had a fiancé. "Why would you want to see me again?"

"Because, Ms. Lady, I want to know that story behind those dark eyes."

Dana smiled nervously as the bartender set their drinks in front of them. She picked up her club soda and drank it slowly, trying to calm her racing heart.

"What if I hadn't nearly smashed your truck? Would you be sitting here with me?"

"Probably not, but sometimes things are just meant to be," he

said. "I saw you looking at me in the backyard. Hell, I was looking at you too. And I was thinking; maybe she's his sister. Then I
saw the rock of ages on your finger. I was ready to let it go. But
after you almost ran into me, I figured the least I could do was
get a date out of an almost tragedy." Chris flashed his pearly
whites again, making Dana's heart flip flop.

Dana looked down at her ring. She knew her mother had
picked it out. It had her style written all over it. The ring was too
much for Dana's taste. She would have liked a simple baguette-
styled ring. A smaller diamond wouldn't have hurt either. She
twisted the ring on her finger.

"You know, I don't even like this ring," she said.

"What?" Chris said. "Women love big rocks, don't they?"

"I don't want to get married."

Chris furrowed his brows. "Then why are you wearing that
ring?"

Dana picked up her glass and turned her back to the bar.
"Because I'm one of those people you were talking about."

"Huh?"

"I let other people tell me what I should do. I follow the rules
that people say I should."

"So, this is about breaking the rules?"

Dana nodded. "I guess. I wanted to do something for Dana
for a change."

Chris put his hand on top of hers. "What else does Dana
want to do?"

The heat from his hand sent chills down her spine. "I think
I'd better go," she said as she slid her hand from underneath his.
Dana didn't want to do something she was going to regret. Right
then and there, she might have been open to a night of steamy
passion in Chris's bed, and she still didn't know his last name.

She reached into her purse and pulled out enough money to
cover Chris's beer and her soda. He grabbed her hand.

"I can't let you pay for my drink. Not this time. This means you still owe me a drink."

Dana smiled. "So, I have to see you again?"

He picked up a napkin and tore it in half. Then he snatched a pen from the other side of the bar and wrote his number down on the paper. He pressed it into Dana's hand, then stood up.

Draining the rest of his beer, he smiled at her.

"You know you want to." He dropped seven dollars on the bar.

He was right, but Dana didn't want to be that transparent. She tucked the number into her pocket.

"You think a lot of yourself, don't you?" she asked.

"If I don't, who will?"

"When and if I want to see you, I'll give you a call."

Chris smiled as if he knew the game Dana was playing. "All right, Ms. Lady."

Dana walked away, putting a little extra twist in her hips.

A sly smile spread across Chris's face. He sat down. If only she didn't belong to someone else. Chris had been there before. So why was he there again? Because there was something about Dana, the innocence in her eyes, the curve of her lips when she smiled. She had a shy sexiness about her that quickened his pulse. But she's getting married, he told himself. *All of the good ones are always taken.*

He ordered another beer and thought back two years ago to when he'd met another intriguing woman who'd stolen his breath. Chris had thought Rosalyn Harper was his soul mate. She was the color of creamy caramel and her legs would have put Tina Turner to shame. They'd met at Myrtle Beach during the Bike Fest. She was walking down Ocean Boulevard with two of her friends. She was wearing a pink bikini that showed her beautiful legs and taut behind. He'd pulled his gold Honda Ninja motorcycle to the side and waved for her to come over. She'd sauntered over to him with a seductive smile on her face.

"You look good, girl," Chris said, not trying to run a smooth player line.

She smiled. "You know, I would love to ride your bike." She ran her hand down the fender.

"Hop on," he replied.

They rode down the crowded strip. Rosalyn squeezed Chris's waist tightly and leaned against him. He whipped around a corner to get away from the crowd. After he parked his bike near the Boardwalk, they talked about everything. The backdrop of ocean, a salty sea breeze and a setting sun that hung streaked across the sky set the mood. The natural light seemed to make Rosalyn glow like an angel. Chris knew fate had a hand in their meeting since they were both from Columbia. The next thing either of them knew, the sun was starting to creep over the horizon, turning the sky a faint pink and yellow. Love colors, Chris called it. They exchanged numbers when Chris dropped her off at her hotel.

The moment Chris and Rosalyn got back to Columbia, they began talking on the phone for hours at a time. She would come to his place, but she never invited him to her house.

Then the strange calls started. Someone would hang up every time he answered the phone. Chris ignored the situation until Rosalyn's husband showed up at his door. That night Chris had told Rosalyn that he had fallen in love with her and wanted future with her. When she started crying, he'd thought they were tears of joy because she felt the same way.

But a few hours after Rosalyn left, her husband pounded on his door. "Leave my wife alone," he warned when Chris opened the door.

"Wife? What are you talking about?" Chris threw his hands up in confusion.

The burley man pushed his way inside the apartment. "Rosalyn is my wife and I'm not letting some punk like you take her from me."

Chris threw his hands up. "I didn't know she was married. I

don't want or need the drama."

The man snorted and shook his head as he poked Chris in the chest. "Remember that."

Chris grabbed the man's finger and bent it back. "You need to get the hell out of my house! If you satisfied your wife she wouldn't have sought me out."

Chris pushed the man out the door, then dialed Rosalyn's number.

"Hello?" she said.

"It's me."

"Chris, *hi*," Rosalyn said cheerfully.

"Don't hi me. Your husband just left my house."

"I'm sorry, I wanted to tell you, but I was afraid—" Her voice quivered as if she were crying.

"Afraid of what? That I would leave you alone? Look, if you can cheat on your husband with me, there's no telling what you would do to me. I told you I loved you and you've been lying this entire time! Do us both a favor. Lose my number."

"But Chris, I love you—"

He slammed the phone down, then plopped down on the sofa and dropped his head into his hands.

Chris had to wonder if he was in for the same thing with Dana. *I just won't get close. We're adults; it's just a fling,* he thought as he waved for another beer.

Dana walked into her house and took a deep breath. She couldn't believe she'd gone out with Chris. What would her mother think? What would Andre think? Dana knew she was in trouble, because she was certain she would see Chris again.

Maybe the thrill of getting caught added to the attraction. The gleam in his eyes when he looked at her made her tingle inside. Something about him shook her sleeping soul awake. But what kind of man was Chris? He'd already admitted to having an affair with a married woman, and now he was making moves on her, knowing she was engaged and making wedding plans. And what about herself? She couldn't string Andre along, letting him think that she was going to marry him when she knew she didn't want that. And what if this thing with Chris was just lust? A quick fling? Could she risk being alone?

*It would be better than being in a loveless marriage that looks good on paper,* she thought as she climbed into her four-poster bed.

Dana was about to drift off to sleep when the phone rang.

"Hello?" she asked, hoping it was Chris.

"Have you gotten over your little temper tantrum?" Denise demanded.

"Mother, I don't have time for this."

"When are you going to make time to plan your wedding? Andre wants to marry you and you're dragging your feet. What's the problem?"

"I'm not sure that I want that right now," she said.

"That's nonsense. Andre is a good man. He's smart, he's established, and he's in love with you. What more are you looking for?"

*Some passion and excitement for starters,* she thought as her mother droned on and on about Andre's qualities. Maybe Chris would be the man to bring that into her life.

"Are you listening to me?" Denise asked.

"Yes, Mother," Dana replied flatly.

"If you don't marry Andre, someone else will and you're going to be hurting. And I'm not going to listen to you whine and cry."

"Mother, have you ever thought about what I want?"

"Oh, is this about that silly notion of yours to be a cook?" Denise laughed haughtily.

Dana narrowed her eyes. She wished she could shake her mother until she got her point. Dana wasn't planning to flip hamburgers at a fast food restaurant. She wanted to be happy, and the only time she was happy was when she was in the kitchen with flour underneath her fingernails.

"I'm not sure I want to get married," Dana revealed.

"It's just a case of the cold feet. You'll get over it," Denise said in a tone that was more suited for an unruly student.

"I'm going to bed." Dana rolled her eyes at the ceiling.

"We need to talk after you get off from work tomorrow. I have some plans for the wedding I want to go over with you. And you can tell me a date that is more suitable for you."

*Did she hear anything that I just said?*

"Fine, I'll try to make it," Dana said. "Goodbye, Mother."

"And you might want to call Andre and apologize to him. He is very confused by the way you're acting."

"Andre is a big boy. He can call me if he wants to talk."

"I don't understand you, Dana. Most women your age would be grateful that a man wanted to marry them. You're not a teenager, your choices are limited. Remember that."

The dial tone sounded in Dana's ear. She slammed the phone down and stared at the ceiling. *Why do I always let her get to me?*

# CHAPTER THREE

Chris got to Andre's house about seven a.m. His crew was down two men, which meant he was going to have to put in more hours on the pool than he wanted to. "Hernando, hurry up," Chris called out.

The man mumbled something in Spanish as he grabbed his tools from the back of the truck. Hernando was difficult to work with because he thought he should have been made foreman instead of Chris. But unlike Chris, he didn't have the experience or patience to work with men who had different personalities.

"I don't have time for your crap today," Chris said as he rang the doorbell.

"*Si, señor.*" He managed to make those three syllables sound insulting.

"And you've been in this country long enough to speak English." The day had just begun and already Chris was seething. Hernando just rolled his eyes.

Andre opened the door and smiled at the two men as he straightened his tie. "Gentlemen, you're early."

"Two of my men are sick and I need to finish this job today," Chris said. "I said it was going to be done, so it will be."

Andre nodded. "Good, I'm hoping to have my wedding reception out here this spring."

Chris smirked, but Andre took it as a congratulatory smile.

"We'll have it pretty for you," Chris replied, swallowing his sarcasm. He wondered how a man could be so blind to the misery of the woman he supposedly loved. Chris had known it the first moment he'd seen Dana.

"I'll have my fiancée come over and lock up the house this afternoon. I have a staff meeting."

Chris hid his happiness. Seeing Dana again would be the bright spot he'd need after working with Hernando. On the other hand, he wondered if it would be awkward.

Andre dashed out the door and Chris headed to the pool with Hernando. The men worked in silence. All Chris could think about was Dana in those red leather pants.

⚬⚬⚬

"Dana, you have a phone call in the main office," the secretary said over the PA system.

"I'll be right there," she replied, laying down her ink pen. Even though she should've been using her planning period to grade book reports, Dana was instead sketching the shape of a layer cake for Zariah. She was going to try a technique she'd read about in *Martha Stewart's Living* magazine. Dana was trying to figure out how to make the cake in the shape of a wide brim straw hat, similar to the ones the women in Charleston wore on Foley Beach when they were out crabbing.

Walking into the office, Dana picked up the phone. "This is Dana."

"Hey, babe," Andre said.

"What is it? I'm working." His call annoyed her. Didn't he realize she was at her place of business? How would he like it if she called him at USC on a whim?

"It's your planning period, isn't it?"

"Yes, but I have work that I do during this period," she replied in an exasperated tone.

"We need to have a long talk about last night," Andre said

sternly.

"What about last night?" Did he know about her date with Chris? Nervous beads of sweat beads popped out on her top lip and her heartbeat quickened. Then the thought struck her that if everything were out in the open, things might be better. Their farce of an engagement would be over and she wouldn't have to pretend anymore. She'd be free to live her life her way.

"The way you tore out of my house. Look, we can't get into that right now and that's not why I'm calling. I need a favor."

"Uh-huh." *You always need something.*

"Do you think you can stop by my place after work and lock up when the pool workers leave? I have a staff meeting."

Chris was there! Of course she would go. Dana smiled inadvertently. "Okay, fine."

"Will you wait for me so we can talk?" Andre asked, nearly begging her.

Dana sighed. "I'll wait, but I can't stay long. I have to bake a cake tonight."

"All right. I should be home no later than seven."

"Bye," Dana said, then hung up. She scowled as she thought about the conversation ahead. As usual, Andre would do all of the talking and she would struggle to stay awake, pretending to hear him out.

As Dana walked out of the office, her thoughts turned to Chris. What if he was just looking for a one-night stand? Did it matter? Dana didn't know exactly what she wanted from Chris. Was it a simple case of lust or something more? The bell rang as she reached her room, signaling class change. Dana shook her head and shifted her attention to *The Diary of Anne Frank* as her third period class began pouring in the classroom.

Dana told the kids to sit down and she pulled out her study questions about the book.

The students groaned. "What's the problem?" Dana asked.

"This book is boring," a girl called out.

"You just can't read," another girl yelled.

"Your momma!"

"Hey, hey!" Dana said as the two girls leapt from their seats and began pummeling each other like prizefighters. The other students began cheering as if they were ringside at the WWE. Dana rushed over to stop the fight, but instead got knocked to the floor. She wanted to smack both of them as she stood up but she held herself back because she didn't want to risk a civil lawsuit.

"Corey," Dana called out. "Go get Mr. Anderson."

The boy nodded and dashed out. Dana tried unsuccessfully to pull the girls apart again as they toppled three empty desks in the back of the classroom. The fight progressed to the bookshelves, which went flying. As they crashed to the floor, they broke into ricocheting shards and the students sitting in their desks had to duck the missiles flying across the room.

"Damn it!" Dana yelled as she yanked one of the girls by the arm, nearly getting punched in the process. "Stop it right now! I will not have this in my classroom. Look at the mess you've made. Why? Over words?"

As one, the class held its breath. Ms. Ellison had cursed and lost her temper. They had never seen her this way. Her nostrils were flaring, sweat covered her forehead and she had a dust print on her behind from where she had sprawled onto the floor. Her hair was standing wildly up as if it had been styled by Don King.

"You go stand by the window," Dana said to one of the girls. "And you stand by the door. The rest of you, take your books out and read."

Mr. Anderson, the assistant principal, walked in. "What happened, Ms. Ellison?"

"Get these two out of my classroom. Look at this." She waved her hands at the destruction.

"Some fight. Come, ladies," he said. "Have you written the referrals?"

"No, I haven't. I was busy making sure Tyson and Lewis didn't kill each other."

Mr. Anderson smiled at Dana, but when she didn't return his smile, he gave the girls a stern look.

"Looks like someone is going to have about 10 days at home to think about this," he said as he led the girls down the hall.

Dana dashed to the door. "Can I get someone in here to help me clean this mess up?" she called to his back.

Without turning around, Mr. Anderson nodded and waved his hand in acknowledgment.

Dana closed the door and sat at her desk. She turned her icy glare on the class. "I don't want to hear a word from anyone until the bell rings. I suggest you read carefully because there will be a test tomorrow."

Groans and mumbles rippled through the class.

Dana raised her perfectly manicured eyebrow at them. "It's not too late to join Alicia and Rhonda in the office," she snapped. "One more word and we'll have a test today."

A tense silence fell over the room. Dana was too mad to care what her students thought about her attitude. Today she had become the teacher she had hated most. When she was in middle school, she'd had a teacher who used tests as punishments. As much as she didn't want to admit it, the method worked to calm the students down. Dana picked up the book reports she had been putting off grading and started reading as well. She couldn't wait for the day to end.

The bell finally sounded and the 15 students stampeded out like a herd of buffalo. As two janitors walked in and began cleaning up the aftermath of the fight, Dana took a deep breath, closed her eyes and prayed her next class would just sit down and shut up. Only the thought of seeing Chris later comforted her.

By mid-afternoon, the word had gotten around school about the fight and Dana's fall, leaving her open to ribbing from her students.

"Ms. Ellison, why you let them girls take you out?" chubby-faced Tommy Parker asked.

The rest of the class snickered.

"Ha, ha," Dana said sarcastically. "Well, Tommy, if I had fought back, I wouldn't be here to teach you this afternoon. Now, let's talk about *Romeo and Juliet*. Tommy, since you have so much to say, tell me about Juliet's death."

"Uh," he stammered.

"That's what I thought. Instead of being a wise a—, instead of being a smart aleck, do the reading. There will be a test tomorrow."

"Aw man!" the class said collectively. The bell sounded and the class filed out of the room. Finally it was over. If she had to rate her day, Dana would definitely put it in the hell category. Her rump was a little sore from her spill and tension had her body in knots. She closed her grade book and then massaged her shoulders. Remembering that she still had to talk with Andre, Dana groaned and dropped her head onto the desk.

"Knock, knock," Principal Mason said as he walked into the classroom. "How are you doing?"

Dana sat up and smiled at him weakly. "I've had better days."

"I'm sure you have." He placed his hand on her shoulder as a comfort.

"Those kids were out of control," Dana complained.

"Do you think you need to go to the hospital? I heard you

took a nasty fall."

She shook her head. "My bookshelf needs a doctor."

"I'll see if we can get you another one."

Dana nodded as she rose to her feet.

"We have to meet with the girls' parents in the morning."

"Great," she mumbled.

Mason patted Dana on the shoulder again. "They're going to be in my office at eight. Dana, it's not that bad. Middle-schoolers get a little wild sometimes. Just consider yourself lucky. Some teachers have to deal with this every day. Tell your father I said hello."

"All right," she said, turning to walk out the door. Dana wondered if she would be a third-year teacher teaching honors English if her last name weren't Ellison. All of the other honors teachers had at least five or ten years of teaching experience. She pushed the thought out of her mind as she adjusted her briefcase on her shoulder. Draping her brown leather trench coat over her shoulders, she headed down the hall. When she got outside, she saw thick gray clouds hiding the sun and threatening to drench the city. Dana dashed to her car, hoping to beat the impending storm, but by the time she reached Andre's house, the rain was coming down in thick sheets. Though she pulled her coat over her head when she got out, trying to shield herself from the downpour, water seeped through her coat, running down her back and saturating her shirt. She fumbled with the door lock, then walked in, kicking her boots off and hanging her coat on the banister of the stairs.

"Hello?" she called out as she walked down the hall.

When she got in the kitchen, she saw Chris and an Hispanic man standing under the covered patio. Dana knocked on the window and beckoned them in.

"Hello," Hernando said as he stepped inside.

"Hi," she replied, never taking her eyes off Chris.

"That's some rain out there." Chris stared at the way Dana's shirt clung to her breasts. The water made her white shirt transparent and he could see the creamy tops of her breasts peeking over her beige demi lace bra. As wicked thoughts of taking her breasts into his mouth danced in his head, he turned away quickly.

"Did you finish up?" she asked.

"Right before the bottom fell out," Chris said. "We didn't want to track water and mud in the house, so we stood outside and waited for you."

"Let me get you two some towels." Dana turned toward the basement. Chris followed her as Hernando stepped outside to smoke a cigarette. She didn't hear his footsteps behind, only the loud drumming of her own heart.

"Hey you," he said when she reached the bottom step.

Dana turned around, shaken at his voice. "You startled me."

"I didn't mean to."

"This is weird." Her voice was a breathless whisper.

"I thought it would be," Chris's gaze fell on her breasts. When she noticed, she self-consciously covered her chest by folding her arms, then turned her back, leaned over and opened the drier. She handed Chris a plush towel.

"What are you doing tonight?" he asked.

"Baking."

"She cooks too. Andre is a lucky man."

Dana clucked her tongue against her teeth and held back a sarcastic comment. "Anyway, I'm baking a cake for a friend's party," she said.

"What kind?"

"German chocolate."

"My favorite."

"Really?"

Chris nodded.

"I've been told it's my specialty."

"You're going to have to let me sample it so I can be the judge of that."

Dana smiled. "Are you free later?" *What am I doing?*

"What about you? I mean, your man wants that backyard finished so you can have your wedding reception out there."

Dana sighed. "That's not going to happen," she whispered. *I can't marry Andre when I want to feel your lips against mine,* she thought wantonly. When she took the towel from Chris's hands his fingers touched hers like a butterfly brushing its wings against her cheek. She swallowed hard.

He stepped closer, nearly touching her lips with his. Dana stepped back, holding on to the edge of the dryer for balance. Chris ran his index finger down the side of her cheek.

"Dana, I want you," Chris whispered. "The first time I set eyes on you, I wanted you."

"B-but—"

Chris boldly kissed her. It didn't matter that they were standing in her fiancé's laundry room. He pulled her against his body, molding her against him. His hands roamed her supple body. He squeezed her hips as he pushed her back on the drier. Dana finally mustered up enough strength to push him away.

"I have to go," she said as she bolted up the stairs.

Chris followed her. He touched her elbow. "I'm sorry. I didn't mean—"

"Chris, I just can't do this here. This is Andre's house and I can't disrespect him like that."

Chris appreciated how she felt, but it made him want her even more. "I'd better leave," Chris said. "Will I see you later?"

"I'll call you," Dana replied.

Chris knocked on the window and motioned for Hernando to head to the truck. "Tell Andre everything is finished," he said.

Dana walked Chris to the door and fought the urge to kiss

him again as they stared deep into each other's eyes. Chris backed down the steps, never taking his eyes off Dana. She wondered if he wanted only sex. Dana knew she wouldn't be satisfied with just a physical relationship.

Andre drove up as Chris and Hernando backed out of the driveway. Dana sighed as she watched him get out of the car. He opened his black umbrella over his head and tucked his briefcase under his arm. Dana pushed the front door open.

"Hey sweetie," Andre said as he kissed her on the cheek. She recoiled from his embrace.

"They said the work in the backyard is finished," Dana said as they walked inside.

Andre followed her down the hall. "Dana, can we talk?" He dropped his brown briefcase on the floor in the foyer, then shed his wet coat, which joined the briefcase in the middle of the floor. Dana frowned. He never picked up after himself, which was another reason why she didn't like staying over. Andre seemed to confuse the word *girlfriend* with *maid*. Yet another reason for her to run from this so-called relationship.

Dana looked up from the mess on the floor and at him. "What do you want to talk about?"

Andre led her into the kitchen. Dana sat down on a bar stool as he fixed himself a drink.

"I get the feeling that you don't want to get married," he said, setting his scotch down. "Want a drink?"

She shook her head, then planted her hands on the bar, slightly drumming her fingers on the Formica top.

"Baby, what's going on?"

"I'm not sure that I'm ready to be a wife," she admitted.

"I'm willing to wait, but I need to be sure that we're on the same page," he said. "When you left the way you did last night, I had to wonder if that was the end of our relationship."

*It should be,* she thought. She looked at Andre. With his lip poked out and the gleam of tears in his eyes, he seemed like a little boy who was asking his parents not to get a divorce.

"Dana, I love you and I want to marry you. But if you feel like this isn't what you want, tell me."

"Andre," Dana said. "I—"

He cut her off, an annoying habit of his. "You mean the world to me, Dana. I've never loved anyone the way I love you."

"Maybe we should just wait," she declared. With those words, the weight of her impending nuptials floated off her shoulders.

Andre nearly stumbled. His drink sloshed in his glass. "Wait? Why?"

"I'm going to start baking. Zariah has a contact at Capitol City Bakery and I'm going to see if I can sell some of my desserts there."

Andre shook his head. "That's a pipe dream. You're a teacher. I know baking is a side thing that you do for friends, but that's not your future. I'm your future."

Dana dropped her head in her hands. "It isn't a pipe dream. The only time I feel happy or satisfied is when I'm in the kitchen. If you love me as much as you say you do, then you would support me!"

"What do your parents think?" he asked, placing his hands on his hips.

Dana sighed. "They don't know and it isn't their business. I'm a grown woman."

"Dana, I know that. I know you're an adult, even though you're acting like a child. What kind of future is baking cakes?"

Dana leapt to her feet. "This is pointless. I have to go cook."

Andre grabbed her arm as she turned to walk away. "Dana, please. I need you. I feel like you're slipping away from me." His golden eyes searched her face for a sign that he was wrong.

She rolled her eyes. "Did you hear anything that I said?"

Andre nodded. "I heard you, but this isn't about baking. This is about me and you, us."

*There is no us. My mother wants us to be together, not me,* she thought as she looked at him. Then she took a deep breath and said, "Andre, I need out of this relationship."

"What?"

Dana took her engagement ring off and pressed it into Andre's hand. "This is for the best," she said, then dashed out the front door.

# CHAPTER FOUR

It didn't take long for Dana's phone to start ringing once she arrived home. The first few calls were from Andre. When she saw his number on the Caller ID unit, she didn't pick up. The next calls came from her mother. Dana had known Andre was going to call Denise. That was so like him. All of the problems between them had always ended up in Denise's ear. Dana poured her cake batter into a pan before picking up the phone.

"Hello?"

"Have you lost your damned mind?" Denise shrieked.

"Hello mother."

"Don't *hello mother* me. Andre said you gave him back the ring because you want to work for some bakery. Your father and I did not—"

"I gave him the ring back because I don't want to marry him," Dana said, stopping her mother's tirade.

Denise snorted. "Why not? You can't do much better than Andre. He's educated—"

"I don't have time to listen to you, I'm cooking. And for the record, I don't want a miniature daddy as my husband. I'm not you. This is my life and I'm finally going to start living it for me."

"What? You're being a fool. You need to be—"

Dana slammed the phone down. She'd finally done it. She'd stood up to her mother. Now, she wondered what the consequences would be.

A few minutes later, the phone rang. Dana snatched it up without looking at the caller ID.

"I've made my decision and I'm not changing my mind. If

you can't deal with that, then there is nothing—"

"Hold on," Chris said. "I have no idea what you're talking about."

Dana laughed nervously. "I'm sorry. I thought you were my mother."

"Y'all must be having a hell of an argument."

"Yeah, we are. But don't worry about it. What's up?"

"I know you said you were going to call, but I couldn't get you off my mind."

Dana blushed. "Really? And just what were you thinking?"

Chris chuckled low and sexy. "There was some cake batter and frosting involved. But I'm not ready to share that right now."

"I know where your mind is." Dana's face flushed. She had been having the same thoughts and feelings.

"I'm a man, what can I say? So what are you doing?"

"Baking."

"I'm not disturbing you, am I?"

Dana smiled. He actually cared if he was keeping her from something. All of her other callers could care less. They said she was wasting her time and talent, as if she were striving to be a fry cook at a fast food restaurant.

"Well, I'm actually about to put the cake in the oven."

"So, I guess I won't see you tonight?"

"You will if you want this German chocolate cake."

Chris laughed. "All right. Where do you want to meet?"

"Why don't you come by my place," she said, then immediately regretted the invitation. She bit her bottom lip. What if he took it the wrong way? She wasn't trying to bring him to her house for a night of hot sex.

"Are you sure?" he inquired.

"Yes, but you're just coming to get the cake. That's it."

Chris chuckled. "I know."

Dana gave him directions to her place as she slid the pan in the oven.

"I'll see you in 20 minutes. I don't live that far from you."

"All right, see you then," she said and hung up the phone. Dana ran into the bathroom and fluffed her hair. She splashed cool water on her face and dried hurriedly.

Looking down at her cut off jean shorts, she considered changing into a pair of slacks, but she didn't want to look as if she was trying to impress him. *He knows I'm cooking,* she thought. *No need to try to look like a fashion plate.* She dusted a few specks of flour from her tank top. When Chris knocked on the door, Dana was putting her layers on a wire cooling rack. She wiped her hands on her "God Bless the Cook" apron and opened the door.

"Hi," she said.

Chris handed Dana a bottle of white wine. "My momma always said never show up at a beautiful woman's house empty-handed."

"You really didn't have to do this," she replied as she accepted the bottle.

"I know," he said as he walked in. Chris looked around, taking note of the artwork hanging on the walls. "Synthia St. James?" He pointed to a colorful painting of six black women.

"It's a knock off," she said. "I wish I could afford a real one." Dana was impressed Chris knew the famed artist's work.

"You will once you open your bakery. So, you like baking and art?"

She nodded as she led Chris into the kitchen. "It smells like a bakery in here," he said. He looked at the cake layers cooling on the counter.

"I hope you like it," she said. "I just have to put the frosting on."

"Is the frosting homemade?"

"Is there any other way to make it?" she asked with a laugh.

"Just checking. Some people, not me, think that stuff in a can is good."

Dana opened the refrigerator and pulled out the metal bowl with the frosting in it. She handed him a long-handled wooden spoon so that he could sample the sweetness.

Chris dipped the spoon in the bowl, then licked the brown icing. He smiled approvingly as he savored the taste. "Damn, girl, you're trying to make a brother fall in love."

Dana smiled wistfully. Her baking was making many of the people in her life fall out of love with her. And here was Chris, showing appreciation for something she loved to do. If anyone fell in love, it would be she. Nevertheless, it was too soon to entertain those kinds of thoughts. Dana wasn't one to believe in love at first sight, but there was something about him. She ran her hand down her throat and looked away from him.

"I need to let the frosting warm up," she said.

"Good, we can have a glass of wine." He took the bottle and headed for a barstool.

"Do you want to sit in the living room?" she asked, getting a corkscrew out of her utility drawer.

"Nah, you look comfortable in the kitchen and that's refreshing to see."

"Meaning?" Her eyebrow shot up as if she were expecting a sarcastic comment from him.

"Most new millennium women don't use a kitchen for anything but heating up a Lean Cuisine meal and pouring a glass of water. You know, microwave chefs."

Dana laughed. "Well, I love to cook."

"Obviously. Look at your appliances. Stainless steel fridge and stove. Look at this bar. What is this, marble?" He ran his hand across the smooth top. "Looks like something off the Food Network."

"Stop," she said as her cheeks grew hot.

"What else do you cook?"

"Everything, but I love baking. My grandmother was from Charleston and when I was growing up, I spent the summers at her side as she baked pies, cakes and cookies. She taught me how to roll the dough for tender, flaky biscuits. I used to try to cook for my parents when I would return home, but my mother told me that I wasn't going to be in anyone's kitchen because I was going to be a teacher."

"Your mother planned your life, huh?"

"You could say that. But I'm finally taking my life back."

"Really?"

Dana nodded. "A friend of mine has a contact with a new bakery in town. I'm going to send some samples over next week."

"Wow, you're really making things happen. Good for you."

Dana set two wine glasses on the bar. "Well, if I don't make it happen, I'm going to be a middle school teacher for the rest of my life."

"If you don't want to teach, why do you?" Chris filled the glasses and offered one to Dana.

Dana shrugged. "Why don't you tell me about yourself?" she asked, focusing the spotlight on him.

He smiled. "There's nothing much to tell. I went to New York right after high school because I wanted to get the hell out of South Carolina. But I learned the hard way that New York is a tough town. I stayed there for a year, then ran out of money."

"What were you doing in New York?"

"This and that. Construction, working on the docks. I even worked as a waiter for a few months."

"What brought you back here?" Dana wanted to leave Columbia, but she'd never had the nerve to do it. She knew that if she left she wouldn't come back unless she was in a pine box.

"My uncle started his landscaping and pool company. I needed a job and he offered me one. I didn't mean to stay this long, but I got comfortable."

"Do you want to go back to the Big Apple?"

"That was the plan. But plans change," he said as he sipped the wine.

Dana picked up her glass and sipped it. "I've always wanted to live some place else. Maybe if I make a name for myself with my baking, I can head down to Atlanta or New Orleans."

"The Big Easy. I've gone to Mardi Gras a few times."

"Really? You travel a lot."

"You seem surprised. Don't let the work boots fool you."

"I'm not surprised, just in awe. I've never been half of the places I want to go."

"Now I'm surprised. I would have thought you spent the summers in Europe on the French Rivera or something. You have a classy air about you."

Dana smiled. "Don't let the Nine West boots fool you," she joked.

"Okay. So, Dana, what's your last name?"

"Ellison. And yours?"

"Johnson."

Dana set her wine glass down and began stirring the frosting.

"So, do you want to take a trip this weekend?" he asked.

"What? I can't just pick up and go on a moment's notice." *And I can't be alone with you; there's no telling what I might do.*

"That's why you haven't been half the places you want to go to. We can make it a short trip. We can go down to Atlanta and hang out in Buckhead all night."

Dana bit her bottom lip as she mulled over his invitation.

"Come on," Chris urged. "You only live once."

Dana dipped into the bowl with a rubber spatula. She smoothed the brown icing on one of the cake layers. "All right, I'll go," she said. Her eyes gleamed with excitement as she smiled.

"You know you need some time to get away from those kids."

She nodded in agreement. "Especially after the day I had."

"What happened?" His voice was filled with concern.

Dana was taken aback. She couldn't remember the last time someone showed interest in what happened to her. She smiled. "There was a fight in my classroom."

"Really? What was it about? A girl?"

"Actually, it was two girls. They were cursing and screaming. They ruined my bookshelf and knocked me down in the process."

"Girls?" he asked incredulously.

Dana nodded.

"Were you hurt?" he asked.

"Huh?"

"When they knocked you down?"

Dana shook her head. "I was too angry. I mean, these are honors students. They should know better."

"What does that have to do with anything? They're still kids, y'know."

"I know that, I just expect more from my students. It seems as if I'm losing them."

Chris sipped his wine and looked at Dana. He didn't want to tell her, but he could see she was meant to be a teacher. No matter how she tried to down play it, he could tell she cared about those kids. It came across in the way she spoke of the kids and the disappointment that shrouded her eyes.

"You sure you want to give up teaching because you don't like it? Or are you just trying to spite your parents?" he asked.

"Excuse me?"

"Well, I don't think I stuttered."

"I know what I want," she said. "And I don't want to be a teacher anymore."

Chris threw his hands up. "All right, I was just wondering."

Dana flipped the cake layer on top of the other one. She looked up at Chris and smirked. "You've known me for a day and some hours. You really think you can read my mind?"

"I never said that. It's just the way you were talking about those kids." He dipped his finger in the frosting bowl and Dana smacked him on the back of the hand.

"Sorry. I can tell you cooked with your grandmother." He rubbed his hand as if she had hurt him.

"And she smacked me just like that too," Dana said.

Chris watched Dana as she constructed the three-layer cake. Her movements were quick and smooth as she slid the spatula around the cake. She didn't drop a spot of frosting on the counter.

"*Voilà,*" she said as she finished frosting the cake. "Are you ready for your sample?"

"Just hand me the knife." Chris eyed the cake like Homer Simpson looking at a doughnut.

Dana opened the utility drawer and pulled out a cake knife. "Have at it," she said.

Chris took the knife and cut a huge hunk of cake. Dana handed him a paper towel.

"If you weren't so fast, I would have gotten you a saucer," she said.

"I told you, German chocolate is my favorite." He pinched off a piece of the moist cake with his forefinger and thumb.

Dana handed him a fork. "Don't bite your fingers," she said.

Chris shoveled the cake into his mouth, savoring every morsel. "Girl, you can cook," he said in between bites of cake. Dana wiped crumbs from his chin with the edge of her dishtowel. Chris grabbed her hand.

Once more Dana felt an electric charge at his touch. They stared deep into each other's eyes. She wanted to kiss him and he wanted to kiss her, but neither of them could move. It was as if time stood still. Dana slipped her hand from underneath his.

"Um, I can wrap this up for you," she said once she found her voice.

"Thanks. How much do I owe you?"

She shook her head.

"I know you're not cooking for free."

"Just think of it as a sample. Next time, I'll charge you."

Chris laughed. "I guess I'd better go." He stood up and wiped his hands on his pants.

Dana wrapped the cake with wax paper. "You can keep the plate," she said.

"Nah, I'm going to wash it and bring it to you this weekend when I pick you up."

Dana smiled. "All right." She handed Chris the cake. Again, their fingers touched. Dana swallowed hard and stepped back.

"Until this weekend," he said as he kissed her hand. Dana walked him to the door and watched him get into his truck. She leaned against the door a moment before skipping into the kitchen and beginning her next cake. She could still smell the faint scent of Chris's Nautica cologne. She inhaled deeply as she cracked her eggs in the mixing bowl. The phone rang as Dana poured the milk in the mix.

"Yes?"

"Dana, it's me," Andre said.

"I'm busy."

"I'm not going to give up on us."

"Andre, please, I have to finish this cake."

"Is there someone else?"

"What? Why would you say that?"

"What else is there? We were so happy and now it's like you're a different person."

"Andre, this is me. This is who I am. We never should've been together in the first place."

"Where is this coming from? Your mother says you have cold feet and I agree with her," he said in an annoyed tone.

"Oh really," Dana said. "If you and my mother have so much in common and you value her opinion so much, why don't you marry her? Let's get real. Andre, you want to be married into the Ellison family."

"That's not fair. I love you, not your last name. I could care less about who your parents are."

"I wish I could believe that," Dana said. "Look, I have to finish my cake."

"Dana, please, I need you in my life."

"It's not working for me, Andre. No matter how hard I try, this is not working. I would rather know that now and not wake up 20 years later in a marriage I never wanted."

"I'm not going to beg you to marry me. There are other women who would be happy to have a man like me."

Dana rolled her eyes. *Well, go find one of them.*

Andre continued. "I thought you were different. I thought you had some goals, something going for yourself."

"You know what, Andre," she snapped. "I do have goals and guess what. They don't include you."

"What?"

"You heard me. Now hang up and call my mother." Dana slammed the phone down. She didn't feel like baking anymore.

# CHAPTER FIVE

The next morning, Dana woke up feeling liberated, until she remembered work. Then she felt the shackles again. She didn't want to meet with those parents. Not today, not when she had a new lease on life.

She climbed out of bed and headed into the bathroom to shower. After her shower, she wrapped up in a plush towel and walked into her bedroom to get dressed. Dana pulled out a black and white stripped ankle length Liz Claiborne dress. She laid it on the bed, then headed for the kitchen to brew a pot of coffee. She was going to need caffeine to get through the meeting with those parents.

The main thing Dana detested about being a teacher was dealing with parents whenever a student messed up. Most of the time, they blamed the teacher for their children's actions. Somehow this was going to be turned around on her. It was just the way things went when it came to discipline problems. Dana poured herself a cup of coffee, dumped in two teaspoons of sugar and sipped it. Then she set the mug on the counter. It was nearly seven a.m. If she wanted to get to Mr. Mason's office on time, she was going to have to leave in 20 minutes. Dana dashed into the bedroom and stepped into her dress. She grabbed her black leather knee boots from underneath the bed because she didn't feel like putting on stockings.

Taking the rollers out of her head, she fluffed with her fingers and was ready to go.

It was about five minutes to eight when Dana arrived at Mr. Mason's office. Alicia and her mother were standing in the hallway.

"Good morning," Dana said.

Neither of them spoke; they just eyed Dana scornfully. Dana walked into the office and found Rhonda and her father sitting across from Mr. Mason.

"Ms. Ellison," Mr. Mason said. "This is Mr. Thomas."

Dana extended her hand to him and he shook it.

"Sorry we're meeting like this," he said. "Rhonda knows better than to fight in class."

"I think there was a reason for the fight," Dana said. "Rhonda, do you want to tell me about it?"

"No," she snapped.

Her father glared at her. "Watch your tone, young lady."

"Well," Mr. Mason said. "Although Rhonda has never been in trouble before, she and Alicia did some serious damage in the classroom, and they knocked Ms. Ellison down."

"I'm sorry about that," Mr. Thomas said. "Rhonda has been having a rough time since her mother passed away."

Dana furrowed her brows. She hadn't known about that. She remembered sending Rhonda's assignments during a two-week absence, but she hadn't checked on her and her other students hadn't say a word.

"Why didn't you tell me?" Dana asked.

"Because it's my business."

Rhonda's father glared at her as she crossed her arms over her chest. Rhonda rolled her eyes and sucked her teeth.

"I don't know why you're pretending you care now," Rhonda spat out.

Dana inhaled sharply. "I do care, Rhonda. Is this why your grades have been slipping?"

"Grades slipping?" Mr. Thomas asked as he looked from Dana to Rhonda.

"I sent letters home," Dana said. "I thought you were aware."

Rhonda dropped her head.

"I never got them," he replied, glaring again at his daughter.

Mr. Mason cleared his throat. "I know the low grades are serious but we're here about the violence in the classroom. Ms. Ellison, maybe you and Mr. Thomas need to set up a parent-teacher conference at a later date. Because of Rhonda's previous record and these circumstances, I'm going to cut her suspension to five days."

"Thank you," Mr. Thomas said. "Ms. Ellison, I'll give you a call so we can talk about Rhonda's grades." He gripped Rhonda's arm and led her out of the office.

Dana leaned against the wall. *How could I have missed this girl's pain?*

Mr. Mason looked at Dana and read her expression. "You can't blame yourself. You aren't expected to know everything that goes on in kids' lives."

"But her mother died. How could I have missed that? I didn't check on her when she was out those two weeks."

"Dana, you have more than a hundred students in and out of your classroom. You can't drop what you're doing to check on each and everyone of them. Now pull yourself together. We still have to talk to Mrs. Bennett and Alicia."

Dana took a deep breath as Mr. Mason walked outside and returned with Alicia and her mother. Both mother and daughter had frowns and attitude written all over their faces. They sat down and glared at Dana.

"Mrs. Bennett," Mr. Mason began.

Mrs. Bennett leaned over the desk and pointed her finger in his face. "Don't you sit up there and Mrs. Bennett me. This woman has no control in her classroom and she cursed at the students. Why is my child being punished?"

"Your child started the fight," Dana said. She tried to keep her voice even and steady, but Mrs. Bennett was rapidly pissing her off.

"She was attacked, I know she was. You should be suspended," Mrs. Bennett retorted.

"This isn't going to settle anything," Mr. Mason said. "We have to—"

"It isn't going to be settled! I want this woman suspended and my child reinstated in school today. This will damage her chances at getting into college."

Dana snorted. "Have you seen her grades? I don't think this will do as much damage as her grades."

Mrs. Bennett leapt from her seat. "Do you hear that? Is that how she talks to my daughter in class?"

Dana stood up and put her hands on her hips. "And I wondered where Alicia got her nasty disposition from. Why don't you just take your child out of my class?"

"Mrs. Bennett, Ms. Ellison, calm down," Mr. Mason said. "We need to take a step back and look at this objectively."

Mrs. Bennett looked at him and rolled her eyes. "Alicia, come on. This meeting is over. I'm taking this to the school board."

They blew out of the office. Dana sat down and looked at Mr. Mason, who stood there with his mouth open.

"That went well," she said sarcastically.

"Dana, you were out of line."

"Excuse me?"

"We were trying to calm the situation. You inflamed it."

"You know what, I'm sick of these parents teaching their children bad habits. Then we're expected to turn around and kiss their behinds."

"Dana!"

"What? I'm tired of this," she said. "If you want to suspend me or fire me, go ahead."

The words shocked her as much as they shocked Mr. Mason.

"Why don't you take the day off and calm down. I'm really

surprised at you, Dana. Your father would never—"

She stood up and pulled at her dress. "I'm not my father, okay?" Dana flew out of the office and down to her classroom. She grabbed her briefcase and stomped to the parking lot. When she got into her car, she pulled her cell phone out of the glove box and dialed Chris's number, not expecting him to be home. His voice startled her when he answered.

"I didn't think you would be home," Dana said, all of a sudden feeling nervous.

"My job was canceled because of the weather. What are you doing? Shouldn't you be educating the children?"

"I was given the day off. Let's go have brunch."

"Okay. Is everything all right?"

"Yeah, everything is great," Dana lied.

"Uh-huh."

"Why don't I come to your place?" she suggested.

"All right, but I'm not as good a cook as you are."

"Do you at least have food in the fridge?"

"Of course."

"Well, you pull out the pots and pans and I'll whip something up."

"I could get used to this," Chris said. "A beautiful woman coming to my house cooking for me."

"Don't, I'm not Hazel the maid."

"I was joking. Hell, when you start at the bakery, I'll be lucky to see you. And after the wedding, I'll never see you again."

"Ah, give me directions to your place," she said.

Chris rattled off the roads she should take to get to his apartment.

"You live that close to USC?" she questioned.

"The rent is cheap over here. Especially when you tell them you're a college student."

"So you lied?"

"At the time I was thinking of going to college."

Dana shook her head and wheeled her car out of the parking lot. "I'll see you in a little bit."

As she drove, she started to question the kind of man Chris was. He knew she was engaged, but hadn't stopped him from pursuing her. *I wonder what kind of woman he thinks I am?* she thought. *After all, I'm the one who's engaged.*

When Dana got to Chris's, he was standing on the balcony of his apartment waiting for her. Her breath caught in her chest when she glimpsed the way his wife-beater tee shirt clung to his muscles. His gray sweatpants hugged his biscuit booty. He looked delicious. And Dana wanted to take a bite. She walked up to the second floor unit, trying to keep her knees from giving out on her, and knocked on the door. Dana couldn't believe she was here. What was going to happen inside that apartment?

"It's open," he called out.

Chris took note of her outfit as she breezed past him. "This is how you dress on your day off?" he inquired.

"I was sent home," she said as she looked down at her watch. "I didn't last an hour and a half at work today."

"What happened?"

Dana sat on his butter soft leather sofa. She sank into the thick cushions. Running her hand across the seat, she said, "This is nice."

"Don't try to change the subject." Chris closed the front door and walked over to the sofa, his face full of concern.

"I went off on a parent. Remember those girls that I told you fought in my class yesterday?"

Chris nodded.

"One of the girls, Rhonda, her mother had died and I didn't know it. She basically told me I didn't care. I saw her grades dropping, but I didn't follow up on it and I didn't call her father."

"That's still no excuse for her to act like she's Lala Ali," Chris replied.

Dana shook her head. "Even with all that's going on with that family, her father was calm. He was cordial. But the mother of the girl who started the fight, she tried to blame it all on me."

"How is it your fault that her child was acting a fool?"

"She said I didn't have control in my classroom and I should be suspended," Dana recounted.

"Come here," Chris said.

"What?"

He wiggled his index finger as if to say, "Come over here." Dana slid closer to him.

"Turn your back to me," he said. "You need a massage. Tension causes wrinkles."

"I need a lot more than that," she whispered.

"What else can I do for you?" Chris asked seductively.

Dana smiled and closed her eyes. "Tell me that I don't have to go back to E. L. Wright Middle School."

"You don't have to go back today," he said as he began massaging her shoulders.

His hands sent tingles down her spine and she could feel Chris's warm breath on her neck. She closed her eyes as his hands moved down her shoulders to her back.

"Relaxed yet?"

She moaned appreciatively.

Chris grinned when he saw the satisfied smile on her face. "Lean back," he said.

To Dana, Chris's voice was like a snake charmer's pipe. Her body responded to the music. He spread his legs so that Dana's back could rest against his broad chest. His hands were on her shoulders again. Then he slowly moved them down her sides. Dana held her breath as his hands moved to her thighs.

"How does that feel?" he asked.

"G-good."

Chris reversed his hand trip, slowly moving up her legs, sides and back to her shoulders. Dana opened her eyes, desire clouding her vision.

"What are we doing?" she asked after a rational thought formed in her mind.

"I don't know. But whatever you want to do, we can do it."

She turned around and placed her left hand on his chest. "I gave Andre his ring back."

"Really?"

"Yeah, I can't marry him and I'm not trying to make you his replacement. But Chris, I've never felt this way before."

"It's only been two days since we met."

"You don't know what my life was like before I met you. I did what I was told because that was all that I knew."

"And what's different now?"

"You've opened my eyes."

"In two days?"

Dana nodded. "It's like I've seen another side of life. I hung up on my mother last night. I never would have done that if I hadn't thought about what you said about letting other people set rules for your life. When I took that ring off, it was like taking off a shackle."

Chris laughed. "You're too much. I'm going to be totally honest with you. I'm not looking for a serious relationship. And I definitely don't want to be a rebound for you."

"Chris, I just ended a relationship. I'm not trying to hop into another one."

"But you know what," he said, leaning in close to her ear. "I want to kiss you again."

Dana smiled. "No, I have to cook." She tried to sit up, but Chris held her close to him. They looked into each other's eyes. The attraction was there; neither of them could deny it. The air around them was charged with energy. Dana felt a tingling in her panties.

"Just one kiss?" he pleaded gently.

Dana leaned into him and he captured her lips with his. His tongue searched the deepest crevices of her mouth and Dana melted against him like butter on a hot yeast roll. She wanted to rip his clothes off and make love to him on the sofa. But she couldn't. Sex would change everything. Sex would make whatever they were building fuzzy. Dana pulled back. "Uh, I'd better get into the kitchen."

Chris let her go. "Yeah. Let me know if you need anything."

He prayed she would move before his erection became more apparent. Why had he told her he wasn't looking for a relationship? Why hadn't he told her the truth? Chris wanted to be with Dana in the worst way, but the last thing he wanted to do was fall in love with another woman who belonged to somebody else. Sure, she'd given the ring back and said all of that stuff about living her life, but what if she woke up tomorrow and decided that she wanted to be with Andre? Where would that leave him?

*Sitting in this apartment craving her kiss,* he thought.

"It's well-stocked in here," she called out.

"Yeah. I have to eat. Sometimes I do cook."

Dana laughed. "That I would like to see."

Chris walked into the kitchen. "Step aside, Ms. Lady. But I'm warning you, it won't be IHOP."

Dana threw her hands up and let Chris take over. He grabbed a knife and two onions from a woven basket hanging above the sink. "Hand me a bell pepper from the fridge," he said.

Dana handed it to him and watched as he chopped the onion and the peppers, then tossed them into the frying pan.

"You can put those eggs back," he said.

"What are you making?" she asked.

Chris walked over to the refrigerator and pulled out some chicken sausage. "I don't eat pork," he said as he showed her the package of meat.

"Really? Neither do I."

"Good." Chris opened the package and cut the tube-shaped meat into four pieces. Then he opened the cabinet above the stove and pulled out a box of grits. Dana handed him a pot that she had filled with water.

Chris took the pot from her hands and said, "Tell me you like grits."

"Didn't I tell you my granny was from Charleston?"

"All right," he said as he measured two cups of grits. Then he put a cast iron skillet on the stove for the sausage.

"Is there anything else I can do to help?" she asked. "I don't feel right just standing around in the kitchen."

"Why don't you grate the cheese?"

Dana took out a brick of sharp cheddar cheese and looked around for a grater. Chris opened the utility drawer next to the refrigerator and pointed at the grater.

Dana grabbed it and shredded the cheese. Chris handed her a saucer to put the cheese in.

"Is this enough?" she asked when she had shredded half of the brick.

He nodded as he grabbed a handful of cheese.

Chris added salt, sugar and pepper to the grits in the boiling water. Then he tossed the cheese in with the grits. Chris was a messy cook. He dropped cheese on the stovetop and dribbled grits from his spoon as he stirred the pot. Dana wanted to wipe the mess away, but she just watched.

Chris turned the sausage, making sure it was brown. "You know what? I do need those eggs," he said. "Some cheese eggs would be great with this."

"Yeah, if you want to be constipated for a week."

"Good, more for me. I just need two eggs and some of that cheese."

Dana handed him the eggs.

"I'm not sharing, either," Chris said as he grabbed another frying pan from the oven drawer.

"I'll be fine," she said. Dana pulled a carton of orange juice out of the refrigerator. "Where are your glasses?"

"Above the sink," he said. She grabbed two glasses as Chris flipped the eggs in the pan. Dana handed him some cheese and chopped vegetables, then grabbed two plates from the dishwasher and set them on the counter.

Chris put the grits and sausage on Dana's plate. The aroma made her mouth water.

"This looks good," she said as she inhaled deeply.

"Wait until you taste it."

"Hand me a fork," she said.

Chris loaded up his plate. "We have to bless the food."

They bowed their heads and said a silent prayer. "Let's eat," Chris said as his head snapped up.

Dana bit into the sausage. "Umm, this is good. Oh, this is so good."

Chris smiled proudly. "So, I meet the Dana Ellison standard of cooking?"

She nodded in between bites and flashed him the thumbs up signal.

"Let's go sit down," he said as he headed into the living room. Dana followed him and they sat on the sofa and ate in silence. Dana savored every bite. No one had ever cooked for her before or made her feel this special. It was as if Chris had cast a sensual spell on her.

"Maybe you should cook too," she said when she finished her breakfast.

Chris shook his head. "Nah, I got about three dishes. They would get old real quick."

Dana smiled and stretched her arms above her head. "So,

what's next?" she asked.

"Well, when I used to cut school, after breakfast I would go to the movies."

"Okay, that sounds like a plan. Or we could rent a DVD or something."

Chris shrugged. "Whatever you want to do, Ms. Lady. I'm your genie today."

Dana just smiled at him.

"Just let me get dressed and we can go," he said.

"All right," she said as she unzipped her left boot and rubbed her left calf. Chris caught a glimpse of her bare leg and felt a stirring in his groin. He dashed into the bathroom to take a cold shower.

# CHAPTER SIX

Dana and Chris walked into Blockbuster video laughing as if they were high school students on a ditch day. The store was practically empty. Chris picked up a new action flick starring Jet Li.

"What do you think?" he asked.

Dana shook her head.

"All right," he said as he put it back on the shelf. "What kind of movies do you like?"

"I don't like mindless action movies. I want something with substance."

"Also known as a chick flick."

"Excuse me, Mr. Chauvinist." She pinched his arm playfully.

Chris laughed and picked up an African American family drama starring Alfre Woodard.

"How about this?"

Dana took the box from his hands and nodded. "*Down in the Delta*. I've been meaning to watch this movie," she said.

"All right, now I get to pick one," he said as he walked over to another aisle. "This is a good movie." Chris held up *The Siege*, starring Dana's favorite actor, Denzel Washington.

"Is that Denzel?" she asked as she squinted her eyes to see the box.

"Yep. Don't tell me that you're a Denzel groupie like most women I know."

"I wouldn't call myself a groupie, but if stalking wasn't illegal…," she joked.

Chris laughed. "This should keep us busy for a while."

They walked to the register. "My place or yours?" he asked.

"I was getting kind of comfortable on that big sofa of yours."

Chris smiled. "Yeah, it sucks you right in, doesn't it?"

*Much like you're doing,* she thought. Dana turned away from him. "You know, since you cooked breakfast, I'll get the movies," she said.

"Nah, I can't let you do that. If I pay, then you owe me a drink and a movie," he said with a wily smile on his face.

"Why do you want me to owe you so badly?"

"Because I do," he said as he pulled his Blockbuster card out of his wallet. Dana stood back and admired the way his Levi jeans fit his muscular legs. He looked like a runner. She closed her eyes and imagined his hips pressed into hers, her arms wrapped around his broad shoulders, pulling him closer, deeper, closer, deeper—

"Dana, are you all right?" Chris asked, ending her passionate fantasy.

Her face flushed and she prayed her eyes didn't betray her. "I'm fine," she said. "I was off in another world."

"Thinking about your students and what happened this morning?"

She nodded because she was afraid that if she opened her mouth she would tell him exactly what had been on her mind. Chris put his arm around her shoulder and gave her a reassuring hug.

"Everything is going to work out just fine," he said.

Dana smiled. That was the least of her worries. She wondered if she would be able to sit in the room with Chris for four hours and not fall further under his spell. His walk was hypnotic, his voice melodic, and his eyes seemed to look into her soul. Dana felt naked around him. It was as if Chris saw the real Dana, not the woman people had shaped into her father's image. The Ellison magic didn't impress Chris as it did many in Columbia.

The clerk handed Chris the movies and Dana picked up two jumbo-sized boxes of Goobers.

"We can't have movie day without these," she said as she paid the clerk.

"You're all right with me," Chris said. "I love those things. That's probably why I spent so much time in the dentist's office when I was growing up."

"What was it like for you when you were growing up?" she asked as they walked out the door.

"Normal," he said, then got a far-off look in his eyes. "Just a South Carolina upbringing."

Dana took note of his look but let the conversation drop. By the time they got into his truck and headed back to his apartment, it was almost noon. If Dana had been at school, she would have been on lunch duty. She smiled as she thought about the smells and noises she was missing out on.

"What's that smile for?" Chris asked.

"It's corn dog day at school and I was supposed to have lunch duty. Thank God for small miracles," she said.

"Are you sure you want to give up teaching?"

"Yes, my psychic friend, I am. You don't know what it's like to be the daughter of a myth and a legend."

"Huh?"

"Nothing, I'm not thinking about it today. Let's just watch these movies and eat Goobers," she said rattling the bag at him.

Chris shrugged as he pulled into the apartment's parking lot. "Ms. Lady, your theatre awaits you."

They hopped out of the truck and walked into his place. Dana unzipped her boots at the door and stepped out of them. Chris looked down at her legs. They were shaped like a woman's legs ought to be shaped, he thought. Thick calves, shapely thighs. And her feet. Her toes were perfect. The cherry red polish on her toenails made her feet look edible. "I hope you don't mind me taking my shoes off," she said when she caught his gaze. "I just can't sit down with shoes on unless I'm going somewhere."

"It's fine," he said. "Let me get a bowl for the candy."

Dana sat on the sofa and curled up in a ball. She closed her eyes, only meaning to rest for a few minutes, but she drifted off into a deep sleep. In her dream, Chris took her in his arms and kissed her slowly. He lifted her shirt over her head, then took her breasts into his mouth, making her nipples stand at attention. Then he eased down her body, using his tongue as a guide. Dana moaned as he headed to the source of her heat and pleasure with his tongue.

"Dana?"

"Um."

"Dana, wake up," Chris said.

She sprang up on the sofa. "What?"

"You okay?"

"Yeah, I'm fine. How long have I been sleep?"

"About an hour. You looked so comfortable, I didn't want to disturb you."

"What time is it?" Her face was flustered as she looked at Chris.

"Almost two."

Dana stretched and yawned. She looked at the half empty bowl of Goobers. "I see you've been busy snacking."

"Yeah, I was getting hungry, but I didn't want to be rude. Let's order a pizza for lunch."

"All right."

"What were you dreaming about? You were tossing and turning like you were having a nightmare or something."

*It wasn't a nightmare, not by a long shot,* she thought.

"I don't remember," Dana said.

Chris smirked. "That good, huh?"

Dana laughed nervously. "What are we getting on the pizza?"

"Extra cheese, olives and green peppers."

"Are you walking around in my head or something? I love that on my pizza."

"We have a lot in common, Ms. Lady."

Dana looked at him and prayed that she hadn't uttered anything in her sleep. *Oh my God,* she thought. *If he knows I was fantasizing about him I will die!*

Chris picked up the phone book and looked up the number of Papa John's. Dana stood up and walked into the bathroom. She splashed water on her face as Chris ordered the pizza. She had to get herself together before she went back into that living room. She resolved to go home after they ate. All Chris had to do at this point was breathe to arouse her. Dana was afraid that she would act on it.

"Are you all right in there?" he asked.

"I'm fine." She walked out of the bathroom.

"Okay. The pizza should be here in about 30 minutes."

Dana nodded. "Let's watch a movie."

He smiled and walked into the kitchen. "Want something to drink?"

"Water," she said as she sat down on the sofa. Dana sat up straight and made sure she didn't fall asleep again. Chris came back the living room and set her glass of water on the table in front of her. Then he popped the Denzel movie in the DVD player. Sitting beside her, he slipped his arm around her. Dana leaned her head on his shoulder as the movie started. Chris glanced at her. He wanted to kiss her again. As he'd watched her sleep, it had taken everything inside of him not to lift her dress and make love to her. But he knew it was too soon for that.

Dana looked up at Chris, catching him staring at her. "What?"

"Nothing, just making sure you're not going back to sleep."

She pinched his side. "I'm wide awake now, okay?"

Chris tickled her nose. "I hear you talking, but you'll be snoring in five minutes."

"With Denzel on the screen? I don't think so."

"Oh, so it's all about Mr. Washington?"

"Uh-huh."

They both focused on the movie and the rest of the world disappeared. It felt right, being there with Chris. He felt it too and the feeling startled them both.

∽∾⁂∾∽

After they polished off the medium pizza, Dana went home. She wished she could stay in the comfort of Chris's drama-free home, but it was time to face reality. Not to her surprise, she saw her mother's car in her driveway. Dana sighed as she got out of the car. Denise was standing on the porch with a stone face.

"Mother," she said.

"Are you trying to throw your life away?"

"What are you talking about?"

"William Mason called your father and told him how unprofessional you were today. And just where have you been?"

Dana rolled her eyes, but didn't answer. She wasn't a child, no matter how much her mother wanted to treat her as one.

"Dana, are you on drugs?"

"Mother! Go home. Leave me alone."

Denise grabbed Dana's arm. "I am still your mother. Your father and I busted our butts to make sure you had an education. We didn't do all of this to watch you throw it all away to sell damn cakes."

Dana snatched away from her mother. "I'm 29, not nine. You don't run my life anymore. I will do what I want to do. And you might as well hear this from me: I'm quitting my job at the end of the year. I'm not marrying Andre, ever. And I'm going to sell my damn cakes, even if I have to set up a wooden stand in my front yard. And there isn't a damn thing that you can do about it."

Denise reared back and slapped Dana. "Don't you dare talk to me like that!" she hissed through clenched teeth.

Dana touched her cheek. It burned and stung from her mother's blow.

As Denise stormed off the porch, she turned and faced Dana. "You're an Ellison. Start acting like it."

Denise got into her car and sped out of Dana's driveway. When she was gone, Dana broke down in tears. Her perfect afternoon was ruined. With shaking hands she unlocked the front door and walked into her den and flung herself on the sofa. She sobbed into a throw pillow. Who was her mother to judge her? All of her life she'd dealt with her mother's judgment. Her grades, her style were never good enough. Not a single one of her choices was right, according to her mother. But never before had Denise raised her hand to her. Why was it so important for her to be a carbon copy of her parents? If they really cared, they would support her. *You would think I'd told them I want to be a stripper,* she thought bitterly as she stared off into space.

Dana lay on the sofa until the sky was pitch black. Then she got up and went into her bedroom, stripped down to her underwear, and crawled under the covers. She was about to drift off to sleep when the phone rang.

"What?" she snapped, not caring who was on the other line.

"Dana, are you all right?" Zariah asked.

"Yeah. I was in bed."

"Everyone has been looking for you. Your mother called me at the hospital, Andre called my house and even your father called me. What's going on?"

"I don't want to get into it tonight," she said. "I'm tired." Dana wanted to put the afternoon from hell behind her and rehashing it with Zariah was not a part of her plan.

"All right, but if you do want to talk, you know I'm here for you."

"Thanks, Z."

"Whatever is going on will pass, okay."

"You always know what I need to hear," Dana said, starting to feel better.

"What are best friends for? Oh, Dana, Josh from the bakery called. It's time to put up or shut up."

"Tell him I'll have some samples for him the beginning of the week."

"Great. When he gets a taste of your rum brownies and German chocolate cake, you're going to be hired on the spot, I know it. I'm going to let you get some rest. And don't let your parents, Andre or whoever, get to you."

"All right. Bye."

Dana hung up and stared at the ceiling. What if Josh didn't think her cooking was all of that? What if Andre and her parents were right? Could she be chasing a pipe dream? Dana shook her head to clear the negative thoughts. She had to take this chance and make the most of it. She was going to prove to her mother and father that she could be an Ellison without being a teacher.

⤚✤⤙

Morning rolled in like ominous storm clouds, despite sunbeams poking Dana in the face. She rubbed her temples as her head throbbed. *Thank God it's Friday,* she thought as she threw the cover back.

Dana looked over at the red numbers on her digital alarm clock. It was seven forty-five. She'd overslept. She sprang out of bed, took a quick shower. When she got out, she wiped the fog from the mirror and examined her face. It was just as bad as she'd expected. Her eyes were puffy and red from crying and there was a small bruise on her cheek from her mother's blow. She dried her face gingerly, then rubbed cold cream on it. If she put on some foundation, the bruise wouldn't be as noticeable. She grabbed her M-A-C studio FX compact and applied a heavy dusting of the powder. Wrapped in a towel, she went into her bedroom and grabbed a black pantsuit with a silver tunic with ribbon trim from the closet.

Dana checked the clock to see if she had time for coffee and concluded she could have a cup of instant coffee and maybe half of a banana. Then she decided to simply grab a cup of java from the teacher's lounge and dressed with the speed of an Olympic sprinter trying to break a world record. Her briefcase was still in the backseat of her car, so she slipped on black Italian loafers and left.

As she drove to E.L. Wright, Dana thought about walking into Mr. Mason's office and telling him that she was not a child whose parents should be called. But she knew that would create more unwanted drama. She was just going to avoid him. It was October. All she had to do was hold out until May 31. Then she would be free. The thought of freedom made her smile as she turned into the school's parking lot.

# CHAPTER SEVEN

Chris couldn't stop thinking about Dana as he and his crew dug a trench for Joe D'Matto's new pool. He'd thought work would take his mind off her, that the mindless banter between him and his co-workers would get the vision of Dana sleeping on his sofa out of his head. It didn't. He couldn't wait to see her again.

"Yo, man," Tito Rogers said. "Why are you so quiet today?"

"Just trying to get this work done," Chris replied.

"All right, Mr. Foreman. Guess who I saw last night?" Tito grinned, looking like the cat that swallowed the canary.

Chris shrugged his broad shoulders. "Who?"

"Rosie."

"Rosalyn?"

"Uh-huh. She asked about you, too."

"How's her husband?" Chris replied sarcastically.

"She said she got a divorce. She wants you back, man. You better jump on that. I told her to call you."

A deep frown darkened Chris's face. "Why did you do that?"

Tito shrugged his shoulder. "I just did. I know you were digging her. What harm could it cause to hit that one more time?"

"I don't need that drama."

"All right, whatever you say. What are you doing this weekend?"

"I'm going down to Atlanta."

"Yo' ass don't never sit still. What's down there?"

"I'm taking a friend to show her a good time." Chris beamed at the thought of spending time with Dana.

"Ah," Tito said as he bobbed his head up and down. "That's why you don't want nothing to do with old Rosie. I see how you're playing it. I'm not even mad at you."

"It's not like that. I'm done playing games with women. This woman is somebody that's fun to chill with. We're not going to be together like that." *Not right now anyway,* he added silently.

"So, you're going to hit it and quit it?" Tito probed.

Chris frowned. "How about you stop flapping your gums and put the shovel to work?"

Tito threw his hands up. "We all got to be a dog sometime. I know Rosie messed with your head. You deserve this."

Chris started to deck Tito and he would have if he weren't right. And here he was in the same situation again. Dana wasn't his woman. She could easily turn her back on him and go back to Andre. *Maybe this trip is a bad idea.* He wiped sweat from his brow with the back of his gloved hand. Then Chris remembered how much fun he'd had just sitting in his apartment with Dana. *I'm just going to let it flow. Dana isn't Rosalyn and I can't judge her because of what Rosalyn did.*

Chris and his men took a lunch break around noon. While the men ate, Chris went into the house to talk to Mr. D'Matto.

"Sir," Chris said when he saw the man had company.

"Oh, Chris, come on in," the round bodied man said. Joe D'Matto was shaped like a brown walrus. "Frank, when you and Denise need some landscaping work done, call Jones's Pool and Landscaping. Chris and his crew are excellent. You know Charles Jones, don't ya?"

Frank Ellison nodded. Chris looked at Frank. He'd seen him some place before, but he couldn't put his finger on it. He decided to let it go. He was there to talk to Joe, not Frank.

"Mr. D'Matto, the manufacturer said it's going to be a few more weeks before the pool you ordered is available to be shipped. What we're doing out here is the backfill. That way, when the pool gets here, all of the soil will be settled and you won't have to worry about your pool settling after it's installed."

Joe smiled. "See what I'm saying, Frank. This man does good work. Thank you, Chris."

"We're going to cover the hole with a tarp, but please keep kids and animals away from the backyard," Chris advised.

Joe nodded. Frank looked at Chris.

"Young man, have we met before?" Frank asked.

Chris shook his head. "I don't think so. Could I have done some work for you?"

Frank rubbed his chin. "No, I haven't had any work done to my house in a while. As a matter of fact, my wife has been bugging me about our yard. She wants some shrubs planted or something like that. You know how women are. Why don't you come take a look next week?"

"Sure," Chris said. He was happy for the business. "Give me your name and address and I'll be glad to come out."

"Joe, get me a piece of paper," Frank said, still looking at Chris. "Now I know where I saw you. You did some work at the house of my daughter's fiancé. That was an outstanding job. Dana and Andre's reception is going to look great back there."

*What in the hell is her father talking about? She said she gave the ring back.*

"Yeah, yeah, Andre Harrington," Chris said. *I fell for it again. Damn it, Dana! I thought you were different. You just want a little fling before getting married, huh? Well, that's what you're going to get!*

Joe returned to the den with a sheet of paper from a legal pad and a pen. Frank wrote down his information and handed it to Chris.

"I look forward to seeing you," Frank said.

"Thank you, sir."

Chris walked out of the house, the blood in his veins boiling.

Dana was trying to play him for a fool. She'd just taken the ring off for show, and there he was, acting like a gentleman with her, spending money that he needed for things other than movies and pizza. He'd even cooked for her. As bile rushed up to his throat, Chris spat on the ground.

"Yo, you a'ight?" Tito asked when he saw the scowl on Chris's face.

Chris didn't answer. He just grabbed his shovel and started digging. Dana had some explaining to do.

⸙

Dana was about to end her day when she heard the sound of high heels clicking on linoleum. She was hoping it was a passing teacher heading out for the weekend, but when she looked up it was into her mother's face. Dana didn't acknowledge her. She continued to stuff her grade book and spelling tests into her briefcase.

Denise closed the door. "We need to talk," she said.

Dana looked at her mother, but didn't say a word. What could she say to the woman who criticized everything she did or said? For the first time in her life, she wished she were an orphan.

"Dana, I was wrong to hit you. But you were being disrespectful," Denise continued.

Dana stood up. "I have to go, I have plans."

"With Andre?" Denise's face lit up with hope.

"No."

"Dana, what's going on? This isn't like you at all," she said. "You used to—"

"Do everything you said. I treated your word like it was God's truth. But you know what, those days are over. This is my life and it's time for me to start living it."

Denise sighed. "You're breaking your father's heart. I couldn't even tell him that you gave Andre the ring back. He wants this life for you and so do I. You've never had to struggle for anything, Dana. If you leave this job, you will struggle. We're not going to help you if things don't work out. You want to play it this way, then fine, but you will do it without our help."

Dana looked at her mother. "You want me to fail, don't you? You want me to just make a big fool of myself so that you can say I told you so."

"No mother wants to see her child fail, Dana. Maybe this is our fault. Maybe we should have let you cook more as a child. You could've gotten it out of your system by now."

Dana looked at her mother and shook her head. She didn't get it at all. "Even your apology is condescending," Dana snapped. "I'm leaving."

She walked out of the classroom, leaving her mother standing in the middle of the floor with her mouth wide open.

Dana drove home, trying not to think about Denise. She had other things to think about, like her trip to Atlanta with Chris. When she got home, she rushed into the house and began packing. She opened the closet and looked for something special to wear. She was drawn to those red leather pants again.

*He's seen me in those,* she thought as she flipped through her clothes. Everything looked like something a teacher would wear—long skirts, turtleneck sweaters and holiday theme vests.

Nothing was right, except those leather pants. Dana took them out of the closet and laid them on the bed. Then she grabbed a black v-necked body suit. Before she could finish pulling her outfit together, the doorbell rang.

Dana rushed to the door and was surprised to see Chris standing there. "Hey," she said.

"I can't make it this weekend."

"What happened?"

"Dana, why would we go all the way to Atlanta when we can do what you want right here."

She was confused and it was written all over her face. "Chris, what are you talking about? This was your idea anyway."

He nodded. "You're right, but that was before I found out who you really are."

"Chris, what are you talking about?"

"I saw your father today."

"My father? What does my father have to do with anything?"

"Seems like he's still planning a wedding for you and Andre."

"My father doesn't—"

"Don't bother explaining," Chris said as he walked in without being invited. "I've been here before."

"What?"

"Women like you who pretend that they are something that they're not. That's what you did. You made it seem as if you were this nice, wholesome girl who was taking her life back. You're full of it."

"Chris, you're out of line. Get the hell out of my house."

"You sho? I mean, don't you want to get your boots knocked by this thug? 'Cause I know that's what you think I am."

Dana glared at him. "You know what, you're the one who misrepresented himself. I thought you were different. But you're not. Please leave my house before I call the police."

Chris sucked his teeth and walked out the door. Dana slammed the wooden door behind him and dropped her head into her hands. How had everything gone so wrong, so fast? Dana thought about calling Andre, but what would that accomplish? She still didn't love him. *Girl, snap out of it. You knew him only a few days, even if it did feel like a lifetime.* Dana walked into her bedroom and hung her pants back in the rear of her closet. She sat on the edge of the bed, totally dumbfounded by Chris's

180-turn. *At least I found out now.* She picked up the phone to call Zariah.

"What's going on, Dana?" her friend said when she answered the phone.

"Let's go out tonight," she said.

"What?"

"I want to go to the club."

"All right, I'm down with it. I'm off for the next three days."

"Cool beans, Nurse Z! So meet me at my place at 9:30," Dana said.

"Okay."

Dana was going to dance her cares away and not think about Dr. Jekyll and Mr. Chris.

∞⌘∞

It was 10 p.m. before Zariah made it to Dana's. "Late as usual," Dana said when she opened the door.

"Girl, it takes time to look this good," Zariah replied as she whirled around. Dana checked out her friend in her skin-tight black Gucci cat suit and four inch stiletto heel boots. Zariah was about five foot-two, and she always wore high heels. She had a skin tone that looked like creamy caramel. Her hair was cut in a short pixie style. All she had to do was run her fingers though it and she was ready to go. That's why Dana didn't understand why she was always late.

"I like your outfit. Leather pants, I'm impressed," Zariah noted.

"Well, all of us can't be a size four like some people."

"Child, please," Zariah said as she touched her small waist. "I wish I had hips like yours. And don't start with the Jane Fonda-

I'm-so-fat-bull. You're beautiful."

"I know, but losing five pounds wouldn't hurt me," Dana said as she tugged at the tail of her red leather jacket.

"Uh, whatever. If J-Lo can make money from having a big ass, why do sisters complain that their ass is too big? Don't get me started, Ms. Size 12. I mean, if you were wearing a size 48 or something, I'd hook you up with the gastro surgeon at the hospital."

Dana laughed. "Let's go before the line at Dynasty gets too long." She led her through the door.

"Okay. So why are we going to club again? I mean, what is this new attitude?"

"Get in the car and I'll tell you all about it," Dana said as she unlocked the doors.

Zariah slid into the passenger seat. "This is about that man you went out with the other night, isn't it?"

"He's a jackass, but I will give him credit for one thing. He opened my eyes to the life I should be living."

"I've been trying to do that for years," Zariah said.

"Yeah, uh-huh, I know. But he showed it to me. It was so liberating."

"And what else did he show you?"

"That he's a jerk. We were supposed to go to Atlanta this weekend."

"He stood you up?"

"No. He came over, but it wasn't pretty. He ran into my father or something and he got the impression that Andre and I are still getting married."

"Y'all aren't?"

"No," she said, throwing her left hand up.

"Wow, you gave the ring back?"

"I sure did," Dana said, "and it felt like I had gotten out of jail."

"Well, I'm so surprised. I'm sure he went straight to Denise when you gave him that rock back."

Dana nodded, but she didn't say anything else. The last thing she wanted was to discuss her mother. Zariah let it drop and turned the radio on. Rap sensation 50 Cent's "In the Club" began blaring though the speakers.

Zariah nodded her head and snapped to the beat. "I'm chilling in the club, da da da," she sang off key and butchered the lyrics.

"Shut up!" Dana said.

"Girl, get used to it. This is going to be all you hear tonight."

"Then I should turn this car around. I don't want to hear Silver Dollar hollering all night."

"It's Fifty Cent and this is a club banger."

Dana rolled her eyes. "What happened to the clubs where you listened to smooth jazz and R&B?"

"They went out of business because lames like you only go out when they are pissed at the world."

Dana rolled her eyes. "Whatever," she said.

"You know it's true. You usually spend your weekends in the kitchen with flour up to your elbows."

"That's what I'll do tomorrow. Tonight, I'm going to party like it's 1999."

Zariah shook her head. "Don't say that in front of anybody else, okay."

When they pulled up to the nightclub, the line was wrapped around the block. Friday nights at Dynasty brought out everybody who had toiled away during the week in jobs they hated, loved or were indifferent to. Some of the partiers were dressed in clothes that were more suited for a hot summer night or the inside of a bedroom, while others in long dresses and three piece suits looked as if they were going to church. Dana started to feel comfortable in her ensemble. When she started getting the stares from the men in the line, she felt more than comfortable. She felt good. If she saw one of them inside, she might dance with him. It was going to be a good night, despite the way the afternoon had ended.

⚜

Chris and Tito walked up to the door of Dynasty. "Chris," Johnny, the bouncer, said. "What's up, my brother?"

"I know we don't have to stand in this long line," Chris replied. He shook hands with his old friend.

"Nah, but you might want to. Look at the honeys here tonight."

Chris glanced at the line. Then red caught his eye. *Is that Dana?* he wondered. He noticed the legs. It was. *I guess she's out with her man tonight.*

"You see baby girl in the red?" Tito said. "Thick and fine. Damn! Her friend don't look too bad, but she's kind of skinny for me."

Chris looked away from Dana and her friend. He hoped she didn't see him as he and Tito slipped inside. They took up residency at the bar but Chris kept a close eye on the door, waiting for Dana to walk in. What was he going to say? What could he say? His insecurities about Rosalyn made him make an ass of himself. Dana didn't deserve what he'd said and he knew it.

"Man," Tito said as he watched the bevy of women parading around the club. "Why are we sitting here like broke down busters?"

Chris waved for the bartender, then turned to Tito. "I'm not holding you up. Do what you want to do."

"I'm out. Let me see which one of these honeys want to shake it fast for me."

Chris turned to the bartender and ordered a Bud Light. When the man handed him his beer, he turned around and faced the door. Dana still hadn't walked in. Chris had time to form an apology in his mind.

*I was out of line,* he thought. *I should have never snapped at her like that. She doesn't owe me a thing and she isn't Rosalyn.*

What would Dana say if he walked up to her? Would she flip him off or throw a drink in his face? If she were still going to marry Andre, then she would be with him and not out on the town with her girlfriend.

*I hope I didn't blow my chances with her,* he thought as he watched Dana and Zariah walk in.

Dana had taken off her jacket, revealing a provocative black shirt with a neckline that dipped down so low, he could see the valley between her breasts. Chris couldn't take his eyes off her. He watched her and Zariah settle at a table in the corner of the club. Chris waved for the bartender again.

"Another beer, bro?" he asked.

"Nah, I need a Shirley Temple."

"A what?"

"Shirley Temple, Sprite and grenadine," he explained.

The bartender nodded. "And put a lot of cherries in it," Chris said.

"All right." He looked at Chris with a puzzled expression on his face. He handed Chris the drink with six cherries in the bottom of the glass.

"Thanks." He handed the bartender a $10 bill. "Keep the change."

Chris stood up and walked over to the table where Dana was sitting. When he got there, she was dismissing a guy who had been pestering her for a spin on the dance floor. Chris froze in place. Zariah looked at him.

"Dana, there's a guy staring at us."

Dana turned around and caught Chris's gaze.

"Hey, Ms. Lady," he said. "I bought you a drink. Shirley Temple."

Dana looked at him. "You have some nerve." Icicles hung from her words and pricked Chris's heart.

Zariah looked from Dana to Chris. "You two know each other?" she asked.

Dana nodded. Chris set the drink on the table. "I was wrong," he said in a near whisper. "I'm sorry."

"I agree on that. You are sorry."

Chris smiled regretfully. "I deserve that. But can you give me a chance to throw myself on your mercy?"

Zariah nudged Dana and quietly pleaded with her to hear Chris out. Dana rolled her eyes, but Chris sat down anyway.

"Dana," he said.

She looked at him and sighed. "What?"

"Let me talk to you. Come outside with me."

"It's a little cold out there."

Zariah stood up. "I'm going to dance."

"Subtle," Dana said. "Very subtle."

Zariah smiled as she skipped off to the middle of the dance floor. Dana turned to Chris.

"What do you have to say to me that you haven't already said?" she snapped.

The sound of 50 Cent's "In Da Club" began blaring and the club erupted in a chorus of "that's my song!" Dana couldn't hear a word Chris was saying and he stopped talking.

"I'll give you my jacket!" he yelled.

"What?"

"My jacket! Walk outside with me!"

Dana nodded and stood up. Chris wrapped his brown leather bomber jacket around her shoulders and they headed outside.

"Dana," he said. "When I saw you earlier today, I was totally out of line and wrong."

"Yes, you were. I never thought of you as a thug or—"

"Let me finish, please," he said, fighting the urge to kiss her. "You told me it was over with Andre and I need to take your word for it. You don't owe me anything."

"Chris, it is over with me and Andre. My father doesn't know because I haven't told him. Why would you think I would lie to you about that?"

"Because I've been here before. I was in a relationship, in love actually, but I found out she was married."

Dana touched his shoulder. "I'm sorry," she said. "I didn't know."

Chris smiled bitterly. "It seems that I have a thing for women who belong to other men."

"I don't belong to anyone."

Unable to control himself any longer, Chris pulled Dana into his arms and kissed her gently on the lips.

"Do you forgive me?" he asked when they parted.

"You owe me now," she ribbed.

"Let me start paying my debt," he said.

"How?"

"First, we're going to go inside and dance. Then, I'm taking you and your friend out for breakfast."

Dana smiled. "You're still not off the hook."

Chris grabbed her hand and led her inside. "All right, Ms. Lady."

# CHAPTER EIGHT

Chris held Dana close on every song. It didn't matter if it was an up tempo reggae song or a slow R&B jam. She didn't protest either. Standing close to him and smelling his intoxicating Tommy cologne lulled her into a comfort zone. Dana buried her face in his chest as the DJ played R. Kelly's "Slow Dance" to wind the party down.

Chris's hands roamed up and down Dana's back. He couldn't hide his throbbing desire from her this time. Dana held on to Chris's back, enjoying the feel of his hardness against her thighs. Zariah walked over to the couple and tapped Dana on the shoulder.

"I hate to be the party pooper, but I'm ready to go," she said.

"Oh, okay," Dana said as she and Chris parted.

"Do you want to join us for breakfast?" he asked.

"No thanks, I'm way too tired," Zariah replied. "But you two have a great time."

"I'll drop you off," Dana said.

"Or," Zariah said. "Since my car is at your house, why don't you ride with—"

"Chris," he said and extended his hand to her.

Zariah shook his hand. "I'm Zariah."

Dana took her keys out of her pocket and took her house key off the ring. "Leave my keys in the mailbox."

"All right. You two have fun, okay? But not too much."

When Chris looked away, Zariah flashed Dana the thumbs up sign. Chris turned around to catch Zariah walking out of the club with a smile on her face.

"Why do I feel like I just missed something?" he asked.

Dana shook her head, linked arms with Chris, and they headed out to his car. He started driving toward IHOP. He knew Dana could have easily whipped up a breakfast that would have tasted better than the processed food they were about to eat, but if he were alone with her in his house, he wouldn't allow her to leave. He'd lock her up in passion and hold her prisoner until the police came looking for her.

They walked into the restaurant and waited for the hostess to seat them. IHOP was filled with drunken partiers, loud college students and second shift workers having midnight dinners.

Chris and Dana sat down on the vinyl bench and waited for a table in the non-smoking section.

"I'm glad we ran into each other tonight," Chris said. "I thought I'd blown it with you."

"You had. But, luckily for you, I'm a forgiving person."

Chris kissed her hand. "I was wrong, but when I saw your father and he was still talking about your wedding, I was just taken back to my so-called relationship with Rosalyn. I thought you were trying to make a fool of me. So I wanted to beat you to the punch. It was childish."

"It really was," she agreed.

"Come on, I feel bad enough."

"As you should. But I'm going to leave you alone about it," she said as she gently rubbed his arm. "Everybody's entitled to one mistake. This was yours."

Chris grabbed her hand and looked into her eyes. "You see—"

"Johnson, party of two," the hostess called out. Chris and Dana stood up and followed her to a table in the corner.

"So," she said once the hostess left the table, "what happened with this Rosalyn person?"

Chris sighed and started telling Dana the story of Rosalyn and her husband. Dana reached out and stroked his hand. "So, you see what I mean when I say I have a thing for other men's women? It just happens like that," he said softly.

"You're saying you have a thing for me?" Dana asked.

"Maybe. I know I like your style and I want to get to know you."

"Me too," she admitted.

"Let's just move slowly," he said. "You're just hopping out of an engagement and if there is something here, let's make sure it's real. I have to be sure there are no husbands in the closet."

"Well, my mother would love me to have a husband in the closet. But I don't," she said with a terse laugh.

"Good. So what are you doing tomorrow? Maybe we can hang out."

"I'm baking tomorrow. I have to send my samples to Capitol City on Monday."

"I'm excited for you. They are going to love it."

"Why don't you come over and be my official taster. I'll even cook some chicken and shrimp stir fry to go along with the desserts."

"You sure I won't be a distraction?"

Dana shook her head. "Besides, I would enjoy the company."

"All right, it's a date," Chris replied with a smile.

The waitress came over to take their orders. Dana stared into Chris's big brown eyes as he talked to the waitress. She saw the kind of warmth in them that she'd never seen in Andre's eyes. She yearned for Chris's kiss and began to fantasize about the first time they would make love. With effort, she put the brakes on her sexy thoughts. It was a good idea for them to take things slowly. Everything about Dana's relationship with Andre had been rushed, except the breakup. That had been long overdue.

Chris turned to Dana and smiled. "Who knows that you're a single woman now? I would hate for one of Andre's friends to see us together and get the wrong idea."

"His best friend knows that it's over and she was crushed."

"She?"

"My mother."

"What did she say when you told her you gave the ring back?"

"She was pretty upset," Dana said, leaving out the part about Denise slapping her.

"Your father wants me to do some work at their house."

"Really?"

"Yeah, I'm going over there next week to check out what he wants done."

"Charge them double, they can afford it."

Chris laughed, but Dana was serious. She didn't crack a smile.

The waitress brought their food over and set it on the table. "Can I get you two anything else?"

"We're fine," Chris said.

She walked away and Chris turned to Dana. "What time are you going to start cooking in the morning?"

She shrugged her shoulders. "Maybe around 10 or so."

"I'd better get you home then. You don't need to cook tired. You'll be dumping salt in your cake batter instead of sugar," he said.

Dana smiled. "Chris, you barely know me and you've been more supportive about this than my parents or Andre."

"I don't understand why they don't want you to do this."

"Neither do I and I'm not going to try to understand it anymore." Dana picked up her orange juice.

"Don't forget about me when you become a famous pastry chef down in New Orleans."

Dana smiled. *I could never forget about you, even if I tried.*

After they finished eating, Chris and Dana walked outside to his truck. The wind had picked up, sending a chill down Dana's spine.

"Cold?" he asked.

"Yes." She zipped her jacket up to her neck and flipped her collar up over her ears. They slid into the truck and Chris cranked it up.

"We can just sit here until it warms up in here," he said, turning the heat on full blast.

"This is going to be a cold winter," she said.

"What's wrong with that? Maybe it will snow here for a change."

"Ugh, I hope not."

"You know Carolina snow is beautiful," he said. "It doesn't last long and we all get the day off."

Dana laughed. "That's true." She placed her hands in front of the vents to warm them up.

Chris looked at her and smiled. "Warm yet?" he asked.

"Yeah, thanks."

"All right, let's get you home so you can get some sleep before the big cooking event."

"You make it sound like I'm in the baking Olympics or something," she said with a laugh.

"You might as well be," he replied. "Consider me your coach." Chris turned the ignition off. "Let me walk you to the door."

"I can make it, but thanks," she said. Dana looked down at her watch. If she invited Chris in, it would look just like a booty call.

"I'll wait here until you get inside," he said. "I'll see you around two."

She turned around and waved to Chris as she opened the

door.

❧

Chris waited until Dana was safely inside before he backed out of the driveway. As he drove, Chris imagined Dana walking into her bedroom and stripping out of her clothes. He could see her standing in the middle of the floor in a pair of lace panties and matching bra. Chris shook his head so that he could focus on the road. He knew when he got home, he was going to have visions of Dana dancing in his head.

As Chris turned into the parking lot of his complex, he noticed Rosalyn's car parked near his building. He shrugged it off, figuring she had found another fool to be her toy. He parked his truck two cars down from hers, then headed up to his apartment.

"Chris," Rosalyn called out. Chris kept walking. Rosalyn got out of the car and ran to catch up with him. "Chris, please," she pleaded.

"What in the hell are you doing here?" he demanded hotly.

"Waiting for you."

"Don't you have a husband that you need to be home with?"

"Chris, I got a divorce."

"Good for you. Excuse me." He pushed her aside and headed up the stairs.

"Chris, I love you and I know you love me too."

"That's the past. How can I be with a woman that would lie to her husband to be with me?"

"That just shows you how much I care about you," she said, attempting to grab Chris's arm. He snatched away from her.

"Rosalyn, go home. I don't want anything to do with you."

"Chris, we had something special. I thought you loved me."

"Past tense. I don't have time for this." He bounded up the stairs and closed the door. He didn't know or care if Rosalyn was going to leave or sit in her car all night. He just knew he wasn't going to walk into her web again.

*Once bitten, twice shy,* he thought as he dropped down on the sofa.

# CHAPTER NINE

Dana was inside her house for about five minutes before the phone rang. She knew exactly who it was.

"Yes, Zariah."

"D, are you alone?" Zariah asked.

"What kind of question is that? Of course I am."

"Why? As fine as that man is, I'd have him sitting right beside me."

"Goodbye, Zariah!" Dana hung up with a smile on her face. She wished Chris were there.

The phone rang again. "Look, Zariah—"

"It's not Zariah," Andre said.

"What do you want?"

"I've been calling you all night. Where have you been?"

"Out."

"Dana, I still want to marry you, but I know you need time to do this baking thing."

"Andre, it's late and I don't have time for this. Goodbye."

"Why don't we meet tomorrow and have breakfast? We can talk about this rationally."

"There's nothing for us to talk about," she said. "Andre, we're over."

"Your mother said—"

"I don't give a damn what my mother said. This is my life, Andre, mine."

"I thought I was going to be a part of that life. Dana, I love you. How did everything go so wrong?"

"We were never meant to be together. My mother thought

you were the man of my dreams but I never felt that way," she said.

"But what about all of the times we made love and—"

"I have to go. This isn't getting us anywhere."

"Dana, I'm not giving up on us."

"I have." She hung up the phone and walked upstairs to her bedroom.

The next morning, Dana woke up and headed downstairs to the kitchen to start baking. She took the flour out of the refrigerator, then grabbed the brown sugar, baking powder, and three blocks of semi-sweet chocolate. But when she opened the cabinet above the stove she discovered she was out of rum.

"Damn," she muttered. The liquor store didn't open until noon. She walked over to the oven and opened the drawer, pulling out pans and her rolling pin. She decided to make raspberry truffles first. Time got away from Dana as she cooked and she was lost in rolling the chocolate into balls when the doorbell rang. She looked down at her chocolate-stained tee shirt and baggy gray shorts. *That's Chris. I'll probably scare him away looking like this,* she thought as she walked to the door.

"Hey you," he said.

"Chris, come in."

"You look as if you've been working hard."

Dana blushed. "I look a mess, I know."

"I didn't say that."

"Come on in the kitchen and try my truffles," she said, grabbing his hand.

Chris took a seat at the bar. "It smells fattening in here."

"It is. That's why I'm glad you're tasting, and not me."

"I see how you are. You want to keep your cute little shape and have me walking around with an oversized gut."

Dana smiled. Her mother was always on her about losing five or 10 pounds, but Chris seemed to like her womanly shape. "Remember, you did volunteer for this, coach."

"I know, I know."

"And you look like you keep yourself in good shape. Besides, I know how you could burn the calories off."

Chris smiled wilily. "And how is that?"

"You could go to the liquor store and pick me up some Bacardi Dark." She handed him a cooled truffle.

Chris bit into the candy, then closed his eyes as the chocolate melted on his tongue. "This is great."

"I'm glad you like it."

"Bacardi Dark?"

She nodded and reached into the utility drawer to hand him $10. Chris took the bill and laid it on the counter. Dana rolled her eyes. "Chris, take the money."

"Dana, I'm going to eat more than $10 worth of your food. I can buy the rum."

She waved her hands. "Whatever."

Chris winked at her, then headed out the door.

When Chris left, Dana started making her famous seven-layer German chocolate cake. As she cooked, she thought about what the bakery would say about her samples. What if she weren't as good as she thought she was? *If they don't like my food, my mother would be thrilled. That would just make her day.*

Dana stirred her cake batter furiously. She was determined to make a go of things, just to prove Denise, Andre and Frank wrong.

The phone rang as she was pouring the batter into the pans. She set the bowl on the counter and picked up the phone.

"Yes?"

"Dana, it's Dad."

"Hey, Daddy, I really can't talk now."

"Sweetheart, we have to. I spoke with your mother. She told me that you two are having some issues and that you want to quit your job."

Dana sighed. "Do we have to rehash this?"

"What does Andre think about this?"

"I didn't realize I had to clear my life through Andre or you and mom."

"The attitude is not appreciated. You've worked hard to become a teacher. I don't want you to give it up because you're angry."

"I'm busy."

"Dana, you're making a big mistake. Why are you throwing your life away?"

"How am I doing that? Dad, this is something that I want to do and I'm going to do it."

"What about your career?"

"I don't want this career. Teaching has always been your dream for me."

"I want you to have a good life, Dana. All parents want that for their children. What is this baking going to get you? Nothing, Dana, nothing."

"How do you know that? Everyone tells me I have talent. That is, everyone except the people who are supposed to love me. I don't feel like having this argument."

"Please don't do this. You are just budding in your career—"

"I'm hanging up now," Dana said.

"Your mother and I want you to come over for dinner tonight."

"I'll try," she said.

"Dana, please, I don't like this tension between us."

"All right," she said, thinking the quicker she agreed, the faster she could get off the phone.

"Good, we'll see you at six?"

"Sure," she replied with a sigh.

"Great, and bring one of your cakes if you want to," he said.

"Fine. Now I have to go." Dana hung up, then put her pans in the oven.

A few minutes later, Chris was knocking on the door. "It's open," Dana called out.

Chris walked in and handed her a pint of rum. "I hope this is enough."

"It's more than enough. Thanks. I have a cake in the oven, so walk softly."

"All right. What kind of cake is it?"

"My signature, a seven-layer German chocolate cake."

Chris rubbed his stomach. "I can't wait for that one."

Dana smiled as she mixed the ingredients for the icing. "My father called. He wants me to come over for dinner."

"Are you going?"

She shrugged. "I said I would. But I don't feel like being lectured to."

"Don't go then."

"I wish it were that easy. If I don't go, they'll come here."

"Then they will be on your turf and you can put them out."

Dana smiled. "You have all of the answers don't you?"

"It's simple when you look at it. Parents meddle. It's in their handbook."

"Where are your parents?" Dana asked.

Chris cleared his throat. "Florida. They retired last year and moved to Boca Raton."

"Do you visit them a lot?"

Chris shook his head. "Not really. We're not a close-knit family. My uncle and I are closer than my parents and me. I see them on holidays, every other year."

Dana nodded. "Did they try to run your life?"

"No. As a matter of fact, it would have been nice to know that they cared."

"Sometimes they can care too much."

Chris stuck his finger in the bowl of icing. Dana glared at him. "You know I couldn't resist," he said as he licked the icing off his finger. "What do you need rum for?"

"Chocolate rum brownies."

"That sounds like some serious eating right there."

Dana smiled. "They're a hit at parties."

Chris nodded and smiled.

Dana walked over to the oven and took the cake layers out to let them cool. She took the frosting and put it out of Chris's reach on top of the toaster.

"Why do you have to act like that?" he asked jokingly.

"If I don't watch you, there won't be any left for the cake."

Chris smiled. "I'll be good."

Dana started pulling out chocolate she needed for the brownies. "Damn, no eggs," she said.

"Do you want me to go to the store and get some?"

She shook her head. "I have some egg substitute in the freezer."

"You have it covered, don't you?"

"Just about," she said.

When their eyes met, Chris got up from the bar and stepped close. He stroked her cheek, wiping a spot of flour away, his touch sending electric jolts down her spine. Then he kissed her urgently. When she wantonly slid her tongue into his mouth, he wrapped his arms around her waist and lifted her up on the marble counter. Suddenly he took a step back. "Are you sure you want to do this?"

Dana nodded, then ripped his shirt open, exposing his rippling chest. As she ran her palm over his muscles, Chris grabbed her hand, brought it to his lips and gently kissed it before pulling her tee shirt over her head. Dana attempted to cover her upper body with her arms because she didn't want Chris to see the extra flesh hanging over the waistband of her shorts. But he pulled her arms away.

"Baby, you're beautiful," he said. "Just like I imagined."

Dana flushed. Chris wrapped her arms around his neck and kissed her chin, then slowly made a path to her lips with the tip of his tongue. An empty mixing bowl crashed to the floor but neither of them noticed as Dana slipped her hand inside Chris's slacks, stroking his most sensitive muscle, making him harder and longer with every tender touch. Chris threw his head back as Dana's hands began to work faster and harder. Another bowl crashed to the floor, this one filled with flour. The white powder settled on top of them. It didn't stop their passion. Chris pulled Dana's shorts off, then gently pushed her back on the countertop and slid her lace panties off. Dana shivered with excitement as he stroked her inner thigh. Anticipation made her hot and moist.

Chris smiled as Dana closed her eyes. He was in total control and he loved the way she reacted to his touch. When he placed his hand on top of her mound of feminine sexuality, she moaned deeply. Slowly, he entered her with his forefinger and middle finger, gently tickling her clitoris.

Dana closed her eyes, feeling herself lose control. This wasn't her, this wasn't what she had been taught to do.

"Look at me," Chris commanded softly. "Look in my eyes."

Dana opened her eyes and locked them with Chris's. With his fingers still stroking her, Chris reached over to the right for the bowl of frosting. He dipped his hand inside and smoothed a layer of the brown goo across her stomach. Then he licked every enticing bit off.

"You taste so good," he said before kissing down her thighs

and entering her with his tongue. Dana wrapped her legs around his neck, pulling him closer into her hot, wet sexuality. She tasted like honey and Chris hungrily lapped up her nectar.

Dana hadn't noticed that Chris had peeled off his jeans until she felt his burning skin against hers as he pulled her off the countertop. For a split second, they stared into each other's eyes. If either of them wanted to back out, this was the moment. Dana ignored the little voice in the back of her head telling her that she was moving too fast. That voice sounded too much like Denise's. When Chris leaned forward to kiss her lips softly, Dana returned his kiss with a hard, soul-scorching one. She pressed her hips into his, causing his already throbbing manhood to stand at attention. They stumbled into the living room and hastily fell into an armchair.

Dana climbed on top of Chris, digging her knees into the sides of the chair.

Chris gripped her hips, thrusting himself inside of her and she grasped his shoulders, pulling him deeper and deeper into her. He buried his face in her taut breasts, muffling his screams of passion as she rode him, fast, then slow, then faster. Dana was like a wild woman, tightening herself around him. With Dana wrapped around him, Chris eased their party down to her carpeted floor, positioning her on her back. He spread her legs apart and dove deeper. Dana clutched his back and howled out as the orgasmic waves began. Chris thrust on. He wanted to make sure she was satisfied. He ground against her, touching her G-spot, making Dana lose all control. "Chris, Chris!" she exclaimed.

After Chris reached his own climax, they lay on the floor, covered in sweat and totally spent. With her legs still quivering, Dana looked up at Chris, who wore a satisfied smile on his face. She couldn't say anything, didn't really know what she should say or think.

After they lay on the floor a while longer, Dana cleared her throat. "I guess I need to get back in the kitchen."

"Sorry if I distracted you," he said with a smirk.

"I'll forgive you this time." Dana tried to sit up, but Chris wouldn't let her.

"Don't go."

Dana attempted to protest. After all, she still had a deadline to meet. Chris silenced her with a kiss. Then he pulled back and looked at her. "You know this changes everything."

"What do you mean?" Fear and dread tickled the back of her neck. She knew things had happened too fast. They had talked about moving slowly, but here they were in the middle of her living room, naked.

Chris seemed to read the fear in her eyes. "Dana, I don't do one-night stands."

She relaxed instantly, believing his affirmation.

"So," Chris continued, "I'm going to want to see you, a lot more. I'm probably going to steal you away on weekends. Get used to me, because I'm going to be around."

"Yeah, because now you owe me."

"I owe you?"

Dana nodded. "A bag of flour."

Chris grinned like a Cheshire cat. "All right, but you still have the longer IOU list, Ms. Lady."

Dana playfully hit him on the chest. "Whatever. Seriously, I do have to finish baking. As much as I want to lie here with you for the rest of the day, I can't."

"I understand. But give me five more minutes," he said, burying his head in her bosom.

Dana sighed. "All right, five minutes."

# CHAPTER TEN

It was an hour before Dana and Chris pulled themselves apart and individually showered. Chris exercised more self control than he thought humanly possible when Dana walked into the living room wrapped in a plush pink towel to tell him the shower was all his. He swallowed hard and stood up, willing himself not to rip the towel off her and make love to her again.

"Do you want me to throw your clothes in the wash?" she asked when he stepped into the bathroom. "You have flour all over your jeans."

"Sure," he called out.

She changed into a blue tee shirt dress and a pair of white slippers, then headed to the laundry room. Dana peeked into the kitchen on her way to the laundry room. Flour was everywhere, except on her perfectly browned cake layers. She breathed a sigh of relief and proceeded to the washer. When she returned to the kitchen, Chris was standing there in his boxers with beads of water glistening on his chest. Dana turned her head away.

"That was a quick shower," she said breathlessly.

"The water got cold, real quick."

"Ooh, I'm sorry. I must have caused that when I turned the washer on. I have a robe you can put on."

"No, thank you. It's probably pink and has flowers on it."

Dana squeezed his nose. "It's yellow with bumble bees on it."

Chris kissed her hand. "I'll pass. But you can do me a favor."

"What's that?"

"I have another set of clothes in the truck, shorts and a tee shirt. Will you get them for me?"

"Sure," she said as she picked his keys up off the counter.

"Hey," he said as she headed out the door. "Aren't you supposed to have dinner with your parents today?"

Dana shrugged her shoulders. "I haven't decided if I'm going or not."

"You should go. Let them know that you've made your decision. You're going to be a great chef one day."

Dana smiled, then walked out the door. Chris sat at the bar waiting for her to return with his clothes. He closed his eyes and thought about how passionately she made love. She blew his mind.

Returning, Dana handed Chris his clothes. "You can change in my bedroom."

Chris kissed her on the cheek. "All right," he said. "You get back to cooking."

"I am."

When he changed and returned to the kitchen, Dana was fully absorbed in icing her cake. He watched her as she worked. She was deep in concentration, not noticing Chris's intense stare. To him, she looked as if she belonged in the kitchen.

"Looks good," he said.

"Thanks," she replied without looking up.

Chris perched on a barstool. "Remember what I said the other day about you being a teacher?"

"Yeah."

"I was wrong. This is where you belong. I know a lot of people don't think a woman should be told she belongs in the kitchen, but you really like it here."

Dana nodded in agreement.

"Your parents should understand that," he said.

Dana rolled her eyes. "You don't know my parents."

"Maybe they need to taste that mouth-watering cake of yours."

Dana smiled. "It wouldn't make a difference." She covered the cake with the top of the cake plate.

"You never know until you try," he said.

Dana sighed as she started mixing the batter for the rum brownies. "I'm tired of trying."

Chris shrugged his shoulders. "I'm going to check on my clothes. Point me to the laundry room."

"Down the hall and to the right."

❧❀❧

While Chris was gone, Dana thought about what he'd said. She complained a lot about her parents not understanding her, but had she ever explained herself to them without arguing? *Maybe I'm not giving them the same consideration I want from them.*

"Dana," Chris said, breaking into her thoughts. "I'm going to head out. Call me after you have dinner with your folks."

She walked over and hugged him tightly. Chris kissed her on the tip of her nose.

"Make sure you save me a brownie," he said.

"I'll save you more than that," she said with a grin. She walked him to the door and watched him back out of the driveway. Her mind was filled with thoughts of him. She walked into the kitchen and started stirring her batter again. Once she started cooking, she pushed her thoughts of Chris out of her mind. After she finished her batch of brownies, everything would be set for Capitol City. Dana poured the brown batter into a pan, slid it into the oven, then picked up the phone and called her parents.

"Hello?" Denise said.

"Mom, it's me."

"What time are you coming over?"

"In about an hour. I have something in the oven."

"Okay. Well, we're having chicken and rice."

"Really?"

"This dinner is about you, Dana. I thought I would make your favorite."

"Thanks, I'll see you in a little bit."

Dana hung up and walked into her bedroom to change her clothes. She could smell Chris's cologne. She inhaled deeply and smiled. *I hope I didn't make a mistake today,* she thought as she pulled a black sweater dress out of the closet.

After the brownies were done, Dana got dressed and headed to her parents' house. She took half of the brownies with her as a peace offering. But the thought of peace flew out of the car window when she saw Andre's car parked in the driveway. *I don't believe this!*

Dana got out of the car and slammed the door. As she walked into the living room, Andre and her father looked at her guiltily as if she had been the topic of conversation. Dana placed her free hand on her hip. "I thought this was just going to be a family dinner," she said.

"Andre is practically family," Frank said as he stood up and kissed Dana on the cheek.

Dana fought back a sarcastic comment as she turned and headed for the kitchen where Denise was standing over the stove. Dana dropped her pan of brownies on the counter to announce her arrival.

"Mother, what's going on?" she demanded.

Her mother rolled her eyes, but kept silent. Andre walked into the kitchen seconds later, tugging at the collar of his blue Brooks Brothers shirt. "Dana, I didn't think you would mind me being here," he said.

"Andre, you've never cared about my feelings before. Why

would you start now?"

"Enough of this," Denise said. "Dana, we all need to talk."

"You know what, why don't the three of you have a good meal." Dana turned to walk out of the kitchen.

"Now hold on," Frank said. "You and Andre love each other. I'm sure whatever problems you two are having, you can work them out. Dana, you're just—"

"Don't stand there and tell me what I feel. I don't love Andre; you two love Andre." She pointed her finger for emphasis.

"Dana," Andre said.

"What? Didn't I make it clear to you that I wasn't going to marry you when I gave you your ring back? Andre, we were never good together. My mother handpicked you," Dana snapped.

"Dana, you're acting like a child," Denise exclaimed.

"I'm acting like a child? No, but you are all treating me like one. What is this supposed to be, an intervention or something?"

Andre shook his head. "You know, Mr. and Mrs. Ellison, I'm going to leave," he said.

"Don't bother, I'll go," Dana said.

Denise stood up and grabbed her daughter's arm. "Dana Janice Ellison, you aren't going anywhere. We need to have a serious discussion about you throwing your life away."

"It's my life and I'll do just what I want!" She snatched away from Denise and bolted from the house. Denise and Frank stared after their daughter with their mouths hanging open.

Andre ran out the door, catching up with Dana. "Hey," he said, grabbing her arm.

Dana turned around. "What?"

"I'm not going to keep humiliating myself for you."

"Then stop. Andre, we're over. Why don't you stop showing up at my parents' house and stop calling me. If you had half a brain you would see that a marriage between us would never work."

"But I love you."

"You love me? Andre, you don't love me. You're more comfortable with my parents than I am. Why don't you just be their friend?"

"Just be honest with me. Is there somebody else?"

Dana looked away from him.

Andre nodded. "So that's what it is. Who is he? A teacher at your school?"

"You don't need to worry about that. Just know it isn't you and nothing happened until I gave you your ring back."

"I give up, but you should apologize to your parents. You were rude and disrespectful."

"Don't talk to me like I'm some kid, Andre. I'm sick and tired of people trying to run my life, you included."

"Whatever, Dana." Andre headed back inside the house.

Dana walked over to her car and opened the door, then closed it. She did owe her parents an apology. She should have never spoken to them that way and that wasn't the reason she'd come to dinner. She slowly walked up the steps of the house.

When Dana returned to the kitchen, her mother was standing at the sink drinking a glass of wine.

"Mom," she said.

Denise turned around, setting her wine goblet on the counter. She shook her head at Dana.

"I'm sorry about the way I said what I did. But the message is the same. I'm not going to renew my contract at E.L. Wright. I'm going to bake. Andre and I aren't getting married now or ever. You can accept it or I'll be out of your life, too."

"Dana, Dana," she began. "You're making a big mistake."

"So what if I am? I've never taken a risk in my life. I've always done what was expected of me and what was easy. This is what I want to do. Why can't you see that? Have you ever tried any of my desserts?"

Dana looked down at the pan of brownies. She picked it up and pulled the foil back. "Taste this," she said.

Denise picked up one of the brownies and bit into it. Dana watched her mother's reaction. Denise chewed slowly.

"This is my mother's recipe," Denise whispered in between bites. "Rum brownies. She used to make them every Christmas."

"I know. She gave me all of her recipes before she died."

Denise finished the square, then wiped her hand on a dish-towel. "Anyone can read a recipe, Dana. You are a college-educated woman. You don't have to do this."

"I know, but it's what I want to do."

Denise shook her head. "I can't stand by and watch you throw your life away on a pipe dream. And your relationship with Andre—"

"Have you heard a word that I said? I'm trying to talk to you as an adult and you're still treating me like a child."

"You are my child. I'm not going to watch you flush your career and your relationship down the drain."

Dana shook her head and replaced the foil on her brownies. "Forget it, Mother. I'm going to do what I need to do, whether you support me or not."

Frank walked into the kitchen and looked at Denise and Dana. "Are we calmer now?"

"I'm out of here," Dana said.

"You can't keep running away!" Denise said.

"I'm not running. I hope you and Andre are happy with each other."

Dana walked out to her car and headed back to her house. When she was a block away from home, she pulled out her cell phone and called Zariah.

"Hello?"

"Z, what's up?"

"Nothing much. Have you gotten your stuff together?"

"Yes. As a matter of fact, I was wondering if I could take it over today."

"I think Josh is at the bakery today. Hold on, I'll call him on three way."

"Thanks."

"Capitol City Bakery."

"Hi, is Josh in?" Zariah asked.

"Hold on."

"Dana, are you here?" Zariah asked.

"Yeah, I'm here," she replied.

"This is Josh."

"Hey, it's Zariah."

"What's going on?"

"Remember the baker I was telling you about?"

"Andy or something, right?"

"Dana," Zariah corrected. "She's on the line too."

"Hi," Dana said.

"Hey, when am I going to get to sample the desserts your girl has been talking about?" he asked.

"If you're going to be around for a while, I can bring you some samples right now."

"Josh, you want to stick around," Zariah said. "Trust me on this."

"All right," he said. "Come by."

"Great," Dana said. "I'll be there in about 20 minutes."

"Cool."

"Bye Josh," Zariah said, clicking him off the line.

"Z, wish me luck."

"You don't need it. Make sure you bring me the leftovers."

"Bye, girl."

Dana pulled into her driveway, ran inside and loaded up her truffles, brownies and cake. She said a silent prayer as she put the desserts in the car and headed to the bakery. *God, please let him like these samples. Please don't let my mother be right. Don't let me fall on my face.*

❧❦❧

Chris looked at his watch as he sipped a beer. He wondered when Dana and her parents would finish dinner. He wanted and needed to see her again. It had been a long time since a woman stirred his soul the way Dana did. In fact, he didn't think any other woman had touched his heart so deeply. Chris closed his eyes and relived Dana's kiss on his lips, the feel of her hips pressed into his. The phone rang, breaking into his memories. "Yeah."

"Chris," Rosalyn said. "I miss you."

"Rosalyn, I'm not going there with you. Work on your marriage and leave me alone."

"I told you, I divorced Darren. You're the only man in my heart."

Chris sighed, but didn't reply.

"I love you," Rosalyn continued. "We belong together."

"Do you know what love is? Did you love your husband when you were sleeping with me?"

"I-I…"

"Do me a favor and lose my number." He hung up the phone.

Two seconds later the phone rang again. "What?"

"Hello to you too," Dana said.

"I didn't know it was you. I've been getting crank calls," he said.

"I need a word of encouragement. I'm on my way to Capitol City Bakery."

"What about the dinner with your parents?"

"I don't want to think about that ambush."

"What happened?"

"Let's just say my parents still have a problem letting me live my life."

"I'm sorry about that."

"Don't be. They got me mad enough to take my stuff to the bakery early. Now I'm shaking in my boots."

"I don't know why. They're going to fall in love with your food."

"Well, I'm here now. I have to go," she said.

"All right. Good luck and stop by here when you're done. I want to hear every detail about how they loved your food."

"Okay," she said, then hung up the phone.

Chris decided to surprise Dana with dinner and roses. He headed to Carrabba's Italian Restaurant and Grill and picked up two chicken Alfredo dinners and a bottle of white wine. On the way home, he stopped at the florist and picked up a dozen red and pink roses.

"She's going to love these," the clerk said.

"I hope she has something to celebrate after her meeting."

"These will make her feel better if things didn't go well." The clerk handed him a blank card with a straw hat and daisies on the front and a pen.

*To: Ms. Lady,*
*Congrats on a job well done. The Big Easy is next.*
*C-*

He handed the card to the clerk so she could stick it in the bouquet.

"Here you go," she said as she handed him the flowers.

Chris smiled as he took the flowers and headed out to his car. He drove back to his apartment, hoping he hadn't missed Dana's call.

He dashed in the front door and checked his voice mail. No

messages. Now all he had to do was wait.

# CHAPTER ELEVEN

Dana held her breath as Josh took a bite of the German chocolate cake. He hadn't said anything when he sampled the brownies. Dana knew he didn't like them. Her confidence was waning.

Josh nodded his head. "This is good. It's moist but not oily. Is this icing homemade?"

She nodded. Finally, she could exhale.

"I want that cake," he said, licking his lips. Josh waved for one of his clerks to come over. "Taste this."

"What is it?" she asked.

"A slice of heaven," he said. The woman took a small pinch of the cake. She ate it, then grabbed a bigger piece.

"Josh, did you make this?"

"No, she did." He nodded toward Dana. "Dana's going to be joining us on the weekends, for now anyway."

Dana's heart skipped a beat. She was on her way to making her dreams come true.

"We're adding the seven-layer German chocolate cake and Ellison rum brownies to the menu," he announced.

"Wow," Dana said.

"That's a better description for this food. I thought Zariah was just exaggerating, but she was right. I want you to come by Monday afternoon at four-thirty so we can iron out the details."

"I'll be here," Dana said as she reached for her tray of goodies.

"Uh," Josh said, grabbing her hand. "I'll wash this for you and have it ready Monday afternoon."

"They're that good?"

"Oh yeah. You're going to put this place on the map with those brownies."

Dana smiled proudly. Her mother, Andre and her father were wrong. She wasn't wasting her time.

Josh picked up a brownie and bit into it. "Tell Zariah I owe her one."

Dana waved goodbye and headed out, her excitement brimming. She hopped into her car and called Zariah.

"Z! He loved it," she said not bothering to say hello.

"As if there was any doubt. So what happens now?"

"Well, Monday, we're going to iron out the details, but get this. He already added the German chocolate cake and the brownies to the menu."

"Get out of here! Go Dana, it's your birthday."

"Don't start with that Silver Dollar crap."

"Now, you know it's 50 Cent. Anyway, when are you going to rub this in your parents' face?"

"I'm not rubbing anything. They can read it in the papers when Capitol City becomes the best thing since sliced bread in this town."

"I hear you, Ms. Girl!"

"Josh said he owes you."

"I know. He owes me from way back. But that's another story."

"What's up with you and Josh the baker? He's cute."

"We know each other from college. And there's nothing going on with us."

"I don't know, Z. He's your type, tall, chocolate, deep brown eyes—"

"It would never work, trust me."

"All right."

"So how are you going to celebrate?"

"I have to call Chris. He—"

"Speaking of the right type. That brother is seriously fine."

Dana smiled. "Yes, he is."

"So why are you talking to me?" Zariah asked.

"Good point. I'll call you tomorrow. Let's go have breakfast or something."

"If you can pull yourself away from Chris, sure."

"Bye, Zariah." Dana clicked the phone off and dialed Chris's number.

"Hello," his bass voice said.

"Chris, guess what."

"I don't have to guess, I know. They loved it and want you to take over."

"Well, not yet. But they did love everything."

"I have a surprise for you."

"Really?"

"Yep. Why don't you drive over here and get it."

"I'm on my way," she said.

Dana stepped on the gas and sped to Chris's house, disregarding the posted speed limits. She pulled into his complex, checked her makeup in the visor mirror, then touched up her boysenberry lipstick and got out of the car. At Chris's door, Dana took a deep breath, then knocked.

Chris opened the door and smiled. "Hey you," he said.

"Hi."

Chris handed her the flowers. "For you, Ms. Lady."

"Thank you," she said, then hugged him. "This is too much." Dana looked around the living room. The lights were low and two pillar candles flickered in the distance. John Coltrane's sax filled the air.

"Have you eaten?"

She mouthed no as she absorbed the scene.

"Good, I have chicken Alfredo."

"You cooked?"

"No, Carrabba's did."

"I love that place."

"Sit down, Ms. Lady. I'll bring you dinner."

Dana sat on the sofa. "Chris, I am so excited."

He handed her a plate. "This is your dream. You deserve it."

Dana accepted her plate. "I just have to get all the details from Josh and I'll be on my way."

"Did you read the card?"

Dana set her plate on the coffee table and picked up the flowers. She opened the card and smiled as she read it.

"The Big Easy is next, huh?"

Chris nodded. "It's only a matter of time. I can see you with your own show on the Food Network, filmed right in your kitchen."

Dana smiled. "We're getting ahead of ourselves."

"It never hurts to dream."

"What is your big dream?"

"I want to see the world. Then I can figure that out. Whatever I do, I want to be outside. I want to work the land."

"I never would have thought that, Mr. NYC."

"I'm a country boy at heart, you know," he said. "Besides, there's a lot of nature in New York, you just have to find it."

"I'm glad I found you," Dana revealed. "I feel like I've known you for years."

"Maybe we were meant to meet," Chris said.

"Fate?"

He nodded and smiled at her.

Dana wrapped her arms around Chris. "It won't change, will it?"

"Not if I have anything to say about it." Chris kissed Dana on the forehead. "You're stuck with me."

"You say it like it's a bad thing."

He kissed her on the tip of her nose. Dana traced the outline of his lips with her finger. She could love him. Chris kissed the tip of her finger.

"The food is getting cold," she said.

"I'm just getting warmed up." Chris wrapped his arms around Dana and pulled her close. He stroked her back gently and kissed her deeply. Dana closed her eyes and dove into his kiss. She was swimming in passion, ready to drown in its bliss. Chris reached for the tail of her dress and lifted it up to her stomach. He slid down her body, using his tongue as a guide. Dana stretched her arms above her head as Chris's tongue grazed her thighs. He pulled Dana's satin panties off with his teeth. Soft moans escaped her throat as Chris pressed his finger into her mound of sexuality. Then he replaced his finger with his tongue, pushing Dana closer and closer to the edge of an orgasm. She grabbed his back, digging her nails into his shirt. Chris continued his tongue-teasing, sucking and licking Dana's joy until she could take no more. She tried to push him away, but Chris grabbed her thighs and held on tight, savoring every drop of her nectar as it came down. Then he dropped his pants and climbed on top of Dana.

"You feel so good," he said as he pushed himself inside. "You feel so good."

Dana thrust her hips into his, clutching his back, pulling and him deeper and deeper into her. She wanted to feel every inch of him, every throbbing inch. Dana wrapped her legs around his waist, urging him to dig deeper.

She couldn't speak. She was in the middle of an orgasm, one more powerful than she had ever felt before. She hungrily kissed Chris, grinding her body against his. They tumbled to the floor and Dana straddled him. He sat up and took her breast in his mouth and nibbled. She threw her head back in ecstasy. Then he grabbed her hips and rocked her back and forth.

Sweat covered their bodies as they clung to each other, shaking from their powerful climax, each not wanting to let go of the other.

"Is this just a physical thing?" Dana finally asked.

"No, not at all," Chris replied, noting the look of concern on her face.

"This is just happening so fast," she said. "And I don't want you to think that this is all that I want from you."

Chris looked at Dana, remembering what he'd said to her when he thought she was going to marry Andre. "I know I said some messed up things to you earlier, but I didn't mean it."

"I know but—"

"Hey, we can slow down, it's not a problem."

"Okay," she said. Chris let her go and Dana stood up slowly. He turned his head away so he wouldn't be tempted to grab her soft, heart-shaped bottom.

"Do you want to take a shower?" he asked.

"Yeah. I know my way to the bathroom."

Chris watched her walk out of the room and willed himself to calm down. *She wants to take it slow and I've never had it so good,* he thought.

When Dana emerged from the shower, they ate their cold dinners, sitting about 10 inches apart so that they wouldn't touch. Dana exhaled loudly and looked at Chris.

"What?" he asked.

"Nothing."

"Let's get out of here," he said.

"And go where?"

"Come on, you'll see." They stood up and he took her outside to his truck. He drove them to a small park near the Fort Jackson army base.

"Um, don't you think it's a little cool to sit in the park?" Dana asked as they got out of the truck.

"No, besides, this is the best place in town to watch the sunset."

"You like watching the sunset?"

"What? A brother can't be sensitive?"

Dana smiled. "My bad, as the kids say."

"You never told me your story," he said.

"My story?"

Chris nodded.

"All right. My name is Dana Janice Ellison and ever since I was six, I've wanted to be a baker. I still have the Easy Bake oven my granny gave me for Christmas. My mother threw it out once, but I saved it right before the trash truck came. Bored yet?"

"No, go on."

Dana ran her fingers though her hair and looked up at the sky. In the distance she could see a star shining. She felt as if she were that star. Her dreams were distant, but slowly coming into view. She sighed and turned to Chris. "Somewhere along the way, my life became someone else's. Dana got lost, but she's on her way back."

Chris smiled and stroked her hand as they sat on the hood of the truck.

"Your turn," Dana said.

"What?"

"I want to hear your story."

"You must be ready for bed."

"Come on, you sat through my monologue."

"All right, I grew up in Columbia, right around this army base. My father was a sergeant in the army and my mother was a college student. They met, fell in lust, she got pregnant with me, then they got married. My dad was stationed a lot of different places. We were never close. I lived with my mother but we didn't spend a lot of time together. I hung out with my uncle all the time. I learned to work with my hands at a young age, but I always said Columbia would never be my home. I was wrong, because here I am."

"Do you still want to leave?"

"At this moment, not a chance."

Dana smiled. "Why?"

He looked at Dana and smiled slyly. "Do you even have to ask?"

She turned away from him and watched the sky. It had turned burnt orange, but then began to fade into purple. "This is beautiful," she whispered, focusing on the heavens.

Chris looked at Dana. "It sure is."

# CHAPTER TWELVE

It was after midnight when Dana and Chris left the park. They'd been so engrossed in conversation that she hadn't noticed how cold it had gotten. Dana smiled at Chris as he wheeled into the parking lot of his apartment complex.

"Thank you," she said.

"For what?"

"Celebrating with me. Treating me to dinner and the flowers."

Chris winked at her. "I should be thanking you."

"For?"

"The sugar rush I had this afternoon. I got so much done."

Dana leaned over and kissed him on the cheek.

"Why don't you spend the night," he suggested.

Dana shook her head. "I have to go home and clean up. But I'll see you tomorrow?"

"Of course," he said.

"I need to go in and get my flowers and my purse."

He turned the engine off and they headed up to his door. When a female voice called out his name, both Chris and Dana turned around.

"Rosalyn, what are you doing here?" he asked.

Dana looked from Chris to Rosalyn.

"Is this why you won't take my calls?" she asked.

Chris shook his head. Why did she have to show up now? Rosalyn continued talking, even though Chris didn't reply to her.

"Chris, I love you and I know you love me. This," she said pointing to Dana, "is a distraction."

"I'd better leave," Dana said.

"No," Chris said. "Go inside, Dana, and I'll take care of this."

"Are you sure?"

"He said go," Rosalyn snapped, waving Dana away as if she were a child. Dana glared at her before taking Chris's keys.

Chris turned to Rosalyn. "What in the hell are you doing here?"

Rosalyn opened her leather trench coat, revealing her black satin and lace teddy. Chris turned away from her. "Not a good move," he snapped. "I said it was over. I mean it."

"And she's what you're leaving me for?" Rosalyn laughed. "I would have expected better of you."

"She is better, much better than you ever were. She's a real woman. She's not into the games."

Rosalyn rolled her eyes. "Fine, but when this doesn't work out, don't come crawling back to me."

"Not if you were the last woman on Earth." Chris slammed into his apartment.

Dana was sitting on the sofa. "What was that all about?"

"Stupidity," he mumbled, sitting beside her.

"So, that's Rosalyn."

Chris nodded, then dropped his head into his hands. He couldn't imagine what Dana was thinking as she stood silently and picked up her purse.

"Dana," Chris began. "Let me explain—"

"You know what, you don't owe me anything." Dana turned to leave.

Chris grabbed her arm. "Dana, after all that we've shared, I know you don't think that I would lie about this."

"All we shared was some really hot sex. Like I said, you don't owe me anything." Dana stormed out the front door, leaving the flowers from Chris on the table.

The next morning, Dana woke with a heavy feeling in the middle of her chest. Had she made a mistake leaving Chris the way she had? *He could have been telling the truth… I acted like an ass,* she thought as she sat in the middle of the bed. Dana looked over at the phone. She could call Chris, but what if he didn't want to talk to her? The truth was she had no right to get that upset with him. They weren't committed to each other. Dana rolled her eyes up at the ceiling and fell back on her pillows. The phone rang, jolting her out of her stupor.

"Hello?"

"Dana, hello, I thought you were treating me to breakfast this morning?" Zariah asked.

"Oh, yeah. I forgot."

"Is that man there?"

Dana exhaled loudly. "No, and he probably will never be here again."

"What happened?"

"I don't want to talk about it. Let's just go have breakfast at Shoney's or something."

"No. How about I come over there and we have a girls' day in. You can break out those fancy pots and cook something that didn't come from a lab."

Dana sighed, but agreed to get up and cook. But as soon as she hung up she flung the covers over her head. She didn't want to get out of bed and she didn't want to cook.

About thirty minutes later, Zariah was banging on Dana's front door. Dana walked downstairs and opened the door.

"All right, I don't smell food. The only time you don't cook is when you're upset," Zariah said.

"Hello Zariah. I'm fine. How are you?" Dana said sarcastically.

Zariah rolled her eyes and held up a bag of bagels. "Can you at least brew some coffee?"

The two women walked into the kitchen. Dana looked at her "Kiss the Cook" clock. It was almost 11 a.m.

"So, the last I heard you were all happy and excited to see Chris. What happened?" Zariah inquired

Dana sighed as she measured coffee into the filter. "We had a wonderful time. We talked for hours. I told him the Easy Bake story—"

"And?" Zariah interrupted.

"His ex showed up at the end of the night."

Zariah stretched her eyes as she listened to Dana tell her story.

"I don't think I handled it properly. I got mad."

"How deep is this thing with Chris? You haven't slept with him, have you?"

Dana looked away quickly, biting her bottom lip.

"Dana! You've known him for only a week!"

"It felt right. It's like I've known him for years."

Zariah shook her head. "I can't believe you did that, Dana."

"He said he doesn't do one night stands and he bought me flowers."

"Ooh, that means what? Dana, you watch Lifetime. You know how these things turn out."

"I don't need to hear this." The truth was too bitter for her to swallow.

Zariah ran her hand across her face. "What you need is a swift kick in the—"

"Hey! Let's just move on."

Zariah shrugged her shoulders and opened the bag of bagels. "Do you have any jam? Strawberry, preferably."

Dana opened the refrigerator and handed Zariah a jar of apple jelly. "Deal with it."

"You know what? You're a grown woman and I'm not going to sit here and judge you. But if you think you owe him an apology, maybe you do. I'm sure he didn't call that woman over there."

Dana nodded. Her friend was right. She listened to the coffee perk and said, "Why don't I make some eggs to go along with these bagels."

"What you need to do is call Chris. If it is deeper than a one night stand, then you shouldn't be here miserable."

Dana picked up the phone and crossed her fingers. She dialed Chris's number.

"Yeah?" he said.

"Chris, it's me."

"Dana, what's up?"

"I overreacted last night and I'm sorry. I'm usually not this anal."

"Look, seeing Rosalyn here shook me too. But there's nothing for you to worry about. I'm off that drama coaster."

"And you can't control her actions."

"You left the roses. I'm sure they would look better in your kitchen than here on my table."

Dana smiled. "Why don't you bring them over? I'm about to cook some breakfast. I owe you a huge apology for the way I acted."

"All right, Ms. Lady, I'll be right over."

Dana hung up and turned to Zariah. "He's coming over." She smiled brightly.

"Cool. I'll just take my bagel to go. You guys have some things to work out."

"Zariah, I'm telling you, this feels right."

"I hope this works out for you. But if it doesn't, tell me the sex was good."

Dana leaned over the counter. "Unbelievable."

"I'm jealous." Zariah took a big bite of her bagel, then stood up. "I'll see you later."

Dana waved to her exiting friend.

Dana ran upstairs to her bedroom and changed into a pair of boot cut jeans and a white tank top. She put some lotion on her feet, then walked into the kitchen to wash her hands and make two southwestern omelets.

⁐⧳⧳⁓

Dana was in the middle of garnishing the omelets with salsa and cheese when the doorbell rang. Taking a deep breath, she walked to the door and opened it.

"Hey you," Chris said with a bright smile on his face.

Dana smiled. "Come in."

Chris looked down at her cocoa brown feet. Her toes were clear of polish, but they still looked beautiful. He wanted to drop down and kiss her feet, but that would take them away from the breakfast table and straight into her bedroom.

"What's wrong?" she asked, noticing the far off look in his eyes.

"Nothing. I was just thinking I left your roses."

"That's okay. I'm sorry I left them last night. I was wrong."

"Nah, that was a messed up situation. I'm not trying to bring drama into your life."

"And you didn't. I'm just scared, Chris. Everything with us is moving so fast—"

He grabbed Dana's chin. "It isn't a mistake," he said, finishing her thought.

Her eyes searched his face, asking if he was sure.

"You got me hooked, Dana. I want to be with you and it isn't just about sex."

Dana wrapped her arms around Chris's neck and squeezed him. "You know what?" she said. "You're going to love these omelets."

*I just want to love you,* he thought as they walked into the kitchen. "I don't doubt it," he said.

After they ate, Chris washed the dishes and Dana wiped down the counters.

"You were right about the omelets," he said. "Is there anything you can't cook?"

"I'm still trying to master the charcoal grill."

"See, I can help you with that. When it gets hot, I stay on the grill. I'd barbeque corn flakes if I could."

"Typical, men love fire," she said. "Must be your caveman roots."

Chris laughed. "That's true. But my lemon pepper chicken will have you trying to eat your fingers."

Dana put her rag down and motioned for him to follow her into the living room.

"So," he said, sitting down on the sofa beside her. "What are your plans for today?"

"I don't have any."

"Good, because we're going to take a trip."

"What? I have to go to work in the morning and—"

"Shh," he said bringing his finger to her lips. "It's a short trip."

"Where are we going?"

"Orangeburg."

"Orangeburg?"

"I want to show you something."

"Let me get a sweater and some shoes."

"Hurry up," Chris said.

When Dana got dressed, she and Chris hopped in his truck and headed down Interstate 26.

"What's in Orangeburg?" she asked as he drove.

"You'll see," he said.

Dana looked out the window. She'd wanted to go to South Carolina State University when she was growing up, but her parents told her the University of South Carolina was a better choice. She'd believed them, but she'd always wondered what it would have been like to be a regular freshman, not be compared to her mother and father every time she opened her mouth.

"You okay over there?" he asked.

"I'm fine. I was thinking about how I wanted to go to school down here."

"Why didn't you?"

Dana looked at him, shaking her head. "Do you even have to ask?"

"Ah, the parents weren't having it?"

"Not at all."

Chris took the Highway 301 exit. "Remember you asked me about my dream?"

"Yeah. You said you wanted to work with your hands."

"I want to show you what I want to do."

"All right."

They turned into the entrance of Edisto Memorial Garden and Chris parked the truck. They hopped out and stopped at the entrance. "Look at this," he said. "It's closed right now and we can't go in, but I want to build something like this somewhere in the world. Maybe in Columbia, maybe New Orleans. This is what I want to do. Put my mark on nature."

Dana looked at him as he spoke. "You can do it," she said.

"You can build a bigger and better garden than this."

"We're two dreamers aren't we?"

"I wouldn't say that. It isn't like you're dreaming of being an NBA star or me trying to be the next Patti Labelle."

"What? I got skills." Chris pretended to dribble a ball between his legs.

Dana hit him on the shoulder. "Yeah, skills one on one with yourself. Shaq would knock you out."

Chris nodded. "Maybe so, but I could give Kobe Bryant a run for his money. Anyway, think about that park near Fort Jackson. If it had some flowering dogwoods, azalea bushes, a few evergreen shrubs and two big magnolia trees at the entrance, that place would be beautiful."

"I can see that."

From behind Chris wrapped his arms around Dana's waist and rested his chin on her shoulder. "All I have to do is save up enough money, start my own business and convince the city to give me a chance to work on the park."

Dana reached back and stroked his head. "You can do it, Chris. And if you need me to grease some palms with cakes and brownies, I will."

She turned around and faced him, staring into his eyes.

Chris leaned in and gently kissed Dana on the lips. "Let's get out of here before somebody calls the cops."

They hopped into the truck and headed back up the interstate toward Columbia. As Chris drove, Dana watched the pine trees fly by in a haze of dark green and brown.

"Thanksgiving and Christmas are coming soon," Dana said, more to herself than to Chris.

"What was that?"

"Oh, I was just thinking out loud. The holidays are coming up."

"Yeah. You're going to be busy filling orders at Capitol City.

Just tell me you don't do fruitcakes."

Dana laughed. "I like fruit cakes, but they are so expensive to make. And trust me, you would love my fruit cake."

"Ugh, I'll pass on that one," he said.

"What about gingerbread cookies and sugar plums?"

"Damn, girl, you're going to have me 400 pounds in January if you start that."

"Please," she said, cutting her eyes at Chris. "This is for the bakery. I want to really make a name for myself this holiday season."

"Can a brother get some leftovers?" he joked.

"You can have all the fruitcake you want."

"Ha, ha," he said.

"What do you usually do for the holidays?" she asked.

"Nothing really. Maybe this year will be different."

"Maybe so," she said.

Chris stroked Dana's knee. "I hope so," he said.

# CHAPTER THIRTEEN

After their trip, Dana and Chris headed back to Dana's house so that she could whip up a light dinner.

"That was a nice outing. But it wasn't Atlanta. You still owe me a night in Buckhead," she said as they walked toward the house.

"I know," he said. "And I always pay my debts."

Dana unlocked the door and they walked inside. Chris took notice of her house for the first time. It was furnished with rich woods like cherry and oak. Her living room looked as if it was rarely used. As far as Chris could tell, the egg cream-colored walls hadn't been touched since the painters finished applying the last coat of paint. The kitchen, at least in his observation, was the only room that had life in it. Faint chocolate stains dotted the counter, and the wall behind the stove had three grease spots. There was the slight scent of old dinners in the air.

"What do you have a taste for?" Dana opened her well-stocked refrigerator.

"I'm going to assume you're talking about food."

Dana smirked. "Yes, I am."

"Whatever you want to cook."

"How about chicken and broccoli?"

Chris nodded as he sat on the barstool.

Dana turned around and looked at him. "You'll eat anything, won't you?"

"Anything except fruit cake."

"You're going to eat mine. Trust me."

Chris rolled his eyes and made a face as if he had tasted bitter medicine.

Dana pulled her Teflon pots out from underneath the oven and started prepping the meal. She rinsed the chicken breasts, then set them on the cutting block on the counter to let them thaw slightly.

"Do you need me to help?" Chris asked as she dropped a bunch of broccoli in a glass bowl.

"No. I got it. You can go in the living room and watch TV if you want," she said.

"Why? The Food Network is right here."

"Oh, you need to quit."

"You know how I feel about seeing women in the kitchen."

Dana playfully threw her dishtowel at him. "You're such a chauvinist."

Chris smiled and shrugged his shoulders. "What can I say? Now cook me some vittles, woman."

Dana put her hands on her hips. "You're lucky I like to cook, because that right there would cost you quite a few meals."

Chris laughed heartily. Once Dana began cooking, she looked as if she were in "the zone" as she shuffled back and forth between the stove and refrigerator. Chopping the chicken into cubes, she dropped them into the warm oil.

"Rice or noodles?" she asked.

"Rice," Chris replied.

Dana opened the cabinet beside the refrigerator. "Brown or white rice?"

Chris pointed to the brown rice. Dana pulled out a bag of rice down and set it on the counter, then checked the chicken to make sure it was browned.

"Can you hand me that?" she asked, pointing to the bowl of fresh broccoli. Dana sprinkled some onion powder on the chicken.

Chris stood up and handed it to her. "That smells good."

"Thanks. It should be ready in another 15 minutes."

"Good, because I'm hungry."

"Me too," she said, darting her eyes away. Unspoken desire hung in the air between them. They wanted each other with everything inside of them. Dana craved Chris's lips, his touch and the magical feeling she experienced each time he was inside her. But she couldn't tell him that, not when she had told him that they needed to slow down. But moving fast felt so good, a little too good.

"Chris," she said.

"Yeah."

"What are we doing?"

"What do you mean?"

"I don't want to be just your bed buddy," she blurted out.

"You're not. Dana. I've outgrown purely physical relationships. I care about you."

"I don't want to make a fool of myself with you."

He walked over to her and turned her head so that she was looking directly at him. "There is no way you can make a fool of yourself. I'm not trying to play games with you, Dana. I'm not going to lie, I enjoy having sex with you. It feels damn good. But if you think this is too much too fast, then we can take a step back."

"I'm just afraid."

"Why?"

Dana dropped her head. It was hard to put it in words. Her mother had arranged all of her relationships. In fact, she'd never known real love. She'd never experienced dating without her mother's input and approval. "I just am," she finally said. She walked over to the stove and stirred the rice. Chris came up behind her and stroked her back.

"You don't have to fear this or us," he whispered.

The warmth of his breath tickled Dana's neck. She swallowed

hard and continued to stir the rice.

"Dana, let me in."

She dropped the wooden spoon on the spoon rest and turned to face him. "I-I think the food is ready."

Chris stepped back. "All right."

Chewing on her bottom lip trying to think of something to say, some way to explain her feelings to Chris, Dana ran her hand down her slender throat.

"It's okay," he said. "We have plenty of time to talk about this. Rome wasn't built in a day."

Dana handed him a plate. "You can sit down if you want to."

Chris wanted to say something, but he held back. Obviously, Dana wasn't used to expressing her emotions. He wondered what it would take for her to feel comfortable enough to open her entire heart to him.

As they sat down to eat dinner, the doorbell rang. At first Dana ignored it, thinking it was Zariah. Then the bell chimed again, longer and louder.

"You'd better get that," Chris said.

"I know." She stood up and headed to the door. Pulling the curtain back, Dana saw her mother standing on her front step.

Dana opened the door halfway. "What are you doing here?"

"We need to talk. Whose truck is in your driveway?"

"Now isn't a good time, Mother." Dana attempted to close the door.

"What's going on?" Denise asked, putting her hand on the doorframe.

"I have company."

"So, is this 'company' the reason you've been acting like a fool lately?"

"Mother, move your hand. I would really hate to slam this door on it."

Denise didn't budge. Dana started closing the door to show

her mother she was serious. Denise jumped back as if she had been burnt. "Damn it, Dana."

Dana slammed the door. She felt as if she had lava flowing through her veins instead of blood. Stomping into the kitchen, she sat down.

"I take it that wasn't a pushy salesman," Chris said, noting Dana's foul disposition.

"That was my mother."

"Have you and your mother ever gotten along?"

"When I was a little girl, I looked up to my mother. Then I grew up. She still thinks I'm her little shadow. It makes me so mad." She dropped her head and chuckled. "I can't believe I just threatened to slam my mother's hand in the door."

Chris stroked her hand. "Let's eat and forget about your mother and anything else that puts a frown on that beautiful face."

After dinner, Chris headed home so that he could sketch out some plans for a few yards he was scheduled to start on the next week. Dana walked him to the front door and kissed him on the cheek.

"Thanks for my road trip," she said.

"Anytime."

She watched Chris hop into his truck and back out of her driveway, then returned to the kitchen and started washing the dinner dishes. The phone rang as she dipped her frying pan into hot water. She knew it was her mother, so she didn't answer. But the phone wouldn't stop ringing. Finally, after her head began to throb, Dana picked up the phone.

"Hello?"

"Dana, it's your father."

"Yes, Dad?" she sighed.

"Your mother told me what happened when she came to your house."

"And? Dad, this is my house. I didn't want to be bothered."

"Dana, I'm really trying to understand what's going on with you. First, you get in trouble at work. Then you break off your engagement with Andre. Now you're isolating yourself from your family. Is this what that new man in your life is encouraging you to do?"

"Dad, you don't know what you're talking about," she said flatly.

"Then explain it to us," Denise snapped.

Dana rolled her eyes. She should have known Denise was listening. "I don't have to explain anything, but I will say this. Chris has shown me more support than either of you."

"So this Chris is pushing this foolish notion of yours?" Denise asked. "What kind of man would want a woman to give up a real career to become a cook?"

"It isn't a notion. This has been a dream of mine for a long time and it's about to come true. What do you have to say about that?"

"You're being a fool. Who is this Chris person anyway?" Denise asked.

"Don't worry about that. It's none of your concern and this conversation is over." Dana slammed the phone down.

◈

The next morning, Dana woke up with the flutter of butterflies in her stomach. She couldn't wait to see Josh that afternoon. She wanted to hear the details about her job at the bakery. Leaping out of bed she headed into the bathroom humming the chorus to "I'm Coming Out."

After her shower, Dana fixed herself a toasted bagel and a cup of coffee. The doorbell rang as she walked into the bedroom, munching on the bread. She looked down at the towel covering her body. *Who's at my door this time of morning?*

Peeping out the window, she saw Chris.

"Hey," she said, opening the door.

"I just wanted to bring you these." He handed her a bouquet of daisies and tulips. "I know today is a big day for you."

"Thanks," she said. "Do you want to come in for coffee?"

"I have to go pick up two of my men for a job. But I didn't want the day to go by without me telling you how proud I am of you."

Dana opened the door all the way and hugged him. "Thank you."

"You'd better get dressed," he said when they separated.

"I know."

"I'll stop by when I get off from work."

"All right, I'll cook dinner."

"Why don't I bring us something over? You have a long day ahead of you."

Dana kissed him on the cheek to thank him again.

Chris stepped off the porch and waved to her. Dana closed the door, feeling happier than she had when she woke up. Not only did she have her meeting with Josh to look forward too, she was going to spend the evening with Chris.

❧❧❧

Chris pulled up at Denise and Frank Ellison's house. He felt strange being there, knowing what he knew about them from Dana. But this was business and he had to separate his personal feelings from his business. Chris rang the doorbell.

The door opened. "Yes?" Denise asked.

"Good morning, ma'am. I'm here to see Mr. Ellison about some yard work."

"Come in," she said, stepping aside.

Chris took a good look at Denise. She looked like Dana, only with more fine lines on her face. Her raven hair was sprinkled with gray strands and it shook with body as she walked. "You can wait in the kitchen."

"Thank you, ma'am," Chris said.

"And you are?"

"Chris Johnson. I work for Jones's Pool and Landscaping."

Denise nodded and walked down the hall, disappearing behind a closed door. Chris didn't know if he should sit down in one of the high back oak chairs at the dining room table or remain standing. He felt as if he were in a museum; he didn't dare touch a thing.

"Chris," Frank's voice boomed.

Turning around, Chris extended his hand to the older man. They shook and Frank nodded for Chris to sit down.

"Do you have any idea what you want to do to your lawn?" Chris asked.

Frank folded his hands underneath his chin. "Not really. I know Denise was saying she wanted to get rid of the azalea bushes."

"Does she want to replace them with some evergreen bushes? They're really easy to take care of and if you want a green-looking lawn, that's the fastest and easiest way to get there. And some tulips or some other flowers would be nice in the middle of the lawn, maybe in a brick flower bed."

Frank nodded. "I like the way that sounds."

Chris smiled. "I can draw you a diagram to show you how it would look once I take a look around."

"That sounds good." Frank watched Denise walk into the

kitchen.

"What sounds good?" she asked.

"I'm finally doing something about the lawn."

"Great. I'm going into my office early," she said. "Young man, I don't care what he says, I want those azalea bushes gone."

"Yes, ma'am," Chris said with a laugh.

"Frank, please try and talk to your child today," Denise said as she walked out of the side door to the garage.

Frank looked at Chris and shook his head. "Do you have children?"

Chris shook his head.

"Married?"

"Nope."

"Be smart, don't ever get married."

Chris didn't know if he should laugh or not so he stood up and headed outside to take a look at the yard. Crabgrass covered half of the front yard and all of the back, except for several spots where no kind of grass grew. Chris knew he would need a full crew to sod the lawn and it would take a full year to get the lawn in *Better Homes and Gardens* shape. But with the right winter grass, he could make it look presentable until it could be reseeded in the spring.

Frank came outside. "I know it looks bad. I've never been one to do much yard work. I just cut it and move on."

"You have a serious crabgrass problem. We need to sod the lawn with some winter grass and then next spring we overseed the lawn so that next fall it will stay lush and green until October when grass dies anyway."

"All right."

"I'll come by in the morning and show you my sketches."

"Great. Denise will be happy," Frank said with a smile on his face.

*Is that woman ever happy?* Chris wondered as he and Frank shook hands.

# CHAPTER FOURTEEN

Time ticked away slowly. Dana watched the clock like an anxious child waiting for recess. She went through the motions of assigning silent reading to the students but all she could think about was her meeting with Josh.

"Ms. Ellison," a boy said, interrupting her thoughts.

"Yes?"

"Can I go to the bathroom?"

"Jacob, if you wait three minutes class will be over."

"He just wants a running start," another boy yelled out.

Dana sighed. "What's this all about?"

"Nothing," Jacob mumbled.

"Stephon said he was going to beat Jacob up after school," the other boy said.

"Steven, who is Stephon?" Dana inquired.

"An eighth grader," Steven replied.

"Jacob, come with me," Dana said, standing. The last thing she wanted was a fight holding her up from her meeting.

"Ms. Ellison, it really isn't a big deal," Jacob said as he trudged to the door.

"Yes, it is," she said, looking at the boy's small frame. "We're going to talk to the principal about this."

"Aw man," he mumbled under his breath. Dana looked away from Jacob. She couldn't understand why this boy would rather face suspension and a beating from a bigger student than get help from the principal.

Dana sighed. "Jacob, I like you. You're one of my best students and I don't want to see you getting in trouble."

"Whatever."

Dana stopped in her tracks. "Fine. If you don't want to talk to Mr. Mason, then take your chances with this eighth grader. Go back inside."

Jacob chewed on his bottom lip. "I'll talk to Mr. Mason."

Dana escorted him to the office and sighed with relief. The crisis seemed averted. Now she had only two more minutes of class before she could cut out early to make her meeting.

She smiled happily when the bell rang. Without a word she watched her students dash out the door, leaving papers on the floor and books on their desks. Usually, she demanded that they leave the classroom in an orderly fashion. Today, she didn't care. Dana was about to leave the empty classroom when Mr. Mason walked in.

"Dana," he said. "We need to talk."

"Okay," she said glancing at her watch. It was three-fifteen. If she were lucky, she'd be out the door at three-thirty and no more than five minutes late to her meeting.

"Mrs. Bennett went to the school board about you."

"I'm sure she did."

"Dana, they want to review you."

"What? On what grounds? I mean, her child started the fight in my classroom and destroyed property. She should be reviewed, not me."

"The school board wants to review your performance. There's also going to be a hearing to determine if you should be disciplined for the way you acted in my office."

Dana tossed her head back and closed her eyes, the wind knocked out of her sails. She wanted to leave this job on her own terms, not because someone thought she wasn't good enough.

"When?"

"Day after tomorrow. I'm going to put you on administrative leave with pay until the board reaches a decision about your future here. I hate to do this, but my hands are tied."

Dana shrugged her shoulders. What could she say?

"A substitute will take over your class starting tomorrow. I'm really sorry about this, but Mrs. Bennett is adamant."

"And you have to cover your behind, huh?"

"That's not fair. I've supported you from day one, but this is out of my hands."

Dana turned to leave the room.

"Dana, is everything all right?" he asked. "Do you still want this job? You used to be a great teacher, but now it's as if you don't even care."

"The grade book and my lesson plans are in the desk." She walked out of the classroom fighting the urge to tell Mr. Mason where he could stick her job, even if the school board stood behind her. She drove slowly to the bakery. The joyful attitude she'd had all day had vanished. *Josh better have good news for me, because I don't know if I can take anymore crap today,* she thought. She parked in Capitol City's lot, then walked into bakery and stood at the counter. In spite of everything, she was a few minutes early.

Dana nervously told the clerk that she was there for a meeting with Josh. The 20-something clerk nodded, then disappeared behind a dark wood swinging door.

Dana looked up at the menu and there it was, Ellison rum brownies. She knew her grandmother would have been proud. Checking the display case, she saw there were no brownies left over from the weekend. She smiled. The sun was beginning to shine on her again.

"Dana, darling," Josh said when he walked to the front of the bakery.

"Hey."

"Your brownies were a hit. Can you make me a batch of 36 dozen for this weekend?"

"Sure," she said.

"I'm going to pay you $500 a weekend. You're welcome to use the kitchen here to bake."

"I could come in tomorrow morning and bake them," she said. "I've been given some time off from school."

Josh clasped his hands together, his eyes sparkling with excitement. "Well, in that case, I want four German chocolate cakes and some of those truffles too."

"What time should I get here in the morning?"

"Six."

Dana grimaced. Morning was not her favorite time of the day. "I'll be here," she said.

"Make it seven. I saw that look you gave me."

"Thanks," she said. "I'd better go."

"Dana, I'm really looking forward to working with you."

She waved to him as she walked out of the bakery. Maybe being suspended from work was a blessing in disguise. Now she would have a chance to put her all into baking. Dana hopped into her car and smiled as she switched the ignition on. From the radio came Diana Ross singing Dana's new theme song, "I'm Coming Out." Cranking up the volume she sang along with Ms. Ross. It was a good day after all.

❦

Chris pulled into Dana's driveway with two barbeque chicken dinners from the Rib House and a six-pack of beer. He was hoping to get something a little classier, but after dropping his men off from their last job of the day, he didn't have time to stop by Carrabba's. Chris got out of the car and rang the bell.

Dana opened the door with a bright smile on her face. "The

most amazing thing happened to me today," she said.

"Really?"

"Get in here so I can tell you about it." Dana pulled him in, careful not to make him drop the dinners he had in his hands.

"All right, what's going on?"

"Put the food on the table," she said as they walked into the kitchen.

"Okay. What happened, did you win the lottery?"

"I got suspended from work."

Chris furrowed his brows. What was so good about that? "Continue," he said.

Dana smiled again, revealing her pearly whites. "I'm starting at the bakery in the morning."

"What? Baby, I'm so happy for you," he said, hugging her tightly and lifting her up off the floor.

Dana went on to tell Chris how Josh had carried on about the brownies and how it felt to see her name on the menu as she handed him two plates for their dinners.

"Dana, I'm happy for you, but what about teaching?"

She shook her head from side to side, then grabbed a beer. "Let's toast to my new job."

Chris grabbed a beer and clanked it against Dana's can. "Congratulations."

Setting down his can, he studied Dana as she swallowed the amber liquid. He wanted to kiss her. Could they break the rules, just this once? Would there be any turning back if they crossed the sex line again?

"So what's in the boxes?" she asked.

"Chicken and coleslaw."

"Sounds good. I'll get some silverware." As Dana stood up, Chris grabbed her arm.

"Dana," he said in a husky voice.

Their eyes locked and Chris ran his finger across her petal-

141

soft lips. Dana kissed his finger, then ran her tongue up his fingertip. Chris felt a shiver up his spine as her tongue darted across his finger. He pulled at the waistband of Dana's pants and she fell on top of him in the chair. Dana wrapped her arms around his neck and straddled him, sucking on his neck. Then she darted her tongue in and out of his ear. White-hot passion seeped from their pores, engulfing them in lust. When Chris ripped Dana's silk shirt open and grabbed her breasts, gently squeezing them, Dana pulled back. Breathlessly Chris asked Dana if she wanted to stop. Her reply was to cover his mouth with hers and greedily suck his tongue, savoring the taste of him. Chris unzipped her pants and peeled them off her body.

When Dana broke off the kiss and looked into his eyes, she saw he seemed hesitant, unsure of her consent. Slipping her hand inside his pants, she stroked his member slowly until it stood at attention. As she moved her hand faster and faster, Chris threw back his head and closed his eyes.

Chris grabbed her hips, feeling as if he were going to die if he didn't feel her around him. Dana ground against him and he leaned forward, burying his head in her breasts. The dinner he'd bought was forgotten. He wanted to feast on her.

They tumbled out of the chair onto the hardwood floor. Chris hovered over Dana as he unbuttoned his jeans and pulled them down. She clutched his back, drawing him down on top of her.

"I want you, Chris," she said. Her breath tickled his lip. He slipped his hands into her hair and then retrieved her head for a kiss. As his tongue jockeyed for a spot inside her mouth, she wrapped her legs around his waist. Wantonly, she grabbed his manhood, sliding it where she wanted it, deep inside her wet and hot vagina. She dug her nails into his back, wanting more, needing more. Chris was happy to give it to her. He throbbed with excitement as pressed deeper and harder, touching her inner core.

A hoarse moan escaped his throat as Dana tightened her muscles around him. He grabbed her breasts, kneading them like dough as the first wave of an orgasm hit him. After the second wave he collapsed on top of her.

"Damn, baby," he murmured in her ear. "Damn."

She held on to him, hoping to push that nagging voice out of her head. *What are you going to do when he leaves? Your parents aren't going to approve of this.*

Dana closed her eyes tightly. "Chris."

"Umm-huh."

"I need to go take a shower."

He opened his eyes and looked at her, then propped himself up on his elbow. "Are you all right?"

"Yeah, I'm fine," she replied, gently pushing him off her.

"What's going on? I know we said we weren't going to do this, but we're adults who want each other, very much."

"I know that," she said. "Chris, I'm just scared. It seems like sex is the only thing that we have holding us together. What happens when you get tired of it?"

"Who says that's going to happen? Dana, I know that we both have some serious baggage, but I've been open and honest with you. I want you and I've made no bones about it and it's not just your body that I want. It's all of you."

"I don't really know what it feels like to fall in love, but I think that's what's happening. It's scary."

Chris stroked her back gently.

"I don't want to be hurt," she said as she stood up and reached for her discarded blouse. Chris grabbed her hand and kissed it softly.

"I would never purposely do anything to hurt you. I've been on the other side of hurt and I don't want to put you though that."

Dana stroked his cheek. "You mean that?"

He nodded. "With everything in me."

Dana sat down and looked at Chris. Now she was really terrified, because she was going to go for it, no matter what the consequences would be.

"I'm going to shower," she said. "Want to join me?"

Chris smiled. "Wash my back, I'll wash yours." They dashed up the stairs, running like teenaged lovers.

# CHAPTER FIFTEEN

"Stay with me tonight," she whispered as when they stepped out of the shower and he began drying her.

"You don't have to twist my arm," he said.

Dana smiled and pulled him into the bedroom. He looked around the room, realizing Dana had great taste. A four-poster cherry bed, covered with a rose-colored comforter and three jumbo pillows, sat in the middle of the room. The walls were painted honey brown and were empty of artwork. She flicked on the dim lamp resting her dresser, which was on the left wall, then sat on the bed. Chris couldn't take his eyes off her naked body as she smoothed on lotion. Finally he took the bottle from her and squeezed the strawberry-scented lotion into his hands and rubbed them together. Then he glided his hands across her stomach. Dana closed her eyes and smiled as his hands moved down to her thighs.

"So this is what keeps you so soft?" He continued rubbing her thighs even though there was no more lotion on his hands.

"Uh-huh."

Chris stopped stroking her. "What time are you going to the bakery tomorrow?"

"Seven."

"If you don't want me to keep you up all night, you need to put some clothes on."

"What about you?"

Chris winked at her. "I have on my birthday suit. What more do I need?"

"Protection from me if you don't get dressed."

"Hurt me, baby." Chris lay back and pulled Dana on top of him.

"You're so bad," she said, wiggling out of his embrace. Walking over to her dresser, Dana pulled out a black satin and lace spaghetti-strapped gown. As she stepped into it she twisted her hips, inadvertently giving Chris a show more seductive than one by a dancer at a strip club. Chris walked behind her and pulled against him. His breath made the back of her neck tingle.

"I like this."

"The gown?"

"Nah, being here with you. Touching you, feeling you against me."

Dana turned around and kissed him on the cheek. "I like it, too."

Chris ran his finger down the valley between her breasts. Her skin was softer than the satin she wore. As she stared into his eyes, Chris leaned in and kissed her gently on the lips.

"We'd better go to sleep," he said when they broke off their kiss. "We both have early days tomorrow."

"Yeah, and I'm not a morning person."

Just as they climbed into bed, the phone rang. Her first instinct was to ignore it, but she answered anyway.

"Hello?"

"Dana, it's me," her father said. "I'm at Richland Memorial Hospital."

"What? Dad, are you all right?"

"Your mother had a heart attack this evening."

"Oh my God, is she okay?"

Frank's voice dropped. "It's not looking too good."

"I'll be right there," she said, leaping from the bed and dropping the phone on the floor.

"Dana, what's wrong?"

Trembling with fear and dread, she threw open her closet

Chris went over to her and touched her shoulder. "Dana?"

She turned around and hugged him tightly. "My—my mother had a heart attack. She's in the hospital."

"All right, I'll drive you over there."

"No, it's okay, I can make it."

"Dana, look at yourself. You're shaking like a leaf. There is no way you can drive anywhere."

She nodded, unable to protest further and he ran downstairs to throw on his clothes. Although she and her mother constantly bumped heads, Dana didn't know if she could handle losing her. Grabbing a pair of sweats from the back of the closet, she hastily pulled them over her gown, then nearly fell as she raced downstairs.

Chris grabbed her arm when she reached the bottom of the stairs. "Sweetheart, you have to calm down. Your mother is going to need your strength."

Dana nodded and fought back the tears forming in her eyes. "The last time she was here, we were so angry with each other. I said some really harsh things to her. What if I don't have a chance to tell her that I'm sorry?"

Chris wrapped his arms around her and stroked her back. "Come on, let's go."

He grabbed his keys and ushered Dana out the door and into his truck. When he pulled into the emergency room parking lot, Dana jumped out before the truck came to a complete stop and she sprinted through the doors like Flo Jo.

"Dad," she called out when saw her father standing near the nurse's station.

He turned around and pulled Dana into his arms. "I'm glad you're here. They took her to surgery a while ago but no one will tell me anything more."

Dana leaned over the counter. "Hello! I need information about my mother!" she screamed at a nurse who had her back turned to them.

The nurse turned with a scowl on her face. "Ma'am, you need to calm down."

"You need to tell me where the hell my mother is," Dana snapped.

The woman rolled her eyes. "Name?"

"Denise Ellison."

The nurse sat down at the computer and punched some keys. "You need to check with the nurses' station on the fifth floor."

"Let's go," Frank said.

"I have to wait for Chris," she said, turning to the door.

"Chris? Who's Chris?"

"He drove me here."

Dana glanced at the door and saw Chris walking in. Frank looked at him. "Isn't that the landscaper?" Frank asked.

Dana shook her head. "Does it matter?"

"Dana, is everything all right?" Chris asked when he walked over to her.

"I don't know. We're about to go upstairs," she replied.

Before they got on the elevator, Andre rushed through the doors. "Mr. Ellison, I got here as fast as I could."

*What's he doing here?* Dana wondered. Then she immediately thought, *I can't worry about this.*

"Dad, come on," she said.

As Frank, Andre and Chris followed Dana to the elevator, Andre turned to Chris. "What are you doing here?"

"I'm here for Dana," Chris replied.

"It doesn't matter why he's here," Dana snapped. "Why are you here?"

"I care about your mother. I'm surprised to see you," Andre said.

"What the hell is that supposed to mean?" she hissed.

"You aren't exactly your mother's biggest fan."

"Why don't you lay off?" Chris snapped.

"This doesn't concern you," Andre replied.

"All of you shut up," Frank bellowed. "My wife is fighting for her life and you two are having a pissing contest. I'll have both of you thrown out of here if you don't stop this mess right now."

They rode the rest of the way up in silence. When the doors opened, Frank was first off the elevator. Chris held Dana's arm as they joined her father at the nurses' station. Andre hung back. He exhaled loudly as he sat down in one of the chairs in the waiting room.

"I'll let the doctor know that you all are here," the nurse said calmly.

Dana's heart felt as if it were going to jump out of her chest. What if the doctor came in and said Denise was dead? *Don't think like that,* she told herself. *Mom is too stubborn to die.*

Stroking Dana's arm, Chris whispered, "Let's go sit down."

She nodded and followed his lead. They sat down underneath the TV and Dana leaned her head on Chris's shoulder and cried silently. He stroked the back of her neck.

A tall, dark-haired white man in a white lab coat walked into the waiting room. "Is the Ellison family here?"

Dana and her dad jumped up and walked over to him. "We're the Ellison family," Frank said, taking Dana's arm.

"Your wife just had triple bypass surgery. There was a blockage but we got it and there was minimal damage done to her heart."

As tears spilled down Dana's cheeks, Frank pulled her closer. "So how is she?" Frank asked.

"She's in recovery. You can see her, but she's heavily sedated. She may come out of it tonight or she may not, but Mrs. Ellison is a strong woman."

Frank nodded. "Come on, Dana."
They headed down the hall with the doctor.

When Chris glanced over at Andre, their eyes met. Andre stood and crossed to Chris. "What's going on with you and Dana?" he asked nostrils flaring.

"Excuse me?"

"Is that how you do it? Plant my yard, steal my fiancée?"

"Dana was never yours. She didn't want you, my man. Why don't you leave? Dana doesn't want you here. She has her father and me. She doesn't need you."

"Who in the hell do you think you are?" Andre snapped. "You're the hired help. Dana's flaky, she's going through a phase. First, it was the baking, now it's you. What are you going to do when she drops you on the curb like the trash you are?"

Chris grabbed Andre by the collar. "Get the hell out of here before I toss you out like garbage."

Andre pushed Chris hands away. He smirked and sucked his teeth. "The truth hurts, doesn't it?"

"The truth is, Dana didn't want your uptight ass and she's doing something that she wants."

"And what can you offer her? What can you give her besides some dirt and bushes?"

Chris squared off and punched Andre in the face. Stumbling backwards, Andre knocked over a potted plant before regaining his footing and lunging at Chris, pushing him against the wall. Chris countered with a right hook to Andre's temple. Then Andre tried to kick Chris in the groin, but Chris quickly moved out of the way. Suddenly two orderlies and two security officers rushed into the waiting room. It took all of them to pull Chris and Andre apart.

"You'll be hearing from my lawyer!" Andre threatened, wiping at blood trickling from his nose.

"What in the hell is going on here?" one of the security guards asked. "This is a hospital, not a street corner. Do you both need to leave?"

Chris shook his head. "I'm staying here for my woman. He needs to go."

"Go to hell. You don't even know Dr. Ellison," Andre snapped.

"Dana doesn't want you here," Chris yelled.

"All right, enough," the security guard said. He pointed at Chris. "Get over there." Then he pointed at Andre "Over there. If we have to come back up here, both of you are going to spend the night in the custody of the sheriff."

Chris sat down and glared at Andre on the other side of the room.

❧❦❧

Dana stood at the door of the recovery room and watched her father hold her mother's hand. Denise looked so small and fragile in the bed, like a battered Barbie doll that had been abused by a four-year-old. Dana swallowed hard and clutched her throat. She couldn't breathe and she felt light-headed.

"Dana," Frank whispered. "Come in. Let her know you're here."

Slowly, Dana walked into the room and stood on the other side of the bed. "Mommy," she whispered. "I'm right here."

Frank smiled at his daughter. "You know she's going to be

fine. She's got to be here to run that department at USC and our lives. She does it because she loves us."

Dana gingerly placed her hand on top of her mother's. "I love you, Mama. I know I don't always show it, but I love you so much. You can't leave me."

Denise's eyes fluttered open. She looked from Frank to Dana, then blinked rapidly.

"What's wrong?" Frank asked, leaning in closer to Denise.

"Water," she said hoarsely. "Water."

"I'll get it," Dana said. She had to get out of the room. She couldn't stand seeing her mother like that. Denise was the strongest woman she knew but right now she looked weak and helpless. Dana would rather have her mother meddling in her life than have to watch her struggle for life in that hospital bed. Grabbing a nurse, she said, "My mother woke up. She needs some water."

"I'll bring her a pitcher," she said.

"T—thanks," Dana stammered. When she went back into the room, Frank was kissing Denise's hand.

"The nurse is coming with the water," Dana said.

"Baby, why don't you go home? You have to work in the morning. I'll call you if there's a change."

Dana looked at Denise who nodded in agreement.

"Are you sure it's okay?" Dana asked. "I don't want to leave."

"I'll be here with her. Stop by after school."

"I will," Dana said. She walked over to her mother and kissed her on the forehead. "I love you, Mom."

Denise smiled at Dana, then closed her eyes.

"Go ahead," Frank whispered. "Send Andre in. I know he was worried about her."

Dana rolled her eyes, but nodded. When she walked into the waiting room, Dana did a double take. Chris and Andre looked like prizefighters. Chris had a knot on the side of his head and

Andre's eye was swollen. Both had blood on their shirts.

"What happened?" she asked to no one in particular.

"That thug attacked me," Andre exclaimed.

"Andre, why did you stay? You can't go back there to see my mother looking like your face hit a wall. My parents have enough to worry about right now."

"And I'm sure you don't want them to know you have such a violent man in your life."

Dana rolled her eyes. "Just go home," she snapped.

Chris hid his smug smile as Dana turned to face him. "Let's go," she said.

Chris stood up and walked out of the waiting room with Dana. When they got on the elevator, she lit into him.

"What the hell was that? Do you have that little self-control? You and Andre could have saved this for another time. My mother is in there fighting for her life and you two are fighting for what? To see who can challenge Roy Jones Jr. next? I know that wasn't about me. That was a male ego trip."

"So you're just going to take his word as gospel?"

"Chris, I don't give a damn who started the fight. You're a grown man; you could've walked away. You should've ignored him. My parents like Andre. He's going to be around."

"Why is he going to be around? As your insurance policy, in case your mother doesn't approve of us?"

"Now that's not fair!"

"Oh, it isn't? Then tell me, do you even care what happened?"

"Right now, I don't. And I'm not taking sides either. Both of you were acting childish. You are supposed to be here to support me."

"I am here for you," he said. "But that guy pushed my buttons."

Dana rolled her eyes and stepped off the elevator. Chris had to walk quickly to catch up with her.

"Dana, Dana. Look, I didn't mean to add more stress to your night."

"Well, you did. Just take me home, then you can go."

"I'm not leaving you like this. I was wrong, I'm sorry. But I didn't like the way he was talking to you and I didn't like the fact that he was there. When he got in my face, I just snapped."

Dana climbed into the truck. She knew Andre could rub people the wrong way, but Chris should have been a bigger man. Dana brooded as he started the truck.

They rode in silence. Chris stole glances at Dana, wondering what she was thinking. He wanted to say something to her, but didn't know what to say or how to make her understand that he wasn't the thug that he'd acted like at the hospital. "Dana, please, say something."

"You don't want to hear what I have to say," she replied.

"I do. I know you're upset, but I—"

"Save it Chris, I needed you to be there for me, not fighting, and you couldn't do that. I thought I knew you. But I see that I don't."

He pulled into her driveway and she hopped out. Chris sat in the truck and watched her run inside the house.

"Damn!" he exclaimed, then drove off.

# CHAPTER SIXTEEN

Dana sat on the edge of her bed and tried to calm down. She needed to go to sleep but she couldn't. It was one a.m. *Maybe I should call Josh and tell him I won't be in tomorrow,* she thought as she lay back on the bed and pulled up the comforter. She could still smell Chris's scent on her comforter. Dana tried to think about forgiving him, but she was too angry. How could he act like a barbarian when she needed him? And Andre. That smug so-and-so probably needed his block knocked off, but Chris didn't have to be the one to do it. She sat up, then reached for the cordless phone. She dialed Andre's number.

"Yeah?" he said, his voice groggy with sleep.

"It's Dana."

"Do you realize what time it is?"

"I really don't care. Stay away from my family."

"Or what? You're going to have your thug boyfriend beat me up again?"

"No, I'll do it myself. Andre, we're over. The only reason you were with me was because you wanted to jockey for a higher position at USC. I'm not stupid."

"Dana, I did care about you. But I guess I didn't have enough hood in me. So, you met him in my yard and now you're sleeping with him?"

"That's none of your business. You just stay away from my family."

"Your mother is my friend and I'm concerned about her."

"Whatever."

"Dana, the sun doesn't rise and set on your ass. This isn't

about you."

She slammed the phone down in the charger and fell back onto the bed. Closing her eyes, she tried to go to sleep, but Chris kept invading her thoughts. She tossed and turned until the sun rose and her alarm blared.

Dana was so tired. Moving stiffly and mechanically, she got in the shower. She ran her hand through her hair when she got out. It felt like broom straw. Grabbing a jar of gel, she rubbed it through her hair, then plugged in her bumper curlers. While they were heating, she walked into the kitchen and started brewing a pot of coffee. Maybe it would wake her up. The coffee dripped slowly into the pot, filling the kitchen with the pungent aroma of the Colombian beans. It was six-thirty and she knew she needed to get a move on. Dana grabbed her favorite mug from the dish rack, dumped in two teaspoons of sugar and when the coffee finished brewing poured the hot liquid into her cup and downed it, ignoring the burning in her throat.

Running into the bathroom, Dana flipped the ends of her hair with the curlers. Then she pulled out a pair of black Express jeans and a black and purple Express shirt and hastily dressed. At six forty-five, she walked into the kitchen, grabbed her bottle of rum and headed out the door. She had to do this, no matter what else was going on in her life.

Chris woke up about seven a.m. He was late for his job in Lexington. He started to call in sick, but that had never been his style. Maybe if he got out and worked he wouldn't think about Dana and their fight. He wished he hadn't gotten into it with Andre, but he had and if she couldn't accept his apology, then to hell with her.

*Yeah, right. Somehow I have to make her understand that I wasn't trying to make things harder for her.*

The phone rang, interrupting his thoughts.

"Yeah?"

"Chris, man, where are you?" Tito asked.

"I'm running late. Go have breakfast or something. I'll be there by eight or so."

"All right. You know Hernando is out here talking junk."

"Tell him what he can do for me. Say it in Spanish, if you can."

Tito laughed. "All right, man."

Chris hung up and crawled out of bed. After a quick shower, he dressed in his gray coveralls, then headed out the door, ignoring the rumbling in his belly. As he headed toward Lexington, Dana popped back into his mind and wouldn't go away. He turned his truck around and headed downtown. At Capitol City, he pulled into the parking lot, got out of the truck and went inside. He peeked over the counter, looking for Dana, but didn't see her.

"Can I help you?" the clerk asked.

"Is Dana here?"

"Who?"

"Dana Ellison?"

"Oh, the new girl. Yeah, I'll get her for you." The clerk disappeared through the kitchen doors.

Chris tugged at the sleeve of his coveralls as he waited for Dana. She walked out with a white apron over her clothes. He liked the way she'd done her hair. It showed her entire face. "Hey you," he said.

"What do you want?" Her words were as cold as an arctic blast.

"Look, I just wanted to see you this morning."

"Chris, I'm really busy."

"I'm sorry about last night."

"So you've said."

"Damn, Dana, are you going to cut me any slack?"

"Why should I? Chris, this is my first day here and I don't need to be thinking about you and your drama. I need some time. My mother is in the hospital and I'm starting here. I don't need the distraction."

Chris took a step back. "Distraction? That's what I am to you?"

Dana exhaled loudly. "I didn't mean it like that. Chris, I—"

"Forget it. Don't let me distract you anymore." As he turned toward the door, Dana grabbed his arm.

"Chris, I'm sorry. I didn't mean that you were a distraction. I have a lot going on right now."

"And I'm trying to be supportive of you."

"Is that why you fought Andre? To support me?"

"I made a damn mistake. Either you're going to forgive me or you're going to harp on it. You need to decide what you're going to do."

"Don't you dare try to turn this around on me. I wasn't the one acting like a barbarian in the hospital." Her voice was a tight hiss.

Chris yanked his arm away from Dana. "Don't you have some dough to knead?" He stalked out of the bakery, got into his truck and slammed his hands against the steering wheel. He was about to back out of the lot when his passenger side door opened and Dana slid in.

"Chris, I'm really stressed out right now. And even though I'm pissed off about the way you and Andre acted last night, I don't want you to walk out of here this angry."

He turned to her. "I don't know what else I can say."

"Neither do I. I just need some time to make sure my mother is okay. Maybe we should just cool out for a little while until she's out of the woods. I told Andre the same thing, but I doubt he's going to listen."

Chris shook his head. "So he's still going to be in your life?"

"That isn't what I'm saying. Right now, my focus is this bakery and my mother. I can't be worried about you and Andre pummeling each other every time you're alone in the same room."

"Fine, take all the time that you need, Dana."

"Chris, I don't want to give up on us, but you have to understand where I'm coming from right now. You don't know my mother."

He nodded. "You're right. I don't know her. But I know you and I'm trying to be supportive."

"You have been, Chris, since the day I met you. I just need to handle this on my own. I have to go back inside." She handed him a blueberry bagel wrapped in a piece of wax paper. "You need to eat some breakfast before you go to work."

Chris smiled. If she worried about whether he had breakfast, then there was still hope for the two of them. "I don't want to give up on us either. If you need anything, I'm just a phone call away," he said. Dana nodded and got out of the truck.

Chris watched her walk into the bakery, wondering if they would ever get on the right track again.

As soon as Dana walked into the bakery kitchen, her cell phone rang. *What is it now?* "Yes?"

"Dana, where are you?" Frank asked. "I called the school and they said you weren't in."

"I'm not at school."

"Where are you?"

"Is Mom all right? Did something happen?"

"Your mother is stable, but this isn't about her. What's going on, Dana? Why did Andre leave without seeing your mother?"

"I don't know. Look, Dad, if this isn't about Mom, I have to go. I'm busy."

"Well, keep your cell phone on so I can reach you wherever you are."

"I will," she said, then pressed the end button.

Josh walked into the kitchen. "Is everything all right? Tasha said you and some guy were having an intense moment."

"Sorry, there's just a lot going on today."

"Dana, you don't have to be here if you have something else you need to do."

"No, I need to be here. I have the brownie batter mixed and I'm waiting for the oven to heat up."

Josh frowned as if to ask if she was sure about her decision to stay.

Dana poured the batter for the brownies into the large pans. "Josh, it's cool. All right?" she asked, noting his questioning expression.

Josh dropped a white marshmallow-shaped hat onto her head. "OK, associate pastry chef."

"What?"

"I'm making you an associate chef here."

"Just like that?"

"Please, I've had people begging for your brownies. This is a good move on my part. Of course, if you don't want to do this, you can just work here on the weekends."

"This is a lot to think about. I can't give you a decision right now, but I can say I'm interested. My mother had a heart attack last night and I need to be flexible for her right now."

"Dana, why didn't you tell me? You can go be with your

mother if she needs you."

"That's okay," she said. "I can handle it here. Baking takes my mind off things."

Josh nodded and patted her on the shoulder. "I know how you feel. I'm sure your girl is taking care of her."

"I haven't had a chance to tell Zariah about it."

"Are you sure you don't need a break?" he asked.

Dana shook her head. "I've still got to prepare the batter for my cakes and make the truffles. I'll be fine."

"You don't have to be supercook, y'know."

Dana smiled. "I know."

Josh waved and walked out of the kitchen. Dana started mixing and pouring, clearing her mind of everything going on outside the kitchen door.

&#8766;&#9901;&#8766;

When Chris pulled up to the job site, Tito ran over to the truck. "Damn, man, we thought we could go home. What took you so long?"

"Shut up and get to work. Do I have to stand over you with a whip?"

Tito threw his hands up. "Yes suh, massa, suh."

"I'm not in the mood today. Let's just get this done."

Tito didn't say anything else. Chris was in one of his moods. That meant there would be no playing around today.

Chris walked over to Hernando, who was sitting under a tree sipping coffee from a thermos. "You plan on working today?" Chris snapped.

"You just got here and you talking about me?" he replied.

"Just get up and start digging the trench for the pond. Julio!

Get over here. Why are those shrubs rotting away on the back of the truck?"

The man muttered something in Spanish as he walked over to the truck and began unloading the bushes.

"Be a man. Say it in English so you can hop your behind on the unemployment line."

"Yo, homes," Hernando said. "You need to chill out. We're doing the best we can. You didn't leave us plans for this job."

Chris looked down at the ground. "All right, my bad," he said. "Listen up, guys, I'm sorry for acting like this. Let's just get this done before it gets too cold."

The men mumbled and started digging and planting. They worked for about four hours non-stop without talking. Chris attacked the ground, taking out all of his frustrations on the dirt at his feet. In the back of his mind, he wondered if Andre was going to make good on his threat to call his lawyer. He didn't want go to jail because of that fight.

"Yo, homes," Hernando said. "Can we break for lunch or is that against the rules?"

"Take a break," Chris said. He walked over to his truck and realized that he'd left his lunch on the table at his apartment. Now he was going to be hungry and pissed off.

Tito looked at Chris. "Do you want to share my sub?"

He shook his head.

"What's going on with you?" Tito asked.

"Nothing."

Tito bit into his sandwich. "Whatever you say, man. But you have a bug up your ass about something."

"Just let it go."

"Is this about Rosalyn?"

Chris shook his head furiously.

"So what's the problem? The only time you act like this is over a woman."

"You're a shrink now? The poor man's Dr. Phil or something?"

"Nah, but you need to chill out. Maybe you need to call Rosalyn and let her take care of what ails you."

"Stop bringing her name up."

"All right. So what are you doing tonight?"

"Sleeping. We have another job in the morning."

Tito shook his head. "No, we don't. You talking about that Ellison thang? He called this morning and canceled."

"Yeah, that's right," Chris said. "His wife's in the hospital. I guess he's not thinking about redoing his lawn."

Tito shrugged his shoulders. "I sure could have used that money."

"Oh well, that's life," Chris said.

Tito shook his head. "I hate it when you act like this. You need to take some time away. Go eat or something. I'll keep these people in line."

Chris looked at him and scowled. "All right, I'll be back at three."

Tito saluted Chris as he got into the truck. Chris headed up the road back to Columbia. On the 30-minute ride to his place, he tried not to think about Dana. But she was all he could think about.

He drove into the parking lot and sat in the truck for a few minutes. He shook his head, trying to clear all of the conflicting thoughts that were dancing around in his mind. What if Dana's mother got worse and Dana felt that Andre was the person she should turn to? What would he do then? He felt he was in the same boat he'd been in when he was seeing Rosalyn. *Why am I always second string?* he thought as he got out of the truck.

Chris walked in the door and dropped down on the sofa. He ran his hand across his face. He started to pick up the phone and call Dana, but what would he say to her? *I'm not going to chase her.*

*I said I was going to give her time and that's what I'm going to do.*

Now Chris wondered if he could handle the time that she needed.

# CHAPTER SEVENTEEN

By the time the lunch crowd rolled into Capitol City, Dana had baked 144 brownies, three German chocolate cakes and made four-dozen truffles. She stood in the kitchen and watched as the lunch goers bought brownie after brownie.

She smiled as people wolfed down the chocolate squares. Some customers closed their eyes and moaned as they took big bites. Murmurs of "This is so good" floated around the bakery.

"Dana," Josh said as he walked up behind her. "I told you that you were a hit. Now do you believe me?"

"I see it," she said, drinking in the sight.

"Why don't you take off and go check on your mom?"

"I will after I finish this cake." She turned back to the cooled layers.

"All right. I want you to make sure you get out of here. Can you come back tomorrow?"

"Sure. Same time?"

"Yep."

She quickly smoothed the frosting on the layers and constructed the cake. When she looked down at her watch it was nearly one p.m. She planned to head to the hospital, then go home and take a nap. She knew she was going to have to explain a lot to her father about why she wasn't at school. *Maybe I'll wait until I know how Mom is before I tell him anything,* she thought as she took her apron off. She slipped out the back door of the bakery and headed to her car.

She drove slowly to the hospital. Dana was in no hurry to talk to her father about her problems at E. L. Wright or her work at the bakery, even though she was seeing success. When she got there, she rode the elevator up to her mother's room. Denise had been moved to a private room on the sixth floor. Though she was starting to get the color back in her cheeks, she wasn't strong yet. Her voice, which was usually like booming thunder, was barely above a whisper.

"Hi," Dana said when she walked into the room. Frank turned around and looked at his daughter.

"Hey, come sit down."

"How is she?" Dana pulled up a chair on the opposite side of the bed from where her father was sitting.

"Resting. The doctors said she's doing well."

Dana looked down at her sleeping mother. More gray hairs were showing in her hair and there were perceptible lines running across her forehead. Dana stroked her mother's hair. "Have you gotten any rest?" she asked her father.

He shook his head. "Andre called this morning," Frank said.

Dana rolled her eyes and cleared her throat.

Frank continued. "He said you told him to stay away from your mother."

"I did. He has no reason to be here."

"Dana, he also told me that he got into a fight with that Chris person in the waiting room. I don't want him around here either."

"Fine."

"Dana, what's going on with you?"

"I don't want to talk about that now. Why don't we focus on Mom? She needs looking after, I don't."

"I am focusing on your mother. But what are you focusing on? Has Chris ever hit you?"

"What? Of course not! Why would you even ask me that?"

"If he could pound on Andre like that, there's no telling what he might do to you."

Dana rolled her eyes. "Chris is not a violent man. Why don't you ask Andre what he did to get the ass-kicking he deserved?"

Frank stood up. "Let's talk about this outside."

"I don't want to talk about it at all. And before your buddy Mr. Mason calls you and tells you, I've been suspended from my job."

"What? On what grounds?" Frank sat down and looked at Dana. She could read the disappointment in his eyes.

"A parent had an issue with my teaching style. The school board is going to review my performance."

Frank shook his head, then ran his hand over the day-old stubble on his chin. "I can't believe you're throwing your career away like this."

She sucked her teeth. "This is your career and Mom's career. I never wanted to be a teacher. I didn't want to go to USC, I didn't want to be mini Denise and Frank."

"Is that what you think you are?"

"No, I think you think that I'm a 12-year-old child who can't be trusted to make her own decisions. I started at Capitol City Bakery today. This is something I want to do and I'm good at it. I saw people actually clamoring for something that I cooked. Dad, for once in my life I have two things that belong to me and don't expect me to give either one of them up."

Frank's mouth hung open. "I-I didn't realize you were so unhappy."

"All you had to do was talk to me and not at me," she said. "You two never listen to what I have to say."

"You don't know what you want, Dana. I know you can be so—"

Dana rolled her eyes in disgust. "That's exactly what I mean."

"What are you going to do if you fail?" Frank asked.

"I'm not going into this to fail. Is that what you want me to do? Do you actually want to see me fall on my face?"

"No, but you are setting yourself up for failure. Everything your mother and I have ever done was so that you could have a good life. You didn't have to struggle the way we did. Everything was easy for you. We had to deal with segregation, white teachers trying to hold us back, taking the grades we made and passing them off as grades of white students so they could get into better schools. We never wanted you to suffer. If you do this, Dana, you will suffer."

Dana stood up. "Call me if anything changes with Mom." She bolted out of the room. As she pressed the down button on the elevator, she fought back the tears. Why couldn't her family believe in her dream?

Chris called Tito's cell phone. "Hey, I'm not going to make it back to the site, so why don't you guys take off and we'll start early tomorrow."

"You cool?"

"Tired, that's all."

"Get some rest and come to work with a better attitude tomorrow."

Chris laughed. "All right, man." He hung up the phone and lay back on the sofa, kicking off his boots and reaching for the TV remote. He mindlessly flipped through the channels looking for something to occupy his mind. But the only thing he could think about was that he needed to end his relationship with Dana. Chris wasn't going to play the fool for another woman and be hurt again. *Why does love have to be so damned complicated?* The phone rang, breaking into his somber thoughts.

"Yeah?"

"Chris, it's Dana."

"What's going on?"

"I want to see you. We need to talk."

"I'm at home. You can come by if you want to."

"All right, I'm on my way."

He hung up and sat up, trying not to speculate on what Dana had to say. He was going to let her do all of the talking since she wanted to talk, but he had made his decision. For his sanity, this relationship had to end. If it didn't, Chris knew he was going to be in a world of hurt all over again. When a knock came a few minutes later, he opened the door and Dana walked in. She plopped down on the sofa and they sat in silence as Judge Judy doled out her brand of justice to a group of wayward defendants.

Chris turned the television off and looked at Dana. "What's on your mind?"

"I don't care what happened at the hospital. I need you in my life because you're the only person who believes in me. The least I can do is believe in you. Andre probably needed to get knocked down a peg or two. Do I wish someone else had done it? Yes."

"Dana, I wasn't trying to make things harder for you and I don't usually try to solve my problems with my fists."

She stroked his cheek. "I know that."

Chris smiled, but it didn't reach his eyes. "I was still wrong for acting like my momma didn't raise me any better than that. I'm sure Andre told your father what happened."

"I don't give a damn what my father or Andre thinks. I care about you and nothing they have to say is going to change that."

"So someone said something?"

Dana rolled her eyes. "That's not important."

Chris grabbed her hand and squeezed it. "It is if I'm getting between you and your family."

Dana waved her hands in the air and changed the subject. "I had a great day at the bakery. Josh made me an associate chef."

Chris didn't let the family subject drop. "How is your mother?"

Dana sighed. "She's getting better. I would've stayed there, but my father and I got into an argument."

"About me?"

Dana kicked off her leather mules. "Among other things."

Chris shook his head. "Are you sure you want to be here? Look at what you're risking for this relationship."

Dana looked away from him. "Just let it go. I'm really getting tired of people telling me what I should do with my life."

Chris shook his head. "Dana, I know your family may drive you crazy, but your mother needs you a lot more than I do."

"I can be there for my mother and still be... What is this really about?"

Sighing, Chris stood up and walked away from Dana. Turning to her with a sad expression on his face, he said, "This is about me, Dana. I care for you a great deal, but not enough to risk my own sanity and happiness. You say you want to live your own life and make your own decisions, but blood is thicker than water and one day..."

Dana leapt from the sofa, glaring at Chris. "This was a mistake," she shouted. "I sat here and poured my heart out to you when you had obviously already made your decision about us."

"It's the same decision you made earlier when you said you needed space. I'm not going to let you jerk me around," he replied.

Shoving her feet into her shoes, she turned to him. "I'm sorry I bothered you."

Chris grabbed her arm. "Dana."

She jerked away. "If I recall, you were the one telling me

not to give up on us, but it seems like you have."

"It's just that maybe this isn't the right time for us. I've been thinking about this all day and that's the only thing I can come up with. It would be best if we just stopped this thing before someone gets hurt."

"It's too late for that." Dana stormed out of his apartment fighting back the tears. She slammed her car door, feeling like a fool. She wiped her eyes with the back of her hand. Her cheeks burned and her throat tightened. Maybe she spent too much time fighting her mother. Maybe Andre was the one for her. Zariah had warned her about giving Chris what he wanted too soon. *I should have listened,* she thought. She started the car and peeled out of the parking lot, nearly clipping two parked cars in front of her.

By the time Dana got home, she was a bucket of tears. She couldn't believe things had turned out this way with Chris. She'd thought he was special and they were on their way to building something. She stumbled inside and sat on the bottom stair, burying her head in her knees. Tears seeped through her jeans. She sat there for hours, thinking of the time she'd spent with Chris. The way he'd kissed her, how good it felt to have him inside of her. It reminded her of something her granny used to say.

*"Baby, everything that feels good and tastes good ain't always good for you."*

Dana sat up and wiped her eyes with the tail of her shirt. The only thing she could think to do was go to bed. She stripped down to her underwear and crawled underneath the covers. She pulled her comforter up to her chin and closed her eyes tightly. Tears still flowed down her cheeks. As she was nodding off, the phone rang. Dana rolled over and picked it.

"Hello?"

"Dana, it's Zariah. How are you?"

"I'm okay, just tired."

"I saw your mom today. Why didn't you tell me?"

"Can we do this some other time?"

"Dana, what's going on?"

"I made a big fool of myself and I'm trying to deal with it."

"Is this about Chris?"

"Yes."

"All right, we'll talk later."

"Thanks. Oh, I started at the bakery today."

"Did you? How did that go?"

"Pretty well, considering."

Zariah sighed. "You might as well tell me right now what's going on with you and Chris."

Dana recounted the last 24 hours of her life. She told Zariah about the fight Chris and Andre had, how she'd told Chris she needed space and how he'd shot her down when she reached out to him at his apartment.

"Dana," Zariah said softly.

"I know, I was warned."

"Yes, and it's better that things ended now rather than later when you were deeply in love with him."

"Whatever. Pain is pain."

"But wouldn't you rather know that he's a selfish jerk now than two or three years from now?"

Dana sighed. "He isn't a jerk."

"Then what is he? You were willing to give up your family to be with him and he repays you by dumping you?"

"Zariah, I'm going to bed."

"Fine," she said. "But if you still care for Chris, you'd better talk to him before you close your eyes."

Dana hung up the phone and looked over at the clock.

What could she say to Chris? She picked up the phone and dialed his number. The phone rang and rang. *Where is he?* she wondered as she hung up the phone.

⚮

Chris sat at the bar and sipped his fourth beer. He knew he should've been at home sleeping, but he couldn't shut his mind down. Every time he closed his eyes, he saw the tears streaming down Dana's cheeks as she walked out of his apartment. The last thing he'd wanted to do was hurt her. But he had.

*Why did I tell Dana those stupid things?* he thought. *I don't want to be without her.*

"Excuse me," a familiar voice cooed in his ear.

Chris turned around and looked into Rosalyn's gray eyes. "What the hell do you want?"

"I'm here to save you."

Chris mumbled incoherently.

"Sweetie, you're drunk and you need help."

"Not from you."

"Where's your little girlfriend?"

Chris threw his head back and snarled, "Why are you concerned?"

"Because I knew you and that little pampered princess weren't going to last. She isn't what you need. You know I am."

"Like I need a hole in my head," Chris replied.

"Come on, Chris," Rosalyn said. "Just let me drive you to get some coffee."

"No."

Rosalyn slid onto the stool beside Chris, draped one arm around his shoulder and dropped the other one into his lap.

Chris didn't have the strength to push her away. "Tell me what's wrong, baby."

"I wanted a drink and that's what I got."

She slid her hand across his belt buckle. "Is that all you want?"

Chris closed his eyes and willed himself not to get aroused. Rosalyn's fingers danced around his zipper. It took everything inside him to grab her hand and push it away.

"This isn't going to work. I don't want you anymore," he said.

"Mr. Happy is saying something else. Did I drive you to drink like this?"

Chris turned his back to her after he pushed her arm away. "You know what, I'm not going there with you. I have something special with Dana and you're not going to mess it up."

"If things are so good, where is she?" Rosalyn stood up and got in Chris's face. She leaned forward so he could get a good look at her form-fitting sweater. "Let me take you home and if you want me to leave, I will."

Chris wobbled as he stood up and Rosalyn grabbed his arm. "Put your arm around my shoulder," she whispered in his ear. "I'll take care of you."

Chris didn't reply. He just let Rosalyn lead him out to her Honda Accord.

# CHAPTER EIGHTEEN

Dana couldn't sleep, no matter how hard she tried. When she counted sheep, she saw Chris's face. When she stared at the ceiling, she could see Chris's body dropping down into her bed.

The sheets rustled as she sat up. She wanted to drive over to Chris's and talk to him. But before she got out of bed, she changed her mind. It was almost two a.m. Chris was probably sleeping. Dana exhaled loudly, then grabbed the remote from the floor and flipped on the TV. She surfed through the channels, not focusing on the pictures. Finally, her eyes got tired and she turned the TV off and fell asleep.

The next morning, Dana woke up feeling tired and restless. She picked up the phone and called the bakery to tell Josh she was going to spend the day with her mother.

"Dana, take all of the time you need," he said. "We have everything under control here."

"Thanks."

Dana lay in bed after she hung up the phone, staring at the ceiling. It hurt her to the core that Chris thought she would allow her family to determine who she should be with. Suddenly a thought occurred to her. *Breakfast. I'll take him breakfast and we can work this out.* She leapt out of the bed and headed down to the kitchen. Dana pulled out all of the ingredients—eggs, flour, sugar and berries—needed for blueberry muffins. As she started mixing the batter, she reached over and turned the oven on. When she finished the mixing, she pulled her muffin pan out, sprayed it with Baker's Joy and poured the batter in. As the muffins baked, Dana called the hospital to check on her mother.

"Hello?" Frank said when he answered the phone.

"Hey, Dad."

"Dana, good morning."

"How's Mom doing?"

"She's doing well. The doctors are examining her now. She may be coming home this week."

"That's great. Get me a copy of her diet and I'll make her some meals until she gets the hang of cooking the way they tell her to."

Frank sighed.

"What?"

"Nothing, I just... You know what, let's not get into this."

"I'm going to come by later on this morning," she said, feeling disappointed that her father still viewed her cooking as a problem.

"All right, I'll see you then."

৵৵৽৻

She felt good in his arms. Her soft hair brushed against his cheek as he turned over. But something was different. When did Dana start wearing Chanel No. 5? Chris opened his eyes. He was bare-chested and holding Rosalyn was in his arms. *What have I done?* Pulling the covers back, he saw that he still had his jeans on. Relief washed over him.

"Hey, hey," he said, shaking Rosalyn's shoulder.

"Um," she moaned.

"Rosie, wake up."

Her eyes fluttered open. "Good morning," she said.

"What are you doing here?"

"You don't remember? I drove you home last night. You and

Mr. Budweiser, or whatever you were drinking, got a little too friendly. "

"But why did you stay?"

She smiled slyly. "Because you asked me to."

"Yeah, right. You can leave now."

"Why? You owe me. The least you could do is fix me a cup of coffee or one of your famous omelets."

"There's a Waffle House down the street."

"I drove your drunk ass home and this is the appreciation I get?" She pulled the covers back.

"I have to get my truck."

Rosalyn smiled as she sat up in the bed. "I'll take you to it, even though you don't deserve further assistance from me."

"Thanks. I'll fix you some coffee, but I don't feel like cooking," he said.

She stroked his back. "Well, there are other ways you could repay me."

Chris looked at her. "Keep dreaming." He walked into the bathroom and sighed with relief. He was glad he hadn't slept with her. Dana would never forgive him if he had. As he splashed water on his face, he wondered if Dana would even speak to him again.

"You okay in there?" Rosalyn asked.

"Yeah," he called out. "I'll be right out."

"All right."

When Chris walked out of the bathroom, Rosalyn was lying naked on the bed with her legs spread apart. He turned away quickly. "Come on now, put some clothes on."

"You used to like my body."

"I used to like Fruity Pebbles too, but I grew up." Chris walked out of the room and into the kitchen. A few minutes later, a fully clothed Rosalyn entered the kitchen.

"I don't want the coffee. Why don't I just take you to your truck so I can go home? I've embarrassed myself enough for one morning."

"Fine, I just need to put a shirt on."

"You really care about her, don't you?"

Chris nodded. "I don't cheat like some people I know."

Rosalyn sucked her teeth. Chris turned around and walked into the bedroom to grab a tee shirt. The phone rang as soon as he closed the door.

"Want me to get that?" Rosalyn called out.

"No!"

She picked up the phone anyway so that she could listen in on the conversation.

"Yeah?" Chris said.

"It's me."

"Dana. What... How are you?"

"I was thinking about you last night and this morning. Chris, we really need to work this out. I don't want to go back to my life before I met you."

"You know, I was just trying to protect myself but letting you walk out the door hurt me more that I could have ever imagined. I'm so sorry. I hope you'll forgive me for being selfish and not thinking about your feelings too. Last night, when I went to sleep, the only thing I wanted was to have you in my arms, but I thought I had blown it with you."

"I want to see you, I have some homemade blueberry muffins. Why don't I swing by and we have breakfast?"

"Uh, I have to go to work. I don't have time, but let's do lunch." He knew she wouldn't understand why Rosalyn was at his place. And there was no way she would believe they hadn't slept together. He had to keep her away until he got his truck, even if he did have to stretch the truth. Chris didn't have a job he was going to.

"Are you sure everything is okay?" Dana asked.

"Everything is fine. I'm just running late for a job and have to go. But lunch. I'll meet you at the bakery."

"I'm not going to be there. I'll come to you. I'm going to the hospital to be with my mother."

"Cool, meet me at my place around one-thirty."

"All right," Dana said. "I can't wait."

Chris hung up the phone feeling like a cad for lying to Dana about work. But it wasn't as if he'd actually slept Rosalyn and lied to her about that. He pulled his Carolina Panthers sweatshirt over his head and walked into the kitchen.

"You've always been a horrible liar," Rosalyn said.

"What?"

"You lied to that poor girl. You're not on your way to work. And she baked muffins for you," she said sarcastically.

"See, this is why I can't be with your scandalous ass. Why were you listening?"

She smiled. "It was an accident. But now that I've heard how sappy you are for her, I'm going to let it go. You two deserve each other."

Chris snorted. "I'm so glad you approve."

"Chris, I know what I did was wrong, not telling you about my husband and everything. But you don't know what it's like to be with someone who just wants to control you. You made me feel free. Sure, I meant to take advantage of you last night, but I'm glad now I didn't. You're a class act and if this Dana girl doesn't start acting right, let me know."

"Why don't you just take me to my truck and leave the rest of my life alone?"

She shrugged her shoulders. "Whatever."

They headed out the door without saying another word to each other.

Dana had an unsettled feeling in the pit of her stomach when she hung up with Chris. He'd seemed to be hiding something. *Stop it, little Ms. Paranoia.* Dana grabbed a muffin and took it into the living room. She sat down on the sofa and turned the television on. Before she could go to the hospital for another dose of "you're-ruining-your-life" she needed a few muffins and coffee in her belly.

Dana drew her knees up to her chest as she ate. She watched the *Montel Williams Show*, not really paying attention. Just as she stood to grab another muffin, there was a knock at the door. She sprinted to the front door and pulled the curtain back, hoping it was Chris. She frowned when she saw Andre's face instead.

"Andre," Dana said when she opened the door. "What do you want?"

"Since you've banned me from the hospital, I came by to check on how Denise is doing."

"Why didn't you call my father? You two seem to have a lot to talk about."

"All right, I was thinking about you. Look, can I come in?"

"No."

"I just want to apologize for what happened the other day. I shouldn't have provoked your *boyfriend*."

Dana rolled her eyes. "Done?"

"Yes."

She tried to close the door, but Andre placed his hand in the frame. "Dana, what does he have that I don't? Why him?"

"Andre, just let it go. We're over. Even if Chris weren't in the picture, we'd still be over."

He moved his hand. "Is it all right if I go see your mother? Like I said, Denise and I are friends and colleagues."

"I don't care," she said, then slammed the door in his face. Dana shook her head as she walked into her bedroom. Dressing quickly, she started for the hospital, praying that no one would say anything about school, Chris or Andre. But that was wishful thinking.

As soon as she walked into her mother's room, her father looked at her with questions in his eyes. Denise was sitting up in the bed. "Hey, Mom," Dana said. She hugged her.

"Why aren't you at work?" Denise asked as she kissed her daughter's cheek.

"Because I'm here with you."

Frank coughed. Dana shot him a pleading look. *Don't do this, Dad, not now. I'll tell her about my situation when she gets better.* Frank seemed to read her thoughts and didn't say anything.

"Dana, I'm touched, but your father being here is enough."

She sat down beside her mother's bed.

Denise looked at her. "Is there something going on that I should know about?"

"Honey, the only thing you need to know about is getting better," Frank said. "Since Dana's here, I'm going to go take a shower and get a few hours of sleep." He stood up and stretched his legs.

Denise smiled. "All right, Frank."

When he left, Denise turned to Dana. "Remember how my mama used to say every closed eye isn't sleeping?"

Confusion clouded Dana's face.

"I'm disappointed in you."

"Mom, you're recovering from a heart attack. Don't worry about me."

"You're my only child, I can't help it."

Dana reached out and stroked her mother's cheek. "I'm not a child anymore," she said softly. "And I don't want to fight with you. I want you to get better. Then we can fight."

"It's not about fighting, Dana. Honey, I just want you—"

"To succeed," Dana finished.

"Is that such a terrible thing?"

"No, it isn't," she said. "Have the doctors given you your diet yet?"

Denise shook her head. "I know I'm going to have to learn how to cook all over again. All of this good living just caught up with me."

"This is nice," Dana said.

"What?"

"Us, talking and not yelling for a change. I was so scared when Daddy called me."

"Lord willing, I'm going to be here long enough to see my grandchildren."

Dana rolled her eyes up toward the ceiling. "Let's not go there."

"I hope you and Andre have worked things out."

"Why don't I go get you something to drink?"

"Dana, don't you move. Tell me that you and Andre have gotten back on track, because I have some great plans for your wedding."

"The wedding is still off."

Denise sighed and closed her eyes. "I'm not strong enough to go there with you today. But Andre is a good man. Don't let him walk out of your life."

The room door opened. "I thought I heard my name," Andre said.

Dana sucked her teeth and looked away from Andre.

"I'm glad you finally made it. I thought you had put this old woman down."

Andre laughed. "Never that. I just needed permission."

"Permission? What kind of nonsense is that? You can come see me anytime you want."

Dana stood up. "I'm going to get some air," she announced.

Denise shook her head. "Girl, sit down."

"Don't leave on my account," Andre said, flashing a plastic

smile.

Dana sat down, crossed her legs and stared at the wall as Andre filled Denise in on the latest happenings at the University. She looked down at her nails, trying to tune Andre out.

"Dana," Denise said. "Why don't you and Andre go grab something to eat."

"I'm not hungry," she replied.

"Dana, don't act like that. You've been in here all morning. You need to eat something."

"I'll even pay for it," Andre said.

"I said I wasn't hungry," Dana snapped.

"How are things going with your new job?" Andre asked.

"New job?" Denise inquired. "What new job?"

Dana glared at Andre. *You son of a bitch,* she thought. "It's not a new job. I'm doing some part time work."

"Why?"

"Because I want to. I enjoy baking and this is the foundation I'm going to need when I start my catering company."

"This is the first that I've heard of this nonsense," Denise said.

"Don't get worked up, Dr. Ellison," Andre said. "You know how Dana is with her whims."

She bit back a nasty comment that might have given her mother another heart attack.

"Oh, I know," Denise said.

"Why don't I leave you two in here to talk about me?" Dana snapped.

Andre sneered at her.

"Dana, you have a perfectly good job at E.L. Wright," Denise said. "I don't understand this whole cooking thing. Andre, please talk to her."

"Oh, Dana never listens to me."

"You've never said anything worth listening to."

"Dana!" Denise said.

Dana stormed out of the room. Her shoulders ached and she wanted to punch something or someone. *Chris should have knocked him unconscious,* she thought as rode the elevator down to the parking lot.

# CHAPTER NINETEEN

Chris sat on his sofa staring at the blank TV screen. Guilt was kicking him in the pit of his stomach. *She doesn't need to know Rosalyn was ever here,* he rationalized. *After all, nothing happened.* Still, he couldn't help feeling guilty. He felt relief when the phone rang, interrupting his thoughts.

"Yeah?"

"Hey you," Dana said.

"That's my line."

"What are you doing right now?"

"Nothing."

"What would you like to be doing?"

Chris laughed. "What do you have in mind?"

"I know I'm early, but do you want to have brunch?"

"Sounds good to me."

Chris hung up the phone with a smile on his face. He was looking forward to seeing Dana. He needed to see her, but he hadn't made up his mind about what he was going to say about the previous night.

A few minutes later, there was a knock at the door. Chris opened the door and smiled when he saw Dana standing there with three grocery bags.

"I feel like cooking," she said.

"Well, my kitchen is your kitchen."

Dana walked in and set the bags on the counter. "Chris, I'm sorry."

"For what?"

"For making you feel like I would hurt you or somehow be

swayed by other people's opinion of you."

"Why don't we just start over. All that matters is today."

She looked at him. "I like the sound of that."

Chris pulled Dana into his arms and hugged her tightly. "How's your mom?"

"She's getting better."

"I'm glad to hear that," he said.

Dana started chopping green peppers and onions. "I'm making pepper chicken and rice noodles."

"That sounds wonderful."

"I'm glad someone appreciates my food," she mumbled.

"What?"

"Nothing. Remember I said my mother was feeling better?"

"Same argument?"

Dana nodded. "But this is it. No more justifying my choices to my parents or anyone else."

Chris playfully smacked Dana's behind. "I hear you. Need any help?"

"No. Just give me room to work."

"I'll set the table."

"Ah, no. You know the sofa is our spot," she said with a giggle.

Chris walked into the living room and moved his magazines from the table. "Want to watch a movie? I've got some old videos."

"Like what?" she replied as she rinsed the chicken breasts.

"*Love Jones, Carmen Jones, Purple Rain*—"

"Did you say *Purple Rain*? I love Prince."

"Prince it is," he said as he stuck the tape in the VCR. Chris listened to the sizzle of the chicken and the chop-chop sound of Dana cutting more vegetables. He could get used to this; in fact he wanted too. After pressing play on the video, he walked into the kitchen. "It smells good in here. If I close my eyes, I would swear that I'm in a restaurant."

"You should stop. There's nothing worse than a cook with an ego."

Chris pinched her cheek. "You with an ego? I don't see it."

"It could happen. When I saw those people eating my desserts, I knew that this is what I'm supposed to be doing. I don't need to teach; I need to create," she said passionately.

"And what else do you need to do?"

Dana dumped a cup of onions into the pan with the chicken. Then she whirled around and looked at Chris, her gaze falling on his lips. "This," she said as she wrapped her arms around him, dropping the plastic measuring cup to the floor. She kissed Chris with everything in her. Every fear, every bit of passion, every insecurity and every hope. He responded with the same fury and zest. When they broke off the kiss, Chris wouldn't let her go.

"I have to finish cooking," she said.

"Let it burn. I don't want to let you go."

"Chris, is this for real?"

"Yes, it's as real as you want it to be."

"I want to formally introduce you to my family," she said.

Chris's arms dropped. "Are you sure?"

Dana walked over to the stove and stirred the chicken and onions. "Well, you're a part of my life and they have to know that. I won't hide my love for you."

Chris smiled, but a pang of guilt pricked him in the chest. What if she found out about Rosalyn? Would she still love him? Would she be willing to strain her family ties then? How could he not tell her what almost happened. He cleared his throat and smiled. "Let me get out of your way so you can finish cooking." Chris walked into the living room.

A few minutes later, Dana announced lunch was ready.

"Great," Chris called out.

Dana carried the food plates and silverware into the living

room. Chris stood and took his from her hands. "I hope you like it," Dana said.

"I don't see why I wouldn't," he replied as they sat down. Chris shoved a forkful of food into his mouth. "Dou should box tis up."

"What?"

After swallowing, he said, "You should box this up. This is delicious."

Dana wiped Chris's cheek with her napkin. "Thanks."

He grabbed her hand and looked deep into her eyes. "Dana," he murmured. Their lips touched. The kiss was gentle at first, but then Dana hungrily shoved her tongue into Chris's mouth. Her bold move caught him off guard, but he followed her lead. He sucked her tongue, savoring the taste of it. His body began to erupt like a volcano and he pulled her so close that their teeth clanked. A soft moan escaped Dana's throat as Chris's hands slipped inside the waistband of her pants. Her stomach quivered as his fingers grazed her skin. She pulled back.

"What about lunch?" she asked breathlessly.

"I have a microwave," he said before capturing her lips again. Dana's cell phone rang. She groaned as she reached into her pocket for it. Chris wanted to tell to let it ring, but it could be about her mother.

"Hello?"

"Dana, it's me," Denise said. "I thought you were coming back."

"Um, I will. Are you all right?"

"Yes, honey. I just want to talk to you."

"So, do I," Dana said. "I have someone I want you to meet."

"Who?"

"We'll be there in a little bit."

Chris looked at Dana with his head cocked to the side when she hung up the phone. "What was that all about?" he inquired.

"Come on, you're going to meet my mother."

His eyes stretched to the size of quarters. "Are sure this is the right time?"

"If not now, when? My mother and I need to get some things straight and she needs to see that I'm with the man I want to be with."

"If this is what you want to do," he said as he stood up.

"You're my man and I want everybody to know."

Chris smiled and kissed her on the forehead. "Well, let's go, woman."

They headed out to Dana's car. She drove quickly to the hospital, praying that the few bites of food she ate would stay on her stomach. What if everything backfired? They walked into the hospital without speaking to each other. Dana tried to calm her heart as it pumped overtime. Chris grabbed her hand and squeezed it gently.

"It's going to be fine. Stick to your guns," he whispered as they walked onto the elevator.

"I will," she said, her voice barely above a whisper.

The elevator stopped on her mother's floor. They walked quickly and quietly to Denise's room. Chris wrapped his arm around Dana's shoulder as she pushed her mother's door open.

"Mom," Dana whispered.

Denise sat up in the bed. "Hey. Who is that with you?"

"This is Chris," she said.

Denise squinted her eyes at him. "Do I know you?"

"Yes ma'am. I was at your house to see about reworking your yard."

"Why are you here?"

"Because he's with me," Dana said. "Chris is the man in my life."

Denise's mouth hung open. "I don't understand."

"There is nothing for you to understand, except Chris makes me happier than I've ever been in my life."

"But Dana—" Denise stopped in mid-sentence.

"But what?"

"What about your future as an educator? Did you even finish high school?" she asked Chris.

Chris cleared his throat. "I think I'm going to wait outside," he said.

Dana watched him walk out of the room and then she turned to her mother. "That was so rude!"

"I don't give a damn. What can that *man* offer you? Is this about getting back at me and your father?"

"It's about me wanting someone to love me and everything about me. Not someone who sees a relationship with me as a way to get ahead on his job. That's what it was for Andre and I deserve better than that."

"Oh, please," Denise said.

"Are you saying I don't deserve to be loved and to be happy? Or is it just that I can't be happy unless it meets your standards?"

"Dana, your father and I didn't work this hard to watch you throw your life away."

"How am I throwing my life away? How? Do you think that I'm doing this to spite you? I want to be happy. Chris makes me happy, baking makes me happy."

"There is more to life than being happy. You need to realize that, little girl."

"I'm not a child and I won't be treated as one. You will respect Chris. He's a part of my life and he isn't going anywhere."

Denise shook her head. "You wait until I'm lying in a hospital bed to come and tell me this? Are you trying to kill me?"

"Don't worry, Mother, you and roaches will be here after the nuclear bombs explode." Dana ran out of the room and into Chris's arms.

"I'm sorry about that," she said.

"You don't have anything to apologize for. You can't control what your mother says."

"She didn't have to disrespect you that way."

Chris shrugged. "I'm not sure I'm worth this."

"I'm sure you are. It doesn't matter what my mother thinks."

He wrapped his arms around Dana and squeezed her. "She is your mother."

"She's not acting like it. Let's go."

❧⟡❧

They walked to the elevator in silence. Chris hated the strain between Dana and her mother, but he wasn't going to take too many more of Denise's ignorant comments. How could her family love her, as they claimed, but not support her? Chris knew he wasn't Andre, the man Denise had picked for Dana, but wasn't it enough that he loved and respected her daughter? Was status more important than love to those people? He saw now that Dana's family would have no problem turning their back on her. Nonetheless, he was committed to his relationship with her. He had never felt this way about a woman before and there was nothing her family could do to make him leave.

"What are you thinking?" Dana asked as the door opened. He shook his head.

"Come on, Chris, I can read that look in your eyes."

"What happens if your family turns their back on you?"

Dana rolled her eyes. "Not thinking about that."

"You have to think about that."

Dana sighed and looked away from Chris. He grabbed her chin, forcing her to face him.

"If this relationship is going to work, we're going to have to deal with this."

"Chris, my family is my problem, not yours. We've been having this battle for years. If it weren't you, it would be somebody or something else."

Chris rubbed her back gently. "I don't want you to resent me if—"

"Chris, everything is going to work out. My mother is just being herself. It's a sign that she's getting better. We were getting along earlier and I thought she was opening her mind, but it was too good to be true."

When they got back to Chris's place, neither of them had an appetite for Dana's lunch. They dropped down on the sofa, feeling as if they were battered and bruised from a street fight. Chris held Dana tightly, nuzzling against her neck like a puppy.

"Last night, I thought I had lost you. I was really worried that I would never hold you or kiss you again. So, like a stupid guy, I went out and got drunk," Chris whispered.

"I really wanted to come over last night. I wanted to say something, to explain—"

Chris brought his finger to her lips. "It's all right. As long as we're here, nothing else matters."

"Can we stay locked in here forever?"

He kissed her gently on the cheek. "We can stay until the movie goes off." Chris grabbed the remote and turned the television on. Dana leaned on his shoulder as Prince's image danced across the TV screen. Before he finished singing "The Beautiful Ones," Dana was asleep in Chris's arms.

❧

Later that evening, Dana went home to prepare for her day at Capitol City. She wanted to try a new recipe and she needed to do something to take her mind off her mother's rude comments to Chris and her own feelings of guilt for the last thing she'd said to her mother. Her mother had embarrassed her, but she knew it was going to get worse when her father put his two cents in. *What is it going to take for them to realize I'm a grown woman entitled to make my own decisions?*

The phone rang as Dana flipped through her recipe box. "Hello?"

"Have you lost your mind?" Frank bellowed.

"Excuse me?"

"Why did you come here and get your mother all worked up?"

"I don't need this."

"Dana, you need to grow up. Everything isn't about you and your mess. Your mother is sick. You shouldn't have brought that delinquent thug in here."

"Chris is a part of my life. If you can't accept that, then you can't accept me."

"So you're going to turn your back on your family when we need you most?"

"That's not fair."

"Goodbye, Dana. When you get yourself together, we'll be here."

She threw the cordless phone on the floor, smashing it against the tiles. She refused to cry. It didn't seem worth it. No matter what she did, her parents were never going to approve. So, the only thing she could do was move on.

*I don't need them anyway,* she thought bitterly.

# CHAPTER TWENTY

Dana's morning began with the shrill ringing of the telephone. She looked at the clock, it was five-thirty.

"Hello?"

"Dana, it's Mr. Mason. I'm sorry to call you so early, but the board wants to meet with you in my office today at eight."

"That was quick."

"I tried to reach you yesterday."

"Well, my mother is in the hospital and I've started another job."

"What?"

"I don't care what the board decides, I'm not coming back to E.L .Wright," she said.

"Dana, don't make a hasty decision that you're going to regret. You're a fine teacher."

"Out of professional courtesy, I'll go to this meeting, but you'll have my resignation at the same time."

"Dana—"

She cut him off, telling him her mind was made up. Dana hung up the phone and sat up in the bed. The gauntlet had been thrown down. Now she had to make sure she could make it without her parents' help and the security of her job at school. After a moment's thought, she called Josh at the bakery to let him know she was going to be late.

"You have a lot going on, don't you?" Josh said.

"Some of it ends today. Then you will have your associate chef full time."

"I like the sound of that. I'll see you when you get here. Your brownies were missed yesterday."

"I'll make up for it today. And I have a new recipe I want you to try."

"Looking forward to it."

Dana hung up, headed for the bathroom for a quick shower. She didn't want to be late and miss the look on everyone's face when she told them what they could do with her job.

For a split second she thought about her students. *They need a teacher who wants to be there,* she reassured herself as she pulled her favorite black and white pantsuit from the closet.

Dana skipped breakfast in favor of composing and printing out her resignation letter.

> *Dear Mr. Mason:*
>
> *Please accept this as notice of my immediate resignation. I appreciate the opportunity you gave me to begin my teaching career at E. L. Wright. However, I'm moving in a new direction, away from teaching.*
>
> *Thank you again for the opportunity you gave me.*
>
> *Dana Ellison*

She printed the letter out and folded it. It was time to move on.

When Dana got to the school, she walked straight into Mr. Mason's office. She looked at the two board members sitting across from Mr. Mason, recognizing them as Tina Jones and Linda Hopkins. They were frequent guests at her parents' summer barbeques.

"Dana," Mr. Mason said when he noticed her standing in the doorway.

"Good morning," she said.

The two women nodded, acknowledging Dana's presence.

"Mr. Quick is on his way," Mr. Mason said. "Have a seat."

Dana handed him her folded note. He didn't look at it, but set it on his desk and frowned.

"I was really hoping you would change your mind," he said. Dana shook her head.

Tina Jones cleared her throat and said, "Dana, I was shocked when the board received this complaint about you. I mean, Frank Ellison taught you the right way to deal with irate parents."

"With all due respect, Tina, this isn't about my father. Not only that, this meeting is just a formality. I've tendered my resignation." She nodded to the folded letter on the principal's desk.

"But why?" Linda asked. "Clearly this situation was a misunderstanding."

"I don't want to teach. This situation opened my eyes to that."

"You're a good teacher. We don't want to lose you," Tina said.

"Are you getting a job with another school system? We can match what they're offering you," Linda said.

"This isn't a bidding war. I'm not leaving for another school."

"What can we do to make you stay?" Tina asked.

"I've made my decision," Dana replied politely.

Tina and Linda stood up. "Then I can see no point in point in continuing this meeting. Dana, we hate to see you go, but your resignation is accepted," Tina said. The two women left.

Mr. Mason shook his head. "What are you going to do now?"

Dana smiled. "Go back to school, maybe start a catering company. At this point I really don't know for sure."

"But you do have another job?"

"Yes. At Capitol City Bakery. This is something I need to do, Mr. Mason. I need to be my own Ellison."

He nodded. "So, effective immediately, you're no longer a teacher?"

"I'd like to tell my students, if that's okay."

"This morning?"

Dana looked at her watch. "This afternoon. I'm late for work. Tell the superintendent I'm sorry I missed him."

She walked out of the office with a smile on her face.

⚜

Chris sat in Capitol City waiting for Dana to show up. He had to make sure she was all right. *Why isn't she here?* he wondered. *Did something else happen with her mother?*

"More coffee?" the clerk asked him as she wiped down a table beside him.

"Do you know when Dana is coming in?"

"Ah, you want some brownies, huh?" she said with a grin.

"You could say that." Chris turned toward the door just as Dana walked in.

"What are you doing here?" she asked when she saw him.

Chris stood up and kissed her on the cheek. "I wanted to make sure everything was okay with you this morning."

"Everything is great," she said. "I quit my job a few minutes ago."

"What?"

"I'm done with teaching. This is my focus."

"Wow. What are your parents going to say?"

Dana shrugged her shoulders. "I don't care." She headed for the kitchen and Chris followed her.

"Dana, I know your family is important to you."

"I'm not important to them, so to hell with them." Dana pulled her apron over her head.

"All right, I'm going to leave it alone. I have to get to a job."

Dana threw her arms around Chris and kissed him on the tip of his nose. "I appreciate what you're trying to do, but I can handle this."

"You don't have to do it alone. You have me." He playfully

smacked her on her booty, then headed out the door.

Chris sat in his truck for a minute, thinking. Though he was-n't close to his family, he couldn't stand by idly and let Dana throw away her relationship with Frank and Denise, especially since Denise was in the hospital. So instead of driving to Lexington, Chris headed to the hospital.

When he got there, he took a deep breath before he got out of the truck. His mind was made up. He was going to talk to Denise and Frank about Dana. He walked to Denise's door and knocked lightly.

"Come in," Frank said quietly. Chris entered and stood near the door.

"What in the hell are you doing in here?" Frank demanded.

"I came to talk to you about your daughter."

"Get out of here before my wife wakes up. She doesn't need this stress right now."

"Sir," Chris said, struggling to keep his voice even and low. "Dana needs her family and you two need her. This isn't the time to let something come between you all."

"You don't know a thing about this family. Why don't you go plant some bushes or something. Your concern is not needed here."

"Is this about me? Are you going to cut Dana out of your life because she wants to be with me?"

Frank snorted and pointed to the door.

"I can't believe you're that shallow. Thank God Dana isn't like you."

Frank got up and pushed Chris in the chest. "What did you hope to accomplish by coming here?"

"You need to get your hands off me," Chris snapped.

"I know your type. You see Dana and the money she comes from and you want a ride on the gravy train. Do you think I haven't seen your type sniffing around my daughter before? Now

199

you want to bring her down to your level. Dana will return to her senses and you'll be left out in the cold."

"You think so? Dana and I have something special and there's not a damn thing you can do about it. Either deal with it or lose your daughter."

"You think you have the power to pull that off?"

"Mr. Ellison, you're doing this to yourself. Dana loves you and her mother, but have you ever tried to see things her way?"

"Don't you lecture me on my relationship with my daughter."

Chris smirked. "What relationship? Dana is finally doing something that makes her happy and all you do is criticize her."

"I'm calling security," Frank said as he walked over to the phone.

Denise began to stir in the bed. "What's going on?"

"Nothing, this man was just leaving," Frank said, dropping the phone.

Denise looked at Chris. "Why are you here? Haven't you caused enough problems?"

"Mrs. Ellison, you need your daughter and she needs you. But if you can't accept who she is, then she's going to be lost to you forever."

"What's he talking about?" Denise asked.

"Nonsense," Frank snapped.

Chris shook his head as he headed out the door. "Young man," Denise called out.

He turned around and looked at her.

"Why don't you leave my daughter alone? Dana can do much more with her life if she has the right people pushing her the right way. Obviously that isn't you."

"It must not be you either," Chris snapped as he stormed out of the room.

He didn't know what he'd been thinking when he walked into that room. Nothing he'd said or could say mattered. Dana's parents were determined to treat her like a child. He got into his truck and headed to his job, trying push the Ellisons' venom out of his mind. But it was all he could think about.

⋘⋙

Dana's cell phone rang as she placed a pan of brownies in the oven. She had just baked 20 dozen brownies but the bakery needed more. "Hello?"

"What were you thinking?" Frank demanded.

"I was thinking that this is my life and I'll do what I want to do. I don't have time to talk to you right now."

"So sending that thug here was supposed to accomplish what?"

"What are you talking about, Dad?"

"Chris came to the hospital and proceeded to tell me and your mother that we were treating you unfairly."

"I had no idea he was coming there. Is that all you want?"

"Dana, I want you to stop acting like a child and start taking responsibility for yourself."

"I'm doing that, but you can't see that, can you? All you see is I'm not the Ellison you want me to be. I'm blazing my own path. Why can't you just be happy for me and support me?"

"Because I can't support your making a mistake."

"I quit E. L. Wright today."

"You did what?"

"You heard me."

"Dana."

"I have to go, my brownies are burning." Dana snapped her phone shut and dropped her head. She was tired of having the same argument with her parents. *This has to stop,* she thought. *I can't take much more of this.*

By lunchtime, her parents were the last thing on Dana's mind. She was up to her elbows in flour and chocolate. Her German chocolate cake was as big a hit as her brownies.

Josh walked into the kitchen. "I love you," he said.

"What?"

"Listen? What do you hear?"

"The cash register."

"That's right. And we're going to be featured in *The State* this weekend. A reporter is coming by tomorrow."

"Wow."

"This place has become a major lunch destination." He walked over to the kitchen door and pushed it open to show Dana. She scanned the crowd and smiled. There were construction workers dressed in dusty blue jeans mingling with office workers in their $500 suits. "This is great."

"Tell me about it," Josh said. "And people said I wouldn't last a year here."

"Did it bother you having so many people against you?"

He shook his head. "The only thing that bothered me was the fact that my mother never got to see this. She was always in my corner. My dad, on the other hand, thought a cooking son meant I was gay or something."

Dana looked away as tears moistened her eyes.

"If things keep going this well, I'm going to have to let you buy in as a partner," Josh continued.

A light bulb went off in Dana's head. "Josh, have you ever thought about doing any catering?"

Josh shook his head no.

"Let me try some catering, only on the weekends. We can start with some small parties."

"If you can line up some parties, I would definitely consider adding a catering service."

"Let me do some research and I'll make sure you do more than consider it."

Josh nodded. "You're persistent, aren't you, Ms. Ellison?"

Dana winked at him.

"I'm out of here. See you tomorrow," Josh said, then bounded out the door.

Dana waved at him, then returned to mixing her truffles. After they were done, she was going to find Chris.

*What was he thinking, confronting my parents like that?* Andre would have never stood up to Frank and Denise. He always took their side. Dana felt comforted and honored to know she had someone in her corner, and Chris was going to know it the minute she saw him.

# CHAPTER TWENTY-ONE

Chris felt a tingle of alarm when he saw Dana's car parked outside his building. *Damn, her father probably lit into her and now I'm going to get it.*

He slowly got out of the truck and walked over to her car, then gently tapped on her window.

Dana opened the door and got out. Her face revealed nothing.

"Look," Chris said. "I know I took a risk going to your mother's hospital room, but—"

Dana pressed her index finger against his lips. "Thank you."

Chris stepped back in surprise and shock.

Dana seemed to read the look on his face. "Yeah, I teetered on being angry with you, but Chris, you're really in my corner. God, you're everything I've ever wanted. Someone who believes in me and my dreams."

"I just wanted to help," he said.

"Don't worry about it. Just get upstairs and unlock that door. I have a special way of showing my appreciation in mind."

A devilish grin spread across Chris's face. "Oh really?"

Dana's smile mirrored his. "Yeah." She reached into the car and pulled out a white box from the bakery. "I brought dessert for dinner."

Chris licked his lips as he walked up the stairs. "I'm ready for my sugar rush," he said.

When they got inside, Dana pulled Chris into the bathroom. "What are you doing?" he asked.

"You need a bath," she said as she began filling his tub with water.

"Dana Ellison, you're asking for trouble."

"No, I'm asking you to strip," she said boldly.

Chris pulled off his work boots, unzipped his jeans and in one motion quickly kicked out of them. Dana lifted his sweatshirt over his head, then ran her hand across his chest.

"Are you joining me?"

"I do feel kind of dirty," she replied.

Chris began unbuttoning her blouse, gently slipping it from her shoulders. He leaned in and kissed her silky skin, then reached back and unsnapped her black demi bra, freeing her breasts. Dana kicked out of her shoes as Chris unzipped her pants. He slid her pants down, stroking her thighs with his thumbs. Dana could feel herself melting against him as he slipped his hand into the waistband of her hi cut bikinis. He pulled them down, then stepped into the tub, holding his hand out to her, urging her to join him.

Dana quickly took his hand and stepped into the water, splashing some of it over the edge. Chris wrapped his arms around her waist, pulling her against him. Her body quivered with anticipation when she felt his hardness pressing against her thighs. As his hands glided down her back to clutch her buttocks, she moaned and wrapped her leg around his waist, giving him the green light to press into her hot and moist body. Chris backed up to the wall, allowing Dana to position herself on top of his throbbing manhood. She teasingly ground her body against him. Then as Chris dug deeper into her they fell down into the tub and water splashed everywhere. Chris was inside of her, touching her most sensitive spot. Dana tightened herself around him, rocking back and forth, riding the sensual sensation. He took her breasts into his mouth, sucking and licking her nipples, all the while pumping harder, faster.

Chris buried his head in her bosom and moaned. In the

throes of her orgasm, Dana wrapped her arms around Chris's back and rocked back and forth, unable to speak. Her body pooled like the water in the tub and she rested against his chest with her eyes closed. Chris cupped his hand and scooped up some water. He poured it over Dana's head.

"Hey!" she exclaimed.

Chris smiled, then kissed her on the forehead. "Maybe I should go talk to your parents more often."

"Don't ruin the moment," she whispered as she tweaked his erect nipple.

"All right, but this is an issue."

Dana kissed him in the center of his chest. "No, it isn't." She grabbed the blue bar of soap in the soap dish, rubbed it across his shoulders, down to his chest, across his stomach, then his legs and feet. Chris took the hint. She didn't want to talk about her parents. He lay back and let her have her way with his body. Her fingers and soft touch turned him on, made him ready for round two and before she could rinse away the soapsuds, he grabbed her arms.

"I wasn't finished," she said.

"It's my turn now," Chris replied, capturing her lips with his and pulling her onto his lap. "Soap?"

She reached into the water and handed him the slippery bar. Chris rubbed his hands together to work up a lather, then glided his hands across her breasts, making slow circles around her nipples with his fingers. Then his hands danced down her stomach to her thighs. He slowly massaged her inner thigh, keeping his eyes on her face. Dana's eyes were closed and her head tossed back as she waited for Chris's next move. He cupped one hand and scooped up more water and poured it over her heaving breasts. Her nipples grew hard like brown diamonds. Chris poured still more water on her.

"I could do this all night," he said.

"Umm."

"But this water is getting cold."

"I'm not." She opened her eyes and looked at him with a devilish grin.

"All right, now," he said as he stood up. "But you know what's better than bathing together?"

"No, what?"

"Drying off." Chris stepped out and grabbed a towel from the shelf and held it open for Dana to wrap herself in.

"What should I do with these?" Dana motioned toward their soaked clothes on the floor.

"We can deal with them later," he said as he pulled her towel open and pressed his body against hers. Dana rubbed his shoulder with part of the towel.

She looked in his eyes and read so much that was unspoken. Dana could feel herself falling that much harder for him.

"What?" he asked.

"Nothing. I'm just getting a little chilly," she said. Despite her feelings, she wasn't ready to declare her love.

"Come on, I'll get you a shirt to put on. Then we can attack that box of dessert in there. You did make a brother work up an appetite."

Dana thumped him on the arm playfully as he eyed her body. She didn't feel self-conscious being naked around Chris anymore.

"Let me get you a shirt to put on before I have *you* for dessert," Chris said.

Dana followed Chris into his bedroom and sat down on the edge of the bed. A sparkling diamond earring on the floor caught her attention as she glanced down. She picked it up. "What's this?"

"Huh?" Chris turned around and looked at her. Dana held the diamond stud up.

"This earring. Where did it come from?"

Chris walked over to her and took it out of her hand. He knew exactly where it had come from. Rosalyn.

"Um, it's Rosalyn's."

Dana's heart skipped a beat. "Your ex?"

"It's not what you think. The other night after we got into that argument, I went out and got drunk."

"So you slept with her because you were drunk? Is that supposed to make it better?" Dana leapt to her feet. "Unbelievable. I can't believe you did this to me. I really thought—"

"Dana, I didn't sleep with her. I was drunk, she drove me home and that's it."

She looked at him, folding her arms across her chest and pouting her lips as if to say "Do you think I'm stupid?"

"Why would I lie to you about this? I told you it was her earring."

"Only because you've been caught."

"Dana, I didn't do anything."

"Why didn't you tell me about this before I saw the damn earring?" Dana snapped.

"It wasn't important. You know how I feel about you. Why do you think I would risk what we have for a meaningless night with Rosalyn?"

"I don't know. Why did you do it?"

Chris grabbed her shoulders. "Dana, if you trust me, if you care about me, you know that I didn't sleep with her."

Dana pushed him away. Tears sprang into her eyes. She wanted to believe Chris, but a voice in the back of head told her he was lying. Chris reached out to her, touching her shoulder and turning her around.

"Tell me you believe me." His voice was barely above a whisper.

"I want to believe you. But—"

"No buts. You can believe in me, in us."

"You should have told me."

"I was embarrassed. I acted like a child. Instead of talking to you about our problems, I went running to the bar and got smashed. I thought I had lost you."

"Don't keep things from me. If we're going to be together, you have to be honest with me. No matter what. I can't have you or anyone else making decisions for me."

Chris sighed and ran his hand over his face. "I didn't tell you Rosalyn was here because I wanted to avoid a scene like this. I'm sorry."

"You know she wants you. She made that clear."

"But I don't want her. I have everything I want and need in you. You're the one I want and need in my life. Rosalyn is nothing to me because I love you."

"What?" Dana nearly dropped to the floor.

"I said I love you."

Dana bit her bottom lip. Did he mean it or was he saying it just to calm the situation?

"I mean it," he said as if he were reading her mind. "The minute I saw you, I knew I could love you and now I do. You're like no other woman that I've ever met before and I'm not going to lose you because of this nonsense."

"I-I love you too," Dana said. "I was too scared to say it and when I found this earring, I just jumped to all of the wrong conclusions."

Chris stroked her cheek. "You don't have to jump to any conclusions when it comes to me. I would never hurt you the way I've been hurt."

"I'd better put some clothes on."

"I could turn the heat up and we could walk around naked, just like nature intended."

Dana shook her head as she grabbed the oversized tee shirt from Chris's hands. "I don't think so."

"I'll throw your clothes in the dryer." Chris wrapped the towel around his waist and walked into the bathroom. Dana took the earring off the dresser and tossed it into the wastebasket near the door. Her insecurities were not going to cost her this relationship. Chris loved her and she loved him. Nothing was going to stop them now.

❦

Dana and Chris snuggled on his sofa. Even though her clothes were dry, she felt too comfortable in Chris's shirt to change or get out of his arms. "Why don't you stay with me tonight?" he asked.

"I'd love to, but I have to get up early and head to the bakery."

"What are you doing this weekend?"

She shrugged her shoulders.

"Remember that trip I owe you?"

She nodded.

"Pack a bag," he said. "We're going to Atlanta."

Dana stretched and smiled. "You're not getting out of it this time," she said.

"I don't want to."

She looked at the clock. "I'd better go. Where are my clothes?"

Chris stood up. "I'll get them. Finish watching the movie. I know the only reason you stayed was because of Prince."

Dana smiled. "You know that's right," she said, focusing her attention on the ending of *Purple Rain*.

Chris walked into the living room and handed Dana her clothing. "All right, you can leave now."

"Thanks," she said as she took her clothes from his hand. "Breakfast in the morning?"

"Sure. I'll meet you at the shop."

Dana dressed, then kissed him on the cheek. "All right."

Chris walked her to the door. "Dream about me, Ms. Lady," he said as she walked out to her car.

"You know I will." Dana waved to him as she got into her car. Love was a wonderful feeling. Dana just hoped that it would last.

# CHAPTER TWENTY-TWO

Time passed quickly after Dana began to put her all into her work at Capitol City. Josh had finally agreed to Dana tackling a few holiday parties. It was a welcomed distraction from her feuding with her family. If things continued to be strained between Dana and her parents, this would be the first time that she and her family would not spend the holidays together.

As it turned out, Dana and Chris spent a quiet day alone at her house on Thanksgiving chomping down on roasted turkey with cornbread stuffing, collard greens, macaroni and cheese, cranberry sauce and pumpkin pie. It was the first time Dana had cooked a Thanksgiving meal her way, which made her happy and melancholy at the same time. Quietly, Dana wished she and Chris could have spent the day at her parents' house. Now, with the attention turning to Christmas, Dana knew she had to find something to take her mind off her parents and their attitudes.

"Earth to Dana," Josh said. "Hello."

"Huh, what?"

"The Scota party. Have you seen what they want?"

"Oh, yes and it's all taken care of."

"Is everything all right with you? You've been acting strange the last couple of days."

"It's just the holidays. They make everyone crazy," she said in an attempt to keep her voice light. But sadness punctuated her words. Josh smiled at her and stroked her arm comfortingly.

"What are you doing for Christmas?" he asked.

"Baking, more than likely."

"Why don't you, Zariah and Chris come to my party on Christmas Eve?"

"Sounds like a plan," she said as she turned her attention to her fruitcake batter.

"Zariah better be there," he said with a grin.

"What's up with you two anyway?" Dana looked up from the mixing bowl.

Josh shrugged, "Nothing yet, but someday, your friend is going to be my wife."

When he walked out of the bakery, Dana was alone with her depressing thoughts. She didn't feel like baking cookies, cakes and pies for other families to share during the holiday. She wanted to be with her family, but only if they accepted Chris. When, for the first time ever, one of her cakes fell, Dana decided to give it a rest for the night. Looking up at the clock, she saw it was nearly seven and the streets of downtown were going to be empty. *Why did I stay here so late?* she wondered after she dumped her flattened cake in the trash. Dana killed the lights in the kitchen and headed for the front door. When she flipped the lock and opened the door, she found Chris standing there about to knock.

"I thought I would find you here," he said.

"You were looking for me?"

"Yes. I was worried about you. Is everything all right?"

She nodded and tried to smile, but she ended up scowling. "Chris, this is not a good time for me."

"You want to spend the holidays with your family?"

Tears pooled in eyes. "We've always been together for Christmas."

"Dana, just go to them."

Angrily, she wiped her eyes. "No. I didn't do anything wrong. While I'm standing here crying about my parents, they probably aren't even thinking about me."

Chris pulled Dana into his arms. "Sometimes, you have to be the bigger person. I don't want you to have a rotten Christmas because of me."

She looked up at him. "This isn't just about you," she said. "It's my parents' attitude about my life."

Chris grabbed her chin and pushed her face upward. "If you

want to be with your family, Dana, go to them."

"What about you?"

He shrugged his shoulders. "Just save me a plate and we can spend Christmas night together."

"But why should you spend Christmas Day alone?"

"It's just a day," he said. Dana looked at him, unable to believe what she was hearing. Chris seemed to read her thoughts.

"Ms. Lady, Christmas and all of the other holidays didn't mean much in the Johnson household. I was the kid who told the others that Santa Claus was a joke."

Dana playfully hit him on the shoulder. "That was mean," she said.

"Eh, it didn't bother me. But I'll tell you what is bothering me—seeing you so miserable." He ran his index finger down her cheek.

"Chris, I—"

"Go to them, Dana. Grill this beef between you guys and have a good Christmas."

She nodded and turned to lock the door. "I need to do something."

"What's that?"

Facing him, Dana stood on her tiptoes and gently bit his bottom lip. "You," she replied.

"Then let's get busy." He wrapped his arm around her waist and led her to the parking lot. They hopped into their vehicles and sped to Chris's apartment since it was closest to the bakery. For the first time in what seemed like forever, Dana was thinking about something other than her family. She couldn't wait to feel Chris's arms around her, his lips against hers and him inside of her stroking her most sensitive area. She shivered with anticipation as she parked her car beside Chris's truck. Her lustful gaze settled on him as he climbed out of the truck. He held his hand out to her, then clasped his wide hand around hers. Electric jolts shot through her body at his touch. They nearly ran up the stairs to his door. Once they were inside, Chris pressed Dana against the wall. Slowly, he unzipped her jacket, then pushed it off her shoulders. Dana reached for his belt buckle, but he grabbed her hand, stopping her. Tonight, he was going to give her pleasure in every way. He unbuttoned her oxford shirt, peeling it from her body. He ran his palms over her breasts then unhooked her lacy bra. Her breasts poured out. Chris bent his head, alternately taking each breast into his mouth, gently biting and licking her nipples, which hardened at his touch.

Dana's back arched as Chris's fingers danced around the waist of her pants. She didn't feel him unbutton and unzip her slacks. The next sensation she felt was his hand gently rubbing her womanhood. Her panties were moist and she was sure steam was coming from her most sensitive area. Chris slid the satin material aside so that he could feel her wetness on his hand. Dana thought she was going to melt when he entered her with his finger. A muffled moan floated from her throat. Chris pressed his finger in deeper. She dug her fingers into his shoulders to steady herself. Chris lifted her leg around his waist and she pressed her hips into his.

"I need you," she whispered huskily.

"In time," he replied as he cupped her bottom. "I want to savor every inch of you. I'm just getting started."

Chris buried his head in between her neck and shoulder, raining kisses onto her neck and collarbone. Then he scooped Dana up and gently laid her on the leather sofa. Spreading her legs apart, he dove into her pool of love face first. His tongue entered her, lapping up her essence that seeped out. Dana's legs shook violently as Chris took her to the brink of climax and her thighs closed around his head, pressing him deeper into her.

Chris's tongue moved in circles, making sure every sensitive area was touched. Dana's breathing was ragged and her cries of ecstasy died in the back of her throat as she struggled for air.

Finally Chris stopped his sensual kisses. Dana's eyes fluttered open. She knew what was next and she reached out for it. She slowly moved her hand back and forth, making him throb. He moaned as her hand moved faster and faster. As Dana sat up on the sofa, continuing to stroke his member, Chris sank back, allowing Dana to climb on top of him. She guided him into her moist valley of love.

When Chris felt her around him, he muffled a scream. Dana pressed her hips against him, pulling him deeper and deeper. Chris fell into her rhythm and the hot friction between them caused sweat to bead on their bodies. Dana rocked hard, fast and furiously. Chris grabbed her around the waist to slow her down, but she continued moving at a frantic pace.

"Dana, Dana," he exclaimed as she tightened herself around him.

Dana clutched his shoulders as she was overwhelmed by an orgasm and she collapsed on his chest.

Chris closed his eyes and hummed the melody to Prince's "International Lover." Dana smiled, then closed her eyes. She ran her hand across his chest as he continued to hum.

"Damn, woman," he groaned. "That was unbelievable."

Chris ran his finger down a bead of sweat running down her back. Dana's silence let him know her sadness had returned. "Baby, are you all right?" he inquired.

"Un-huh," she said.

Chris looked down at her. "Sure you are."

"I'm fine, Chris."

"I know how you look. I want to know how you're feeling."

Dana sighed and buried her head deeper into his chest. "Just hold me. I don't want to think about anything else."

Chris did as she asked, not pressing for an explanation of her mood.

⌘

Chris watched Dana as she lay in his bed. They'd spent the evening making love, but every time it was over, she brooded. It was as if she were using sex to lose her pain. Chris enjoyed making love to her, but he knew there was nothing he could do to make her feel better about her family, no matter how many times they made love.

She turned her gaze to Chris. Their eyes met and he saw tears.

"This is ridiculous," he said.

"What?"

Chris reached over and grabbed his cordless phone. "Call them."

"I'm not. Anyway, do you see what time it is?"

"First thing in the morning then."

Dana rolled her eyes and folded her arms across her chest. "I'm not calling them," she snapped, pouting her lips like a child.

"Damn it, you don't have to do this. I can look into your eyes and see how much you miss your parents. Obviously, family is important to you. If you all don't resolve this situation, it's going to continue gnawing at you."

"You're important to me too. And my family thinks I should-n't have you. If they can't accept our relationship, then to hell with them."

Chris frowned as Dana turned her back to him. He gently stroked her back. "Hey you," he whispered in her ear. "I'm not trying to beat a dead horse, but you've been in a funk since Thanksgiving."

She turned around and faced him. "Chris, just let it go. I'm trying to get some sleep."

She leaned her head against his chest and fought back the tears. After Chris gently kissed her on the forehead, she closed her eyes and drifted off to sleep.

The next morning, Chris woke Dana up with breakfast in bed, cheese omelets and turkey sausage. "Morning," he said as he set the tray on the bed.

"What time is it?" Her voice was thick with sleep.

"Eight. When are you due at the bakery?"

"This afternoon. I've started working past closing so I can sleep in."

"I'm glad you decided to sleep in here," he said as he cut into the fluffy omelet and lifted a forkful to her mouth.

"This is so good," she said as she chewed.

"I didn't know if you wanted coffee or tea, so I brought both."

"What did I do to deserve you?"

Chris smiled as Dana spooned sugar into her mug of tea. He dropped his cordless phone on the tray.

"Don't start that again."

Chris didn't say anything but he continued to stare at her.

Dana sighed. "How long are you going to sit there staring at me?" she asked. Annoyance peppered her words.

"Until you pick up the phone." Chris casually sipped his coffee. Dana picked up the phone, then dropped it on the tray again.

"There. I picked it up."

"Dana, call your parents."

"What if I don't?"

Chris sighed heavily. "Then I will and we know how well that will go over." He walked out of the room, leaving Dana with the phone.

A deep frown wrinkled Dana's comely features as she dropped her fork and picked up the phone. She dialed the number slowly, trying to formulate what she would say when someone answered.

"Hello?" Denise said.

"Mom," Dana answered, her voice timid.

"Dana, it's so good to hear your voice."

Her mother's words shocked her. "You know the phone works both ways," she replied.

"I know that, but your father and I thought you needed time to work out whatever problems you were having. I just didn't think it would take this long."

*So things haven't changed.* "Just what kind of problems did you and Dad think I needed to deal with."

"Dana, I don't want to argue with you. I hope that isn't why you called."

"No, it isn't. I missed you all at Thanksgiving and I couldn't—I don't want to go through Christmas without us being together like family should be."

"I want you here for Christmas. I was worried that I'd have to drag you out of your house."

"Chris is coming with me," she said.

Silence greeted this information.

"Mother, are you there?" Dana asked.

"I'm here," Denise replied. "Doesn't he have his own family to be with on Christmas?"

"Are you saying you don't want him at the house?"

Denise sighed into the phone. "Dana, it's just that your father and I don't know this man."

"Because you've never tried to get to know him. Why don't we sit down like adults and have dinner tonight?" Dana suggested.

"I'll ask your father and I'll call you back."

"Fine," she replied and hung up the phone. Chris had come back into the room in time to hear Dana suggest dinner.

"Why are you trying to force me on your parents?" he asked.

"I'm not forcing anything. We're a package deal and my parents are going to have to learn to accept you."

"And if they don't, you're back to square one."

"Well, at least I can say I tried. That's one of the reasons I want us to have dinner with them tonight. Once they give you a chance, they'll see why I fell in love with you."

Chris looked pensive.

Dana glanced at her watch. "I have to get out of here. I need to go home and change. I'll call you and let you know what time we're having dinner."

"Are you sure we'll be having dinner?"

She nodded. "Trust me, my mother will call me back," Dana said. Hope beamed from her eyes as she scampered into the bathroom.

# CHAPTER TWENTY-THREE

Chris and Dana walked up the front steps of her parents' home. She looked over at Chris, who was decked out in a pair of black Tommy Hilfiger slacks and a gold turtleneck sweater. Dana ran her hand across his chest.

"Nervous?" she asked.

Chris shook his head

"Should I just walk in or ring the bell?"

"Dana, this is your parents' house. Just walk in. I think you're the nervous one."

She shrugged. Nervous didn't describe what was going through her mind as she turned the knob. "Mom, Dad," she called out.

"In the dining room," Frank's voice boomed.

*It's show time,* Dana thought as she grabbed Chris's hand and led him into the dining room. The table was laden with baked chicken, cornbread, string beans, and apple pie.

"This looks good," Dana said, trying to break the tense silence.

"Well, I just threw something together," Denise said. She looked at Chris and forced a smile. "Chris, I hope this is okay for you."

"It's fine, Mrs. Ellison. Thank you for inviting me."

Frank looked at Chris with contempt in his eyes, then sat down without saying anything to him.

"Well, Chris, it's time to for us to get to know you," Denise said as she placed her cloth napkin in her lap.

Dana nodded and looked at Chris. He seemed calm.

"I'm an open book," he said.

"I'll bet," Frank mumbled.

Dana shot her father a warning look. "So," Denise began as she picked up the platter of chicken, "Dana, are you enjoying your new job?"

"I am. We just started doing some light catering."

"William Mason misses you," Frank said. "I saw him at the gym last week."

"The gym?"

"Your father and I are working out more now." Denise smiled proudly.

"I'm glad you're taking care of yourself," Dana said sincerely.

"If only you would do the same," Frank said. "Dana, do you realize what you threw away?"

She rolled her eyes toward the ceiling. "Dad, please give it a rest." Frank was like a pit bull. He wouldn't let go.

"You're behind this, aren't you?" Frank snapped, turning toward Chris.

"Excuse me?" Chris replied incredulously.

"Dana was on her way up and now she's a common baker. Just because you're content in a dead end job, it doesn't mean you have to drag my daughter down to your level."

"Frank," Denise warned. "This isn't the time."

"Then when is the time? This man has ruined Dana's life and I refuse to sit by and watch." He banged his hand against the table, causing the ice in the crystal goblets to rattle.

Dana stood up, nearly knocking her chair over. "This was a mistake. Chris is the best thing that has ever happened to me. Working at the bakery is the most rewarding thing that I have ever done. Why can't you accept that I'm my own woman and I can make any choice that I want? Chris doesn't have any control over me. And neither do you!"

Chris stroked Dana's arm, urging her to sit down with his

touch.

"Mr. Ellison," Chris began. "I know you want the best for your daughter and so do I. I love and respect Dana."

Frank snorted. "I know what you want from Dana," he snapped. "You want to feel like you're something, someone. Class doesn't rub off. You have it or you don't."

Dana looked to her mother for help. Denise just shook her head. "Dana, sit down," she pleaded. Dana ignored her mother's request.

"No, we're leaving," she snapped.

"Please," Denise said. "We need to talk and get everything out in the open. Now I wouldn't have gone the route Frank took, but Chris, this relationship is strange. When you and Dana met, she was engaged to another man."

Chris rubbed his temples. "I'm aware of that. But Dana's a grown woman and she made her choice. The reason we're here tonight is that she wanted to patch things up with the two of you before Christmas. I don't give a damn what you think about me, but Dana loves you. She's been miserable these past few weeks."

"Chris, please," Dana began.

He shook his head, silencing her. "I'm not a college professor, I don't have a college degree, but I have more love and respect for your daughter than either of you have shown her in the entire time I've known her."

Frank banged his hand against the table again. "How dare you! You don't know anything about our family."

"Oh really?" Chris said. Frank didn't intimidate him. "I know that you expect Dana to live your dream and let hers die. That's not fair to her."

"Please stop this!" Denise said. "Frank, the young man has a point."

"What?" Frank snapped.

Dana stared at her mother. She was sure the woman sitting at the end of the table must be a clone. Denise was agreeing with Chris? Dana shook her head as everything sank in. She couldn't remember the last time she and her mother were on the same side about anything.

"Dana, your father and I have been acting very ugly," Denise continued.

Frank opened his mouth to say something, but he stopped when Denise held her perfectly manicured hand up. "One thing that heart attack taught me was that life is too short to be fighting with my only child. No offense, Chris, but you're not the man I would have picked for Dana. But you make her happy and you stand up for her. I have to respect that."

"Ma," Dana murmured. "Wow."

Frank rolled his eyes. "You may have my wife and my daughter fooled, but I see right through you," he snapped before pushing his chair away from the table. "I've lost my appetite."

Frank strode out of the dining room. Dana dropped her head and bit her bottom lip as tears pooled in her eyes.

"I'll talk to your father," Denise said quietly.

"We're going to leave," Dana stated as Chris stood up.

"Dana, Christmas morning, both of you are invited for breakfast. You know it's our tradition."

Dana nodded. As she and Chris walked out of the dining room, Dana turned back to her mother.

"Thank you," she said.

Denise reached out and hugged her daughter. "Your father is just set in his ways. You know how he can be."

She nodded. "We'll be here on Christmas."

"And I'll work on Frank's attitude."

Chris extended his hand to Denise and she shook it. "Keep making my daughter happy and we'll get along," she said.

"I'll do my best."

When Dana and Chris got in the car, she turned to him. "I'm

so sorry," she said.

"Don't apologize. You can't control your father."

"I wish I did. Then I could make him see that he's acting just like the people that didn't want him to be superintendent or the people who didn't want their children being taught by a black man in the early '60s."

"Come on, this isn't the same thing. I know where your dad is coming from. No one is good enough for his little girl."

Dana rolled her eyes. "Whatever."

Chris stroked her knee. "Just give him time," he said. "Your mother seems as if she's on your side."

"But for how long?"

Chris pulled into Dana's driveway. "So, what are we going to do now? We never had dinner."

"You know I can whip something up," she said as they walked up to the front door. Chris smiled.

"Great. The spread at your mother's was looking good, and this brother is hungry."

Dana unlocked the front door and led Chris into the kitchen. "Sit down and I'll figure out what I have in here."

Chris picked up the phone and called Papa John's.

"What are you doing?" Dana asked, looking up from the refrigerator.

"I'm ordering pizza, you don't have to cook," he said, placing his hand over the mouthpiece of the phone. "You deserve a break after that scene at your parents' house."

"Okay," she said. Dana didn't really feel like cooking anyway. She and Chris walked into the living room and sat on the sofa. He wrapped his arms around her shoulders. She liked the calm around them. If only her father could understand how happy she was.

# CHAPTER TWENTY-FOUR

Dana walked slowly up to her parents' front door. She knew Frank was at home alone and this was the best time to talk to him. She used her key and quietly entered. She took her boots off at the door, a habit she'd had since she was a child.

"Daddy," she called out.

"Dana? I'm in the study."

She walked into the one room in the house that had been off limits to her as a child. Frank's study was like a mini library. The oak bookcase on the back wall was filled with leather bound volumes of writings by Richard Wright, James Baldwin, Zora Neale Hurston, William Faulkner, Shakespeare and many other classics. She looked at her father sitting in his leather armchair sipping a glass of iced tea. The newspaper rested on his lap.

"We need to talk," Dana said as she sat down on the leather ottoman in front of him.

Frank smiled. "You've sat there from the first day I let you in here."

She grinned at the memory. "I used to tell my friends there were monsters in here so they wouldn't open this door."

"I remember that. The kids at school said I had monsters in my house." He chuckled softly.

"Daddy."

"I know what you're going to say and I don't want to hear it, Dana. I won't apologize for my feelings."

"You have to hear it," she said, placing her hand on his knee. "I want you to give Chris a chance."

"He's a buffoon. Look at what your life has become. You quit your job, you've been estranged from us and—"

"Daddy, I'm happier than I have ever been and I have a career. Do you realize what an impact I've made at Capitol City?"

"Imagine the impact you could have made in the classroom. Dana, you should be a teacher. There's a need for teachers. Kids need people to look up to other than gangsta rappers and over-paid ball players."

She shook her head. "That was your dream for me, but I never shared it. And why can't I still be a role model? It's not like I'm doing something immoral."

"But you never said a word about doing this before."

"Dad, you and Mom weren't listening to me back then and you're not listening to me now."

Frank looked down into Dana's eyes and put his hand on her forehead, pushing her bangs back, the way he used to do when she was ten years old and sitting in that same spot. "What do you have to say? I'm listening."

Dana sighed. "Dad, I'm never going back to teaching and I love Chris Johnson. He is a part of my life and he will be for a long time. Why won't you give him a chance?"

"Because he isn't the man I want you to be with."

"It isn't about what you want," she said calmly. "You chose to love and marry Mom, why can't I do the same?"

"What kind of man goes after a woman who's engaged to another man?"

Dana stood up and walked over to the bookcase and ran her fingers across the backs of the books. "It didn't happen like that, Daddy."

Frank turned around in his seat. "How did it happen?"

"I saw him and we were drawn to each other. It was innocent at first; I never disrespected Andre. Chris is the only person who's ever supported my dreams and he did it from the start."

Frank sighed, then stood up. "I had no idea that baking was

so important to you."

"That's because you all never asked me what I wanted. You know, I could have gone to Clark Atlanta for college. I qualified for a full scholarship."

"Dana—"

"Let me finish. I've spent the majority of my life trying to make you and Mom happy. Now it's time for me to start thinking about making myself happy. Chris and working at Capitol City make me happy. I would like for my family be a part of it all."

"I can't in good faith support this," Frank said.

"Why not?" Dana asked. Her disappointment toned her voice.

Frank walked over to his daughter and gripped her shoulders. "I just wanted so much more for you."

"This is what I want for myself. And this is enough."

"I'm not making you any promises about Chris, but I'll be civil if you bring him back over here."

Dana hugged her father tightly. "Thank you, Daddy."

"Do you think you can fix me one of those fruit cakes?"

"Sure. Right now, I have to get to work."

Frank hugged his daughter tightly before she walked out the door. "Dana, I love you. Sometimes I don't say it enough and I don't always show it, but I do love you."

"I love you, too," she said, then kissed him on the cheek.

When Dana got to the bakery, she was hopeful about Christmas with her folks and Chris. Maybe things would work out and she could have it all.

Chris walked into his apartment and scowled. He hated winter. All of his usual jobs froze up when the temperature dipped blow 40 degrees. It was a good thing his uncle kept the workers on salary during the off-season. Chris dropped down on the sofa and flipped the TV on. As he channel surfed, he wondered what he should get Dana for Christmas. The phone rang, breaking into his thoughts.

"Hello."

"What's up, man?" Tito asked. "I don't ever see you since you and that girl got together."

"We've been spending a lot of time together, haven't we?" Chris smiled as he thought about Dana.

"Let's hit Dynasty tonight. They're having a winter jam and you know they're always hot."

"Sure, why not? I hadn't been out to the club in a minute."

"Cool. And I can get all the women because you're spoken for."

"That's right. I got a good one this time, bro."

"I'm glad. Now you can stop whining over Rosalyn."

"Man, that seems like a lifetime ago."

"She doesn't ask about you anymore when I see her out."

"She knows that I'm in love with Dana. Both of us have gotten over that whole thing."

"What did she do to you? I mean, you were the one talking about how you were done with women last year. Now look at ya. Your nose is so wide open your brain is showing."

"I'm thinking about marriage," Chris revealed.

"I know she got you all open right now, but marriage? Are you insane?"

"No. I don't need your approval, either."

"I thought she had a fiancé?"

"That's over."

Tito sighed. "You ever wonder why your relationships turn

out the way they do?"

"What do you mean?"

"You rush everything. You've known her a few months and you want to get married."

"T, when something is right, you go for it. Waiting doesn't make a bit of difference."

"Whatever, but think about it before you jump into something. She just gave a man his ring back. What makes you so special that she's going to say yes to you?"

"What time do you want to head out?" Chris asked, changing the subject.

"About ten. You know we have to let the ladies get in there first."

Chris rushed off the phone because he didn't want Tito to know how his words had affected him. What if Dana weren't ready for another marriage proposal? Chris made up his mind as he stood up and grabbed his jacket. He was going to roll the dice and ask her to marry him. *All she can do is say no,* he thought.

Chris walked into Palmetto Diamonds and headed for the glass case holding the diamond engagement rings. He didn't know anything about picking out a ring, but he remembered what Dana had said about the ring Andre gave her. She didn't like it. *Nothing too big,* he thought as he stared at the rings.

"Hello," a tall, caramel-complexioned clerk said in a heavy southern drawl. "Someone is getting married?"

"I'm just thinking about it right now," he said.

"What's she like?"

"She's a warm and caring person. Her smile lights up the room and she has this sparkling personality that makes everyone love her."

The woman reached into the case and pulled out a tray of rings. She picked up a one-karat white gold ring.

Chris took the ring from the woman's hand. "This looks like

her."

"What size is she?"

He shrugged his shoulder. "How can I find out? I've never done this before."

"Well," she drawled. "You can brang one of her rings in or you can just ask her."

"I want this to be a surprise," he said.

The woman nodded. "For Christmas?"

"Right. I know this is the ring that I want." Chris looked down at the price tag. He inhaled sharply when he saw the cost.

"We have an excellent payment plan," she said, noting Chris's expression.

He nodded. "I'm going to need it."

"Well, find out her size and come back. We'll get everything squared away. But this is a popular ring, so don't wait too long," she said.

Chris nodded and headed for the door. Seeing the price tag had given him second thoughts. What if Dana didn't want to get married? He didn't want to be sitting with her Christmas Day and pull the ring out only for her to say no. If he bought the ring, he was going to surprise her on Christmas morning after breakfast with her parents.

*Maybe I need to test the waters first before I just spring a ring on her.*

∽⊗⊘∽

Dana smiled when she saw Zariah and Josh walking into the bakery holding hands.

"What is this I see?" she asked, coming from behind the counter. She had just put a fresh batch of brownies in the display case.

"Oh, you're the only one who can have a good thing?" Zariah kidded.

Dana grinned.

"How did things go today?" Josh asked.

"Pretty good. I put out some fruit cake samples and believe it or not, people loved them."

He threw his hands up. "Once again, Dana was right."

"Aren't I always?" she joked. "Christmas is not Christmas without fruitcake."

"Josh, there isn't anything Dana can't cook, so her fruitcakes aren't the typical door stopper fruit cakes," Zariah said, standing up for her friend.

"I hear you," he said. "I'm going to check the receipts, so feel free to talk about me."

Zariah slapped him on the forearm. "No one is going to talk about you." As Josh disappeared behind the kitchen doors, Dana smiled at her friend.

"I knew this was going to happen."

"It's been building for years, I finally stopped fighting it. Your happiness is contagious," Zariah said. "How is Mr. Wonderful?"

"Good."

"I'm glad I was wrong about Chris."

"So am I."

"Have your parents come around yet?"

Dana shrugged. "Somewhat. My father is still on the fence."

"Chris must be some man to put up with that crap. I know how your parents can be."

Dana nodded. "Enough about me. What about you and Josh?"

"Well, we've been friends for years, you know that. But lately I've seen him in a different light."

Dana smiled. "Love is in the air," she sang.

"Don't make me go Simon Cowell on your non-singing behind."

Dana stood up. "Let me hurry up and get out of here."

"Hot date with Mr. Wonderful?"

"No. I can do things on my own. I'm tired. I need a hot bath and some time with Zora."

"You're reading *Their Eyes Were Watching God* again?"

"It's a December tradition."

"Do you regret what you've done these last few months?" Zariah asked.

"Not at all. I should have stood up for myself a long time ago. Just think, I could be on the way to the altar with the wrong man, stuck in a job I hate and still living in the shadow of Mr. and Dr. Ellison."

Zariah smiled. "You go, girl! I knew you had it in you all this time."

They slapped five to each other and then Dana headed for the kitchen to clean up before she went home.

# CHAPTER TWENTY-FIVE

Chris sat at the bar with Tito watching his friend strike out with every woman he ran his "Hey baby" line on. He wanted to leave, but Tito claimed he was having a good time. Chris didn't understand how. He was just glad he wasn't trolling the club for women. Any doubts he had about asking Dana to marry him flew away as he got a closer look at the single life.

"Hey, Tito, I'm calling it a night."

"This early? Damn, that girl got her hooks in you something deep."

Chris laughed as he drained his beer. "There's nothing out here but trouble and drama. I'm done with all of this."

"So, you're going to do it?"

"What?"

"Ask her to marry you."

"I think so."

Tito shook his head. "I still say it's a mistake. This is happening way too fast."

"Ask me if I care what you think."

Tito picked up his beer and looked at Chris. "If she says no, don't blame me."

Chris looked away from his friend. He knew he couldn't handle it if Dana turned him down. Deep in his heart, he felt as if Dana would say yes. Every time he looked in her eyes, he saw so much love. *Tito doesn't know what he's talking about and I don't know why I'm letting him bother me,* he thought.

Chris stood up. "All right, man, I'm heading out of here."

"Okay, bro. Hell, I might as well leave too. We can kiss club night goodbye once you drop that diamond on home girl."

Chris laughed as he placed money on the bar to cover his drink. "Whatever, man."

When Chris got in his car, he started to drive to Dana's but it was getting close to midnight. *She's sleeping,* he thought as he headed home. Besides, if he saw her tonight, he knew the first thing he'd do was propose. He'd drop by the bakery the next morning.

❧

Dana sipped steaming coffee, trying to wake herself up. *I hate mornings,* she thought as she stirred the batter for fruitcakes.

"Dana," Josie, the clerk, said. "Your man is here."

"Chris?"

She nodded. "Is there another one?"

"Of course not. Send him back here. I'm up to my elbows in dried fruit and nuts."

A few seconds later, Chris was walking into the kitchen. "Is that the dreaded fruitcake?"

Dana tossed piece of pecan at him. "Don't come in here with that. You're going to eat my cake."

Chris scrunched up his nose and stuck his tongue out. "I don't think so."

"What brings you by this morning?"

"I missed you last night."

"Why didn't you come over?"

"I went out with Tito. He claims we don't hang out since you and I have gotten together."

Dana dumped the fruit into the batter and started the industrial mixer. "Where did you guys go? Let me guess, Dynasty?"

Chris nodded and stole a piece of pecan from the counter. Dana frowned at him, then laughed. Chris cleared his throat. "Has your father come around about us?"

"Not really, but he said he would behave Christmas morning." She turned the mixer off and poured the batter into the Bundt cake pans. She slid it in the oven then sauntered over to Chris, wrapping her arms around his waist. "Everything is going to work out for the best."

He kissed her on the tip of her nose. "I hope you're right. I was wondering about something."

She looked into his sparkling eyes. "What's that?" she asked.

"Where do you see this relationship going?"

Dana looked at him thoughtfully. "I've never really thought about it. I'm enjoying what we're doing right now."

"Me too. But when you dream about the future, I know you see your catering company and possibly a bakery of your own. But do you see me?"

Dana took Chris's face in her hands. "Of course I do. Chris, you opened my eyes to so many things. I wouldn't be here if it weren't for you. Where is this coming from?"

He gently kissed her on the lips.

"You're not off the hook," she said.

"Dana, I love you and when I see my future, I see you and me standing at that park near Fort Jackson after I renovate it. The mayor is smiling as he cuts the ribbon and your brownies are being passed out in the crowd."

"It's going to happen," she said. "I know it is."

"Yeah, I think I'm going to take this down time I have between jobs and research that area over there."

"Let me know if I can help. I'm not above using my cakes and brownies to bribe a politician," she ribbed.

Chris let her go and smiled. He was still trying to figure out how to ask her if she wanted to get married.

Dana looked at the pensive look on Chris's face. Deep wrinkles creased his forehead. "What's wrong?" she asked.

"Nothing. I just have a lot on my mind."

"Did something happen that I need to know about?" she questioned. "If it did, just spit it out."

"Nothing like that. Do you think you'll ever get married? I know the whole thing with Andre was something your parents pushed, but did it sour you?"

"Are you trying to tell me something?"

"No. New Year's around the corner and I get a little introspective around this time of the year."

"If you say so," Dana replied. She watched him grab a handful of pecans and shook her head.

"Well," he said. "I've got to go. Let's have dinner tonight."

Dana hid her smile. "Sure," she said. "My place or yours?"

"I was thinking we could go to Carrabba's."

"O.K," Dana said.

"I'll pick you up at seven," he said as he leaned in and kissed her on the cheek.

"I can't wait," she said.

∽⧉⧉∽

When Chris left, Dana could barely contain her excitement. She called Zariah the minute she took her fruitcake out of the oven.

"Hello?"

"Z," Dana said excitedly. "Guess what."

"I just worked a double at the hospital. I don't have time for guessing games."

"I think Chris wants to ask me to marry him."

"What? You guys have only been dating five minutes. You can't be serious."

"It seems sudden, but I know Chris is the one. I knew the moment I saw him."

"Please think about this, Dana. What do you really know about Chris?"

"He hasn't asked yet but he was just talking about marriage today. Z, I know this much about Chris: he's always in my corner. I love him and waiting around to marry him won't change anything."

"I just don't want to see you rush into something. However, you're an adult and you have to do what's right for you. You know that I'm overly cautious when it comes to stuff like this."

"I guess that's why it took you and Josh so long to make that connection, huh?"

Zariah sighed. "Yes, it did take a while. Maybe your way is the right way. What's the point in putting all of these years between a woman and Mr. Right?"

"Are we saying that Josh is Mr. Right?"

"Uh, I have to go."

"Zariah, Zariah, don't you hang up on—" The dial tone sounded in her ear. Dana laughed as she prepared a glaze for her cakes. She wanted to get as much done as she could so that she could leave early. She had a really strong feeling that Chris planned to propose over dinner.

With a high heart, Chris headed back to Palmetto Diamonds after seeing Dana. He was going to do it, no matter what Tito or anyone else thought.

"Good morning," said the clerk from the day before. "I see ya came back."

"Yeah. I want to get the ring I was looking at yesterday."

The woman smiled. "What size?"

"Can I get it sized later? I want to surprise her."

The woman smiled. "She will be surprised and she's gonna love this diamond." She handed Chris a credit application. He filled out the application and silently prayed that he would be approved.

The woman took the papers when he was done and headed over to the computer. Chris looked at the ring in the box. He closed his eyes and imagined the gleam in Dana's eyes when he gave her the ring.

"Sir," the clerk said. "You're approved."

"Great," he said.

"Good luck to you." She completed the sale and placed the ring in a bag.

Chris walked out of the store, got into the truck and tucked the ring into his glove compartment. He could hardly wait for Christmas morning.

⤜⋙⋘⤛

When her day was over, Dana dashed home to get dressed for what she fully expected to be one of the most special nights of her life. The first thing she did was to go into the bathroom and soak her hands in the sink. She wanted to make sure she didn't have any flour or dough underneath her nails when Chris took her hand in his.

Next, she took a hot steaming shower and smoothed a passion fruit-scented body wash over her body. Since starting to date

Chris, she'd developed an appreciation for her curves that she once kept hidden under bulky layers all year long. Chris made her feel sexy, alive and alluring. She would love to be his wife. Dana closed her eyes and lost herself in a fantasy of Chris asking her to marry him. When the water began to run cold, she shut the spray off and got out. In her head, she could hear Chris's melodic voice whispering, *Will you marry me.*

Slowly, with deliberate strokes, Dana rubbed lotion on her supple thighs. It was as if she could feel Chris's hands touching her. *Get it together*, she thought as she walked over to her dresser drawers. Dana pulled out a pair of pink silk bikini panties and a matching bra, because she knew after dinner she'd be Chris's dessert. Then she selected a black wool dress that hit her at her ankles. It showed off her curvaceous figure and ample behind. Chris's appreciation of her behind made her feel like the sexiest woman in the world. After she pulled the dress over her head, she looked at herself in the mirror.

She couldn't believe the image staring back at her. Dana felt as if Chris's love had transformed her. She wasn't the shy, self-conscious Dana Ellison anymore, but the alluring woman Chris saw her as. At seven, she was ready. When the doorbell rang, her heart skipped a beat. This was it. Dana inhaled sharply before turning the knob.

Chris drank in Dana's image, his eyes twinkling as they roamed her body. "You look fantastic."

"Thanks, come in, I just need to grab my coat."

Chris walked behind Dana, mesmerized by her heart shaped bottom and the way her dress hugged it tightly. He pulled at the collar of his white turtleneck.

Dana picked up her leather trench coat and he helped her put it on. "I'm ready," she said.

"Good." Chris opened the door.

"What's so special about tonight?" Dana probed as they

drove.

"I just wanted us to spend some time alone together. You always cook. It's time for you to be served and pampered."

"But you know I love to cook."

"I know, but tonight I want to focus on you."

Dana smiled. "And why is that?"

"Because you deserve it."

Dana leaned over and kissed Chris on the cheek as he turned into the restaurant's parking lot. They walked into the restaurant and waited for the hostess to seat them. Dana felt like a giddy schoolgirl as they were led to a secluded table in the rear of the restaurant. The amber candles in the middle of the table lent a soft glow to the corner. Dana chewed on her bottom lip as Chris looked over the menu. When was he going to pop the question? Before dinner? After? During dessert?

The waiter came over and they ordered their food. When he left, Chris grabbed her hand.

"Are you enjoying yourself?"

"Yes," she said.

"Good. Christmas is a week away, huh?"

Dana furrowed her brows. *Christmas? Why is he talking about Christmas?* She played along. "Yeah."

"Last night when I went out with Tito I realized how lucky I am to have you."

*Here it comes,* she thought happily. "I think I'm the lucky one."

Chris smiled at her, then fell silent.

"Chris, do you want to ask me something?"

"No. Why would you say that?"

Dana felt like a deflated balloon. "No reason." She looked around for the waiter. "What's taking so long with the food?"

"You seem jumpy tonight. Are you okay?"

"I'm fine."

When the waiter brought their entrees over, Dana ate in silence. Chris looked at her with questions dancing in his eyes. "Dana, are you all right?"

"Yeah."

"Why are you so quiet?"

"I guess I'm a little tired."

Chris held her hand. "I guess so. After all, you've been working really hard these past few weeks. I'm so proud of what you've done." He kissed her hand.

Dana smiled weakly. "Thanks." *I guess I was wrong,* she thought. *It's too soon to think that Chris would want to get married. Zariah was right. We've only been together a few months.*

"Do you want to go home and get some rest? You seem beat."

"No, we can finish dinner," Dana said, trying to mask her disappointment.

Dana suffered through the rest of the dinner silently, answering Chris's questions with an "uh-huh" or a "yeah." They skipped dessert and headed back to Dana's place in silence. Even the soulful Christmas music coming through the radio's speakers didn't lift her spirits. Why had she thought he would want to marry her so soon?

"Do you want to come in for coffee?" she asked when he pulled into the driveway.

"I'm going to let you get some rest. I don't like you being overworked like this. Make sure you take care of yourself."

Dana smiled and kissed him on the cheek. "Thanks for dinner."

"I'll see you tomorrow," he said as they got out of the truck and he walked her to the front door. "Go straight to sleep."

Dana winked. "I will," she said as she unlocked the front door. She cursed inwardly when she walked inside. *What the hell was I thinking?*

# CHAPTER TWENTY-SIX

For the next three days, Dana avoided Chris. When he called, she didn't answer. She was too embarrassed. She had taken what could have been a beautiful evening and ruined it because she was looking for an engagement ring.

*I can be such an idiot,* she thought as she prepared the batter for her brownies.

"Hey!" she heard the new clerk call out. "You can't go back there." Dana looked up and saw Chris standing in front of her.

"Dana, I'm sorry," the clerk said.

"Lynn, it's okay."

Chris waited for Lynn to leave before he said anything. "What in the hell is going on?"

"I should ask you that. You're the one who came in here acting like Rambo."

Chris shook his head. "I've been worried about you. I haven't heard from you since we went out to dinner. You won't answer my calls, you don't call. Is there something going on?"

"Chris, I'm just really busy right now. Christmas is right around the corner and—"

"That's bull," he bellowed. "Dana, if you want to end things, then just say it."

She dropped her mixing spoon and turned to look at him. "Chris, maybe you're the one who wants to end our relationship since you're being so introspective."

"What's that supposed to mean?"

"Chris, why were you asking me about marriage?"

"I was trying to wait, thinking that maybe it was too soon,

but I want to marry you. I love you so much it hurts."

Tears welled up in the corners of her eyes. "Chris," she whispered. He pulled her into his arms. "I feel like such a fool."

"Why?"

"At dinner the other night, I kept waiting for you to ask me and when you didn't, I was disappointed. That's why I've been acting this way. I didn't want to set myself up for another disappointment."

Chris kissed her on the forehead. "Dana, I wanted to surprise you on Christmas, but I guess it's all out there now."

"Chris, I—"

"Dana Ellison, will you make me the happiest man in Columbia and marry me?"

"Yes!" she exclaimed. "Yes!"

Chris picked Dana up and spun her around. Then he brought his lips down on top of hers, kissing her with an urgent passion that turned her legs into jelly.

After a moment, Dana pressed her hand against his chest. "I hate to do this, but I have to get back to work."

"I know. By the way, I called the parks and recreation department this morning. We're going to meet after Christmas and discuss me doing some projects."

"That's wonderful. I know they're going to love your ideas."

Chris smiled and stroked her cheek. "I'll see you tonight."

"You can count on it." She walked Chris out to the front of the bakery.

He kissed her on the cheek and squeezed her hand. Lynn looked at her boss with confusion written all over her face. She'd thought that man was a crazy customer. "What was that all about?" she asked.

"That was my future husband," Dana said. A happy smile

spread across Dana's face.

"Wow. Congratulations," Lynn said.

Chris sat in his apartment looking at the ring he'd bought for Dana. He was sure this was the right thing, but he wondered what her family would think. Would they approve of their engagement? *I'm not going to worry about that,* he thought. Grabbing the telephone, he ordered two-dozen red roses. Tonight he was going to focus on Dana and their love. Everything else could wait.

After he ordered the flowers, Chris headed to the year-round farmers' market to pick up some of Dana's favorite fruits, like strawberries, navel oranges, Granny Smith apples and currants. His next stop was the record store. He decided to pick up a CD of smooth jazz to set the mood.

It was late afternoon when Chris finished his shopping. He couldn't wait to see the look on Dana's face when he arrived at her house later. He could hardly believe that Dana had agreed to marry him. Lucky didn't begin to describe how he felt. After years of loving the wrong woman, he had the right one in his life. Tonight, he was going to show Dana how much she was loved and how much she meant to him. In just a few hours, she would be in his arms.

Dana spent the day at the bakery with a smile on her face.

Josh looked at her as she put her last batch of brownies in the display case. "All right, what's going on? You've been too damned chipper around here today and this place has been a mad house."

"Josh, this mad house is lining our pockets. There's always a silver lining in the clouds."

He frowned and rolled his eyes. Lynn cleared her throat. "Dana is getting married, Josh. That's why she's floating around here."

"What? When did this happen?"

"This morning. I haven't told Zariah yet, so don't say anything."

Josh gave Dana a friendly hug. "I'm happy for you. Who's going to bake the wedding cake?"

"You're getting ahead of yourself. We haven't set a date or anything. And I still have to tell my parents."

"I'm sure they're going to be happy," Josh said.

Dana grunted and frowned. "You don't know my parents. Listen, I'm going to get out of here and try to make myself presentable."

"All right, girl!" Lynn said as Dana walked out of the door. She rushed home to prepare for her evening with Chris. Then it hit her. She didn't know where they were going or what the plan was. Dana ran a hot bath, then grabbed the cordless phone and called Chris.

"Hey you," he said.

"You know, I was sitting here trying to figure out what to wear tonight and I realized you didn't tell me what we're doing."

"That's right. I'll say this. Wear something sexy."

"Come on, Chris, give me a hint."

"No. I'll be there in about 45 minutes."

"Chris! I just ran a bath. I need more time."

"You're naked? I'll be there in five minutes."

"Let's be serious for one minute," she said. "Where are you

taking me?"

"To ecstasy. Let's just say you won't be disappointed."

"All right," she said, still confused as to what she should wear. Dana hung up, then got into the bathtub. She sank back into the lilac-scented bubbles and closed her eyes. She thought she had time to take a relaxing bath before Chris arrived, but the doorbell rang in less than ten minutes.

"No, he didn't," she thought aloud. She wrapped in a plush pink towel and walked downstairs to the front door. She pulled the curtain back and there he was, standing on the front step holding an armful of roses.

"Chris, you said 45 minutes," she said as she opened the door.

"And you said you were naked." His eyes hungrily roamed her body as he handed her the roses. Then Chris reached down and picked up two black cases. "Dana, go finish your bath and I'll be right up."

She looked at the devilish grin on his face. "What do you have up your sleeve?"

"Ms. Lady, you are just going to have to find out." Chris headed for the kitchen as Dana walked up the stairs.

Chris opened the cases. One was filled with sensual massage oils and two bottles of champagne. The other case had the fresh fruit in it. Chris just needed to cut it up and put it on a platter. He was trying to have everything together before Dana got out of the bathtub. He pulled the engagement ring out of his pocket and sat it on the edge of the bar as he sliced the apples and oranges into bite-sized chunks. He reached into the cabinet and grabbed an ivory platter and arranged the fruit. He set the engagement ring in the center.

"Dana, are you ready?" he called out.

"Chris, I'm just getting out of the tub. That's what you get for being so fast."

He started up the stairs with the oils underneath his arm and platter in his hands. He walked into the bedroom. "You're ready," he said.

Dana turned around. She was stark naked. "What?"

"Lie on the bed," he ordered.

"I thought we were going out?"

He shook his head. "Tonight, I'm going to make all of your fantasies come true." He set the platter on the dresser and walked over to Dana. He put the bottles of oil on the nightstand beside the bed. "What's your pleasure? Coconut oil or red cherry oil?"

She smiled. "Surprise me." Chris leaned down and kissed her gently on the lips. Dana wrapped her arms around his neck, pulling him on top of her damp body. Chris pulled back. "We have all night and I'm going to take my time with you."

"Lie on your stomach," he ordered softly. Dana obliged him and smiled as she felt the warm coconut oil on her shoulder. His hands kneaded her flesh, making her hot with desire.

Chris looked down at her hourglass-shaped body. She was the perfect woman to him. Her skin was soft as fresh rose petals. He kissed the small of her back as he squeezed the oil onto her body. With his massive hands, he stroked every inch of Dana, starting at her shoulders, moving down to her back, lingering on her bottom, then moving down to her legs and stopping at her feet.

Dana muffled her cries of ecstasy in her pillow. Chris's hot hands were making her body yearn for him inside of her. She turned over and looked at Chris as he slowly pulled his black turtleneck over his head. His muscles rippled in the dim light spilling out of the bathroom.

"Did you like that?" he asked.

She moaned affirmatively.

"You're going to love this." He walked over to the dresser and grabbed the platter of fruit. "I have all of your favorites."

"You thought of everything, didn't you?"

"The champagne is downstairs chilling. But before I get it…" Chris picked up the velvet box and opened it. The diamond was reflected in Dana's dark eyes. "Oh my," she whispered.

Chris pulled the ring out. "I don't know if it will fit, but when I saw this, I knew you were the one that was supposed to wear it."

"Chris, it's beautiful."

"It doesn't compare to you." He slipped it on her finger and it was a perfect fit. "Destiny."

She wrapped her arms around his neck and squeezed him tightly. "I love you so much," she whispered in his ear.

Chris responded by kissing her on the neck. Dana melted against him. She reached down and unzipped his black jeans. Chris immediately hardened at her touch. Dana tugged off his clothing.

Chris climbed into bed beside Dana, taking a strawberry from the platter and teasing her lips with it. He pulled the berry back, then kissed the sweetness of it from around her mouth. Then he bit into the berry and held it out for Dana to do the same. Chris licked his lips as she sensually pulled the fruit from his fingers with her lips and tongue. "Um, I have never wanted to be a strawberry until now," he said.

"You are my orange." Grabbing a juicy piece of orange, Dana straddled Chris's body. She rubbed it across Chris's chest, then slowly licked the juice away. Chris closed his eyes as she traveled his body with her tongue, treating him like the strawberries she'd devoured. Chris sank back into the pillows as Dana's tongue glided across the tip of his penis, then moaned loudly as Dana took him deeper into her mouth. He ran his hands through Dana's hair as she bobbed up and down. When she began her journey northward, Chris grabbed her hips and pulled her down on top of him.

He pushed into her hot valley of love. Dana gasped as he

pushed deeper and deeper into her. She pressed her hands against his chest as she rocked back and forth and Chris gripped her hips, pumping into her. Dana leaned back, grasping the bed sheets. "Oh, oh," she exclaimed as Chris stroked her G-spot. She could feel her climax coming. Her legs shook, her thighs tightened around him and her chest heaved up and down. Chris grabbed her breasts, squeezing them, tweaking her nipples as he began his orgasm.

Dana collapsed on top of him. He clutched her tightly as orgasms rocked their bodies. Chris released a satisfied sigh as Dana buried her head in his chest and he gently kissed her on the cheek.

"Can we stay like this forever?" she whispered.

"If you want to." He stroked her hair.

Dana didn't want to spoil the mood, but she couldn't help wondering what her parents were going to say when she showed up wearing Chris's ring. She ran her finger up and down his arm. "Chris," she murmured.

"Uh-huh?"

"You know we're going to have to tell my parents."

"Let's not think about that right now," he said.

"Okay, but we can't put it off forever."

"But we can for right now."

Dana sighed. Chris picked up a strawberry and fed it to her. She smiled and licked her lips as he reached for another piece of fruit. "You know," she said as she grabbed his hand, "I think I want to taste you again."

"You won't get an argument from me." Dana and Chris kissed and began to make love again.

After hours and hours of lovemaking, Chris and Dana decided to pull themselves out of bed to have dinner. Dana cooked chicken stir-fry over white rice. They ate dinner in the living room and watched the classic holiday movie *It's a Wonderful Life.*

Although Dana tried to take Chris's advice and not think about what her parents were going to say when she told them that she and Chris were getting married, she couldn't help worrying about it.

# CHAPTER TWENTY-SEVEN

The next morning, Chris and Dana decided to sleep in. He knew he should've been working on his plans for his proposal to the park and recreation department, but being in Dana's arms felt too good to think about work.

"Are you playing hooky from the bakery today?" Chris asked, running his index finger across her collarbone.

"Yeah. I made sure everything was well stocked. And today is the day you eat my fruitcake."

"Nah, I don't think so."

"This way you and my Dad can bond over something before we tell him that we're getting married."

Chris inhaled sharply. "All right, I guess we have to do it."

She nodded. "Let me go take a shower."

Chris pulled Dana into his arms. "Not yet. I just want us to lie here. Just five more minutes."

"Okay, baby" she said, kissing him on the cheek.

An hour later, Chris and Dana were on their way to her parents' house. "Nervous?" he asked. She held the steering wheel in a vice-like grip.

"What do you think?"

"If your parents aren't behind us, what are we going to do?"

"Chris, I'm still going to marry you. I don't care what my parents think."

He didn't say anything.

"You do believe me, don't you?" she asked.

"Yeah, but how long will a marriage like that last?"

"We're getting ahead of ourselves. They may surprise us."

Dana pulled into the driveway, then turned to Chris. "I love my family, but I love you too. I know I can have both of you."

*I hope you're right,* he thought as she kissed him on the cheek.

Dana reached into the backseat, grabbed the cake from the floor and headed to the front door. Chris walked two steps behind her. She turned around and looked at him. "Are you all right?" she inquired.

"I'm fine. Just keeping my distance from that cake."

Dana shook her head at him as she unlocked the front door. "Daddy," she called out.

"In the kitchen," he replied.

She and Chris walked into the kitchen. Frank was standing on a stepladder reaching up to change the light bulb in the overhead fixture. He glanced back at Dana and Chris.

"I brought your cake," she said as she set it on the counter.

"Thanks." Frank snapped the bulb in place and climbed down. He didn't look at Chris. "I've been wondering when I was going to get this."

"Where's Mom?" Dana asked.

"She went to get something for dinner." Frank walked over to the refrigerator and pulled out a beer. Chris looked at Dana and shook his head.

"Dad," Dana began, "I have to tell you and Mom something."

Frank looked from Dana to Chris. "What's going on?"

Chris inhaled sharply. "Mr. Ellison," he began. "I asked Dana to marry me."

"And I said yes," she replied.

Frank sighed, but didn't respond. He inhaled and exhaled. "Well," he finally said, "I hope you two aren't here to ask for my blessing. You'll never get it!"

"Dad," Dana began. "Please, don't do this."

"Do what, Dana? Now I said I would give him a chance and

be cordial. But if you think I'm going to stand behind this marriage, you must be out of your mind."

Dana ran her hand over her face and groaned. Hot tears of anger and disappointment sprang into her eyes.

"With all due respect," Chris said, "Dana and I are going to get married and we're going to have a life together."

"So why are you two here? If the decision has been made, why do you need to tell me?"

"Would you prefer that we elope?" Dana snapped. "Dad, for once can you just stand behind me and support my decision?"

"A decision to marry a man you barely know? I can't stand behind that."

Denise walked into the kitchen with two heavy shopping bags in her hands. "What in the world is going on here?"

"Your daughter is getting married," Frank said.

"Married? But I thought you and Andre—"

"She's not marrying Andre," Frank bellowed.

"Dana, what's going on?" Denise asked.

Dana walked over to her mother and took one of the bags out of her mother's hands. "Chris and I are getting married."

"R-really?"

"Is that all you have to say?" Frank asked.

"Frank, what do you want me to say?" Denise asked.

He scowled at his wife. "What?" she questioned when she saw his frown. "Dana, it took me a while to learn this, but I have to let you make your own decisions. If you want to marry Chris, then who am I to stand in your way?"

"Denise, this isn't about standing in Dana's way. Dana, you're not thinking clearly. You barely know this man."

"Dad, this is our decision. Chris and I will be married."

Chris put his arms around Dana's waist. "Mr. and Mrs. Ellison, I love Dana with all of my heart. All I want to do is make her happy."

"And he does make me happy. I'm happier than I've ever been," Dana said.

Frank and Denise looked at each other. "But you two should really think about this," Denise said. "It wasn't too long ago that you were getting ready to marry Andre."

Dana rolled her eyes. "I was never going to marry Andre. That's something you all thought was a good idea. I didn't agree."

"Dana, what did you really expect us to say? Did you think we were going to welcome this news with hearty congratulations? This is the biggest mistake of your life," Frank said.

"I didn't expect this, but it doesn't matter. My mind is made up," she snapped. She grabbed Chris's hand and started to pull him out of the kitchen.

"Wait," Chris said, throwing his hands up and waving everyone silent. "Wait. Dana, the last thing I want to do is come in between you and your family."

All eyes were on him as he continued. "A few weeks ago, you were miserable when you and your parents weren't speaking. There's no way we can have a life together if you have to give them up."

"Chris, what are you saying?" Dana asked.

"I'm not worth this."

"Finally, the voice of reason," Frank said.

Dana's eyes stretched to the size of quarters. "Chris—" She stopped speaking as everything began to sink in. How could Chris just give in to her parents' bullying?

"Whatever is going here is bigger than me. Maybe you all can work things out if I'm not in the picture."

Dana shook her head. "Do you hear this?" she demanded. She focused on her parents. "Chris is willing to sacrifice our love to save this family. Why can't you two support me?"

"Dana, I think we've done a pretty good job of keeping quiet about the turn your life has taken as of late," Denise said. "But this is just too much."

"I thought you were on my side," Dana said.

"Dana, I'm your mother and I'm always on your side. But you don't know Chris well enough to marry him. What kind of life would you have with him?"

"A good one," she snapped. "I'm not going to stand here and argue with you." She turned to Chris, grabbed his hand and led him to the door. "Enjoy the cake," she snapped.

When they got in the car Chris turned to Dana. "I was serious about what I said in there," he said.

"I'm not listening to you about this."

He placed his hand on her shoulder. "You have to. If your parents aren't in your life, you will never be truly happy. I saw that before when your mother was in the hospital."

Dana slammed on the brakes. "So, do you want your ring back now or should I wait a few days?"

The cars behind Dana's car blared their horns. She ignored them. Fire danced in her eyes. How could Chris so easily give up on their love after the night they'd shared when he proposed?

"I don't need you playing with my emotions. I love you. You shouldn't have asked me to marry you if you weren't sure."

"And I love you enough to know that if you don't have your parents' support we're not going to be happy in the long run."

The cars continued to lean on their horns. "Dana, we can't sit here," Chris said, noting the line of cars behind them.

"You're right, I'm going to take you back to my place so you can get in your truck and go." Dana fought back the tears as she sped off.

"Slow down," Chris exclaimed as she whipped around a sharp curve, crossing the double yellow line. "Dana!"

She swerved to avoid an oncoming car. The near accident scared her into slowing down. She refused to look at Chris or talk to him. Anger heated her blood. Finally they arrived at her house.

Dana didn't know if she wanted to slap Chris or toss a bowl of hot grits in his face. She decided to just walk away. Silently, she walked to the front door and unlocked it. Chris stood on the front steps, unsure of what he should do. He'd thought he was doing the right thing when he said they shouldn't get married. In his thoughts he had meant *right now,* that they should wait awhile. But he hadn't said that. He now realized he should have because the last thing he wanted to do was lose Dana. Not when she had brought so much happiness into his life. But as the front door closed in his face, he felt as if he had lost her forever.

# CHAPTER TWENTY-EIGHT

Six weeks after Christmas, Dana was still smarting from her breakup with Chris. She hadn't forgiven her parents or him for the drama they'd caused. At the bakery, she was all business. She didn't talk and joke with the staff and she didn't come out to greet the customers, even when they wanted to meet the woman who made the delicious brownies.

"All right," Josh said one afternoon. "What's going on?"

"What?"

"Dana, for the last few months you've been acting like a beast."

"Josh, look at the receipts. The money is still coming in hand over fist. That's all you need to concern yourself with."

"Hey, I thought we were friends and partners."

Dana sighed. "I'm sorry. I didn't mean to sound like such a bitch. Things are just a little screwed up in my life right now."

"Want to talk about it?" Josh leaned against the counter. Dana closed her eyes as she kneaded the dough. She realized that she had shut everyone out of her life. She hadn't even talked to Zariah since she and Chris had broken up.

"I'd rather cook," she said.

"All right, but Zariah is concerned about you. She says she hasn't heard from you in months."

"I'll call her when I get a chance."

Josh shrugged and wiped some flour from his black slacks. "Maybe you should take some time off."

"Is than an order?"

"No, just a strong suggestion."

Dana rolled her eyes.

Josh walked out of the kitchen and Dana broke down in tears. Her banana nut bread was ruined. Maybe time off would do her good.

Chris walked out of the office of Damon Hinson, the city park director, with a smile on his face. He'd won the contract to renovate two parks and plant the city's memorial garden. The only thing that would've made his day better was having Dana at his side. For the last six weeks, he'd tried to talk to her, but she hung up on him every time he called. He wanted to go to her house, but he knew he wasn't welcome, she he decided to focus on his career. Things progressed quickly after he sent his sketches to Mr. Hinson. The two men became fast business friends and Mr. Hinson showed Chris the ropes on how to get around city government. When the time came for the renovations to start at the area parks, Chris was so well known by other people in the park's department that Mr. Hinson didn't have to do much arm-twisting to make sure Chris received some of the work.

Chris looked down at the contract. He hadn't ever seen that many zeros behind his name. He was going to be able to start his company if everything went well. He knew he was going to bring Tito on board. Chris started the truck and headed toward his apartment but slowed down as he passed Capitol City. Although he wanted to stop and share his news with Dana, he was afraid she wouldn't talk to him.

Chris yearned for Dana. At night he ached to hear her voice, touch her face and feel her kiss. He needed her in his life as much as he needed to breathe. Despite his misgivings, he turned into the parking lot of the bakery. When he spotted Dana's car, he threw his truck in park and hopped out. It was lunchtime and the bakery was crowded with people taking care of their sweet tooth.

He was surprised to see Dana standing at the cash register. Chris stood at the end of the line, waiting for all of the customers to be served.

"May I help you?" she said without looking up.

"Yes."

She looked up and their eyes locked. "What do you want?" she asked.

"Dana, I want to talk to you."

"As you can see, I'm busy and even if I weren't, I don't have a damned thing to say to you."

Chris looked down at her hand. "I see you're still wearing the ring," he whispered.

Dana glanced at the diamond and stroked it absent-mindedly. "Is that what you want to talk about? Getting your ring back?"

"No, Dana, I still love you and I still want to marry you. These last few weeks have been hell."

"Chris, this isn't the place."

"Then where? At least here you can't run from me. You won't return my calls. What else can I do?"

Dana turned to Lynn. "Can you take over?"

"Sure," she replied. Dana walked from behind the counter and pointed toward the door. They stepped outside into the fresh spring-like air. Winter didn't last long in South Carolina, but Chris could feel a frost coming from Dana. He wanted to pull her into his arms and kiss her until the Earth crumbled around them. Dana folded her arms across her chest. "What do you have to say, Chris?"

There had been so many nights when Chris had dreamed of pouring his heart out to Dana but now words failed him.

"Get on with it."

"There are so many things I want to say to you. So many things I've dreamed of saying to you. Dana, I can't go another day without you."

"This was your idea. And you know what, you can't have me when you want me or when you feel like you need me!" White-hot anger peppered her words. Dana's voice rose and fell like an angry rock song.

"Look, things just weren't right for both of us. Your parents—"

"Who were you marrying, me or my parents? Why is it so important for you to be accepted by them? God, Chris, you're no better than Andre. I need someone to love me, Dana, not some flunky trying to make my parents proud of them."

"Dana, do you think I give a damn what your parents think about me? I was thinking of you. I know how much your parents mean to you—even if you try to act like their opinion doesn't matter. I didn't want you resenting me and our marriage if your family never accepted us."

Dana turned her back to Chris. He gently grasped her shoulder. "I never meant to hurt you."

"Well, you did," she hissed. Dana masked her sadness with anger.

"You're not fooling me with the tough girl act, Dana. You know what I did, I did out of love for you."

"So you broke my heart because you love me?"

"No, damn it. I gave you the time and space you need to work things out with your parents so we could be together."

"Oh, that's what that was? And now is the time that we're supposed to pick things up and stroll down the aisle?" she sarcastically asked. "I don't think so." Dana pulled the ring off her finger and threw it in Chris's face. "If there was any doubt before, it's over now!" She stormed into the bakery.

Chris picked it up and looked at it. The night he'd given it to her flashed in his mind like a scene from his favorite movie.

Just as he was about to turn and leave, someone grabbed his arm. He whirled around and looked into Zariah's eyes. Chris exhaled loudly, expecting to be reamed out by Dana's best friend.

"Chris," she said.

"Hi, Zariah."

She glanced around as if she were looking for Dana. "Let's go around the block, I need to talk to you."

Chris threw his hands in the air. "Dana just chewed my head off, I don't need an instant replay."

Zariah folded her arms and pouted. "First of all, that isn't why I want to talk to you. I know you love Dana and she's like a sister to me. You make her happy, Chris."

He snorted. "I messed up."

Zariah nodded in agreement. "Walk with me before she sees us together. Maybe I'm overstepping, but I know why you ended things with her."

Chris rubbed his forehead. "That has to be the worst decision I ever made in my life," he said.

"It sure was, because Dana isn't speaking to her parents either. Nothing has changed. As a matter of fact, Dana isn't speaking to anyone right now. Chris, if you really love her, you'll march into that bakery and win her back. I've known Frank and Denise for a long time and nothing is good enough for Dana. They didn't want her hanging out with me when we were growing up. But Dana chose to keep our friendship. Why don't you let her choose to keep your love?"

Chris stopped dead in his tracks. Zariah was right. If Dana hadn't tried to make things right with her parents, then there was no reason for the two of them to be apart. He hugged Zariah and thanked her.

With a head full of steam Chris charged into the bakery, ignoring the cautious gazes of the patrons. He looked at Lynn when she tried to stop him from walking behind the counter.

"You need to move," he said evenly.

Unsure what do, Lynn stepped aside. She knew something was going on from the way Dana had slammed into the kitchen.

But was this a matter that needed the police or was Dana finally going to come to her senses and take this man back?

"Dana," Chris said.

She was standing near the oven with tears running down her cheeks. "Chris, there isn't anything left say."

"Yes, it is. Dana, I love you too much to let you go."

"You've already let me go."

He pulled Dana into his arms. She struggled to escape his embrace. He held on tighter.

"Chris, get your hands off me!"

"I'm not going to do that. Not until you listen to what I have to say."

She rolled her eyes, but stopped struggling. Chris could feel her heart racing. "Dana, do you remember the night I gave you this ring?"

She closed her eyes and shook her head, as if she were trying to fight that memory. Chris leaned in closely. "I know you remember."

His warm breath caused her skin to tingle.

"Dana, you love me as much as I love you and you know this is destiny. I'm not taking this ring back. Not today, not ever."

She wouldn't look at him, because she knew if she did, she would kiss him and forget about the last six weeks and the pain she felt inside. Chris's lips sought out hers but she twisted her head away from his face. He didn't give up and his mouth finally captured hers. Dana melted against him. She'd missed his kisses, his hands on her body. Her mind was frazzled. Why were they fighting? The ring. The wedding. He'd left her.

Dana pushed him away. "I'm not going to do this," she said, hitting him in his chest. "I'm not going to do this."

"Do what? Admit you still love me?"

"You ripped my heart out and stomped on it. Last Christmas should have been the happiest time of my life. But it wasn't and that's because you didn't or couldn't stand up for our love to my parents."

"I did that for you, Dana. Why don't you understand that?"

"Leave, Chris. Please just go."

"I'm not leaving," he said. "Not until we work this thing out."

"What is there to work out?" Dana pushed him away from her. "Chris, we were a mistake. I shouldn't have taken your ring to begin with."

Chris stood in Dana's face and grabbed her by the shoulders. A yelp escaped her throat and fear flickered in her eyes. He let her go. "Dana, I'm not trying to hurt you."

"Too late."

"I'm going to go." Chris turned to walk out the door but stopped and looked at Dana. "Do you still love me?" he asked.

The question caught her off guard. *Of course I do.* She didn't answer and instead focused her eyes on the pile of dough on the counter in front of her.

"Dana, answer me!"

"Yes." Her voice was barely audible. "I love you, Chris."

"If you love me, why are we hurting ourselves?"

She began kneading the dough. "Maybe this is for the best."

Chris walked over to Dana and reached out to touch her but stopped his hand in mid air. "How can it be for the best when I yearn for you at night, in the morning and right now?" He stroked her hair. "Baby, please. I can't go another day without you. I need you."

Dana turned around, unshed tears gleaming in her eyes. "I need you too. But nothing has changed. If I go to my parents and tell them we're getting married, their reaction is going to be the same."

"I don't care anymore. I love you and I can't live without you."

Dana fell into Chris's open arms and he showered kisses on her face. He tasted her salty tears. "Don't cry," he whispered. "I promise I'm not going to let anything ever come between us again."

Dana raised her head to look into Chris' eyes. She wanted to believe they could make it. She had to believe that.

Chris let her go. "I'll call you tonight," he said. "We can work this out."

She nodded her head, fighting back the tears in her eyes. Chris blew her a kiss and walked out of the kitchen. When he was gone, Lynn rushed in. "Is everything okay?"

Dana sniffed and wiped her cheek with the back of her hand. "Yeah. Is the lunch rush over?"

"Yes. Are you sure that you're all right?"

"I'm going to take off," Dana said. "Tell Josh I don't feel well."

"All right. Dana, did that guy do something to you?"

"No, Lynn. Chris would never do anything to hurt me." Dana sighed as she walked out the back door and got into her car. Dana didn't know if she should be happy that Chris was back in her life or if she was setting herself up for another heartbreak.

Chris stared at the phone. He didn't know what to say to Dana. But he had to say something. He picked up the phone and dialed her number.

"Hello?"

"Dana."

"Hi."

"How was your day?"

"Chris, I think we're past small talk."

He laughed nervously. "I guess you're right."

Neither of them spoke. Finally, Dana sighed and said, "What are we doing?"

"It's hard to do anything over the phone. I want to see you," he said.

"That's not a good idea."

"How are we going to get past this if we don't sit down and talk?"

"All right," she said. "Why don't you come over here? But we're just going to talk, Chris."

"I wouldn't expect anything else."

When they hung up, Chris ran outside and hopped into his truck. He sped to Dana's house, not caring about the posted speed limits. If a police officer had stopped him, Chris would have explained that he was on the way to see the woman he loved. When he got there, Dana was sitting on the front porch with a glass of tea at her feet as she read the latest copy of *Essence* magazine. Chris swallowed hard as he approached her.

Dana dropped the magazine, stood up and ran her hand over her hair. Chris stood on the bottom step, gazing at her quiet beauty. Was this real or would he wake up and be alone in his bed again?

"That was really quick. It feels like I just hung up with you," she said, keeping her distance from him.

"I just couldn't wait to see you," he replied in a low voice. An awkward silence hung between them.

"Want some tea?" she asked.

Chris shook his head.

"So what are we supposed to do now?" Dana asked.

"I don't know, but Dana, I need you back in my life."

"It's going to be hard to go back."

"Do you want to try?"

"Yes. Chris, I never stopped loving you. But you hurt me when you just walked out on us."

"I'll admit I could have handled things differently. I thought I was causing all of the problems between you and your parents. But if nothing has changed, then I know I'm just the tip of the iceberg when it comes to the issues you have with them. I made both of us suffer because it hurt me to say that we shouldn't get married. "

Dana rolled her eyes. "Then why did you say it?"

"Dana, your family was ready to toss you aside. I couldn't stand by and let that happen."

"So what are we supposed to do now? Start over as friends?"

"We're past being friends. The first day I sat in your kitchen, I knew I wanted you to be my wife. I have enough friends."

Dana wanted to melt in his arms.

"Don't shut me out, Dana," Chris said as he held his arms out to her. Unable to deny her feelings any longer, Dana fell into his embrace. She had dreamed of his kiss every night since they'd split up. He was sweeter than she remembered, his hands warmer, his touch more electric. Dana pushed him back. "Oh, Chris," she breathed. "I love you so much."

"I love you too."

She wrapped her arms around him. "I'm scared."

"Don't be." Chris cupped Dana's chin in his hand. "I am going to spend the rest of my life with you, with or without your parents' blessing because I love you more than I ever thought possible. If your parents can't see that, then it isn't our problem."

Dana nodded. She knew her family problems went deeper than her relationship with Chris. If she was ever going to be happy, she was going to have to confront her parents and get it all out in the open.

"Will you stay with me tonight?" Dana asked as they broke their embrace. Chris smiled.

"I'd love too."

Dana led Chris inside, putting her parents out of her mind for the night.

# CHAPTER TWENTY-NINE

Dana woke up with a start. Chris was really holding her; this wasn't another one of her dreams. She stroked his muscular arm. During the weeks they were apart, Dana would look at her engagement ring and tell herself that she was going to take it off. But she never had. Being in his arms again was like coming home.

Dana slipped out of bed and walked downstairs to the kitchen. It was too early to call her parents. Besides, she'd been avoiding their calls for weeks. It was time to stop running and talk in person.

"Hey you," Chris said, appearing in the kitchen.

"Good morning."

He walked over to her and kissed her on the cheek. "Why are you up so early?"

"I couldn't sleep," she said.

"Why?"

Dana tilted her head and smiled bitterly. "I needed to think about what I'm going to say to my parents. I haven't talked to them in weeks."

"Back at square one?"

She nodded as she walked over to the coffee maker. "They need to know that I love you. But I won't live like this anymore. I won't be caught in the middle."

"I don't want you to be. What's really going on? I mean, I understand that your parents wanted you to marry Andre, but—"

"It's hard to understand and even harder to explain."

"I'm listening."

"All of my life, I've been sheltered. My parents tried to have kids before they had me and right after my mother found out she was pregnant with me, the doctors found a tumor in her uterus. She had me and then she had to have an emergency hysterectomy."

Chris nodded as he listened.

"Since my parents could never have another child, they doted on me. I got everything I ever wanted. They pinned all of their hopes and dreams on me. I used to complain to my granny about how overprotective they were. That's when she told me what happened when I was born. I felt so guilty I made up my mind that I would never give my parents any problems."

"So all these years, you've been trying to make your parents happy without once giving a thought to what makes Dana happy."

"Until I met you," she said. "I still love my parents and I want them to be a part of my life, but they can't control my life anymore and I can't live in their image."

"Then that's what you should tell them."

Dana started the coffee maker. "I know what I should say. I just hope they listen."

Chris wrapped his arms around Dana's waist, silently telling her everything would work out. She turned around, feeding off the strength in his eyes. Dana hugged him tightly, hoping to absorb some of his positive vibes.

Chris looked down at his watch. "I'd better get a move on. I have to meet with the city this morning."

"Meet with the city? What's that all about?"

Chris beamed proudly. "You are looking at the man who is going to renovate two parks in the city and plant the first memorial garden in Columbia."

Dana kissed him on the cheek. "I'm so proud of you. It looks like all of your dreams are coming true."

"Not all of them. I still haven't married the woman of my dreams." Chris ran his index finger down Dana's cheek. "That's the only one that matters."

She grabbed Chris's hand and kissed his palm. "Why don't you get dressed and I'll fix you a quick breakfast."

He nodded and dashed into the bedroom to retrieve his clothes. Dana pulled out her frying pan and some eggs. She decided to make Chris an omelet and bowl of grits. She grabbed a package of instant grits and poured them in a bowl as she flipped the eggs into a fluffy yellow fold.

Chris walked into the kitchen, dressed in his jeans and tee shirt from the day before. He stood back and watched Dana cook. The satin robe she wore had slipped from her cocoa brown shoulder. Chris wanted to forget his meeting and take Dana into her bedroom and make love to her. "Uh, I checked the time. I'm going to have pass on breakfast. But I will take a cup of coffee and a kiss."

She sauntered over to him and planted a wet kiss on his lips. "I'm proud of you," she said.

"Thanks. Before I leave." Chris reached into his pocket and pulled out the engagement ring. "Will you take me and this ring?"

"You know I will." She brushed her lips against his. "I love you, Chris."

He slid the ring on her finger, then kissed her hand. "I really don't want to leave you right now."

"But you have to, so go. Wait," she said, going over to the coffee maker. Dana poured the coffee in a mug and dumped in two teaspoons of sugar. "Your coffee."

"Thanks, babe," he said as he took the mug from her hands. "I'll call you when the meeting's over."

She watched him as he dashed out the door. The ping of the

timer on the microwave reminded her she had just cooked break-fast. Too nervous to eat, Dana threw the food in the trash. Her stomach tightened when she put her hand on the phone but she knew she had to pick it up and call her parents. It was time to stop running and face them.

Slowly, she dialed the number. Dana knew her mother would be sitting at the breakfast table reading the metro section of the paper and that her father was probably sitting by the television watching the morning news, waiting for Denise to leave so he could smoke his pipe in peace.

When the phone rang, Dana wanted to hang up. She was get-ting ready to click the off button when she heard her mother say, "Dana, is that you?"

"Yes, Mother, it's me."

"I'm certainly surprised to hear from you."

"Is Daddy there?"

"Yes," Denise said. "What's wrong?"

"We need to talk face-to-face and we need to do it now. And I honestly want both of you to actually listen to what I have to say."

"Dana, we always listen to you," Denise replied.

"No, you don't, but you will today. I'll be right over."

Dana ran into her bedroom and dressed in a pair of jeans and an oversized USC tee shirt. She stuffed her feet into a pair of Italian leather mules, then dashed out the door and sped to her parents' house, hoping to catch her mother before she left.

When Dana arrived at her parents' house, she sat in the car a moment and said a silent prayer. Then she hopped out and knocked on the front door. Denise snatched the door open. "I'm going to be late for work waiting on you."

"Sorry," Dana said as she walked in.

"Well, it is good to see you."

"Where is Dad?"

"In the den."

Dana marched down the hall with her mother in tow. Frank looked up and smiled at his daughter. "Dana."

"Dad, we need to have a serious talk," she said as she sat down on the leather sofa.

"I know. It's been months since we've seen each other," he said.

Denise sat down beside Dana. "Are you done being stubborn?" she asked.

Dana rolled her eyes. "I really love you two and I've had a wonderful life as your daughter. But it has never been my life," Dana began.

"What are you saying?" Frank asked.

Dana stood up and walked over to the fireplace. She picked up a picture of the family that had been taken when she was 12. "I'm not that little girl anymore. You can't shelter me from heartache, failure, and everything else you didn't want her eyes to see. I know how hard it was for you two to have me, but I'm here and I'm a grown woman now. You have to respect that."

Denise and Frank stared at their daughter with puzzled looks on their faces. Dana continued talking. "You two mapped my life out before I was born and when I veered off course, you tried to make me feel lower than dirt. But now I've made some decisions about my life and you can deal with them or you can stay out of my life forever."

"This is about that Johnson boy," Frank snapped.

"I'm going to marry Chris. I know he isn't the man that you would have picked for me. But you don't know Chris. I love him and he loves me. When I walk down the aisle to be his wife, I want both of you there. But if you can't respect our relationship, then I don't want you anywhere around us. Not when we get married, not when we have our children. Never."

Denise put her hand to her chest. "I can't believe you would cut me out of my grandchildren's lives."

"Why not?" Dana snapped. "Chris will be their father and if you have such contempt for him, how are you going to treat my children?"

Frank shook his head. "I'm not going to allow this."

"You don't have a choice," Dana snapped. "I can't carry all of your dreams. I have dreams of my own!"

"Dana, we only wanted you to have the best life possible. That's why we pushed you so hard," Frank said.

"You didn't push," she said, looking at her father. "You forced me into a carbon copy of your life. Did you ever think that I could be my own person?"

"Dana," Denise said, "you're our only child."

"That's not my fault. Since I'm your only child, it would seem as if we would be closer and you would be a little more supportive of the decisions I make. You two taught me to stand up for what I believe in and finally, I'm doing it. You can either support me or leave me alone."

Dana turned to walk out of the den.

"Wait a minute," Frank bellowed. "Just wait. You can't come in here and drop all of this on us and then leave."

She whirled around and looked at her father. He didn't seem larger than life to her anymore. "Dad, I'm going to marry Chris and whatever you have to say isn't going to change that. I'm going to be a partner at Capitol City and one day, I'm going to have my own catering company and bakery."

Denise tapped Frank's shoulder. "She has a point." She turned back to Dana. "I guess we have been overly protective of you for a long time. It's just because we know how hard this world can be on a person."

"I know that too. But some things are best learned on your own," Dana replied.

Frank scowled. "Fine," he said. "If this is what you want to do, then do it."

"And we will s-support your decision," Denise stammered. "It's just that we don't know Chris."

"Because you never took the time to get to know him. When things get tough in this family, we bury our heads in the sand or run from the problem. It's time for that to stop," Dana said.

Frank nodded in agreement. "Does he really make you happy?"

Dana's face lit up. "Yes, he does."

"Why don't you two come over tomorrow for dinner?" Denise said. "And this time, we're going to sit down and talk like adults."

"I'll let Chris know. He's been busy lately."

"Oh, I guess it is planting season," Frank said snidely.

"As a matter of fact, Chris has a contract from the city. He's going to be planting the city's memorial garden and renovating two parks. Chris isn't just some hired hand. He's always had goals and dreams, just like me. That's why I love him so much. We're just alike."

Frank rolled his eyes and crossed his hands over his belly. "All we've ever wanted for you is the best."

"I know that, but I'm old enough to make my own decisions. It's time for you two to believe that and trust what I do." Dana turned to walk out the door.

"Wait," Denise said. "Are you sure this is what you want?"

Dana nodded. She didn't feel like a little girl anymore. She felt like an adult, finally standing on her own two feet. For the first time ever, she was her own Ellison.

"We'll see you two tomorrow then," Denise said. She looked down at her watch. "I have to get to work."

Denise dashed out the door. Frank gazed sadly at his

daughter. Dana kissed her father on the cheek, then also headed out the door.

# CHAPTER THIRTY

Chris drove home silently patting himself on the back. Construction was scheduled to begin on the garden in two months. He couldn't believe that everything was falling into place for him. This was the first time in his life that he was actually going to have everything. Well, almost everything. He wondered if he and Dana would ever have a chance to get their relationship on track. What if her parents still held to their objections to their marriage? Chris pushed the negative thoughts out of his head. Things were going to work out, he could feel it. Everything else was shining in his favor.

He pulled into his apartment complex, parked the truck and said a silent prayer of thanks. Then he asked for things to work out for Dana and her parents. He knew they wouldn't have a chance at being happy if her parents didn't support their marriage. *Love shouldn't be this damned difficult,* he thought as he unlocked his door. Chris walked in and looked down at his answering machine. The light was blinking, indicating that he had a message. He punched the play button and Dana's voice pierced the silence in his apartment, inviting him to her house for dinner. She said she had something important to tell him. *Let it be good news,* he thought as the message ended. Chris dashed into his bedroom and changed out of his black business suit and into a pair of dark blue Levi jeans and a white tee shirt. Grabbing his tan Timberland boots from the foot of the bed, he put them on and rushed down to his truck, hoping for the best.

When Chris pulled into Dana's driveway, the sun was just beginning to set. He could see white smoke coming from the backyard. She was barbequing. Chris inhaled the scent of searing, succulent meat. His mouth began to water and his stomach grumbled. He walked around to the backyard. "Hey you," he called out.

Dana turned from the grill and waved. "Hope you're hungry."

Chris walked over to her and kissed her cheek. "Smells good."

"How did things go with the city?" she asked as she wiggled out of his embrace.

"Great. I'm going to start working on the garden in two months."

Dana planted a juicy kiss on Chris's neck. "That is such great news."

Chris wrapped his arms around her and lifted her off the ground. She dropped her spatula to the ground but she held on to Chris.

"You're going to make me burn dinner," she said.

"Let it burn," he said before capturing her lips with his. Dana finally mustered up enough strength to push him away.

"Chris, let me just get this chicken off the grill. I have to tell you something."

He stepped back from her. "Is it good or bad?"

"It's interesting. We're having dinner with my parents tomorrow night."

Chris couldn't force himself to smile. Images of the last time he had been in the Ellison house danced in his mind. He couldn't help wondering if this was another disaster in the making. He was determined to stand his ground, though. He wasn't going to let anything Frank or Denise had to say keep him from the love of his life.

"So, are your parents going to behave themselves?" Chris asked.

"They really don't have much of a choice. Chris, we deserve to be happy, with or without their acceptance."

Chris stroked Dana's cheek. She held his hand and kissed it gently. "It's going to be fine," she whispered.

He nodded. "I'm going to set the table."

Dana blew him a kiss of thanks as he walked into the house.

Once he was inside, Chris sat at the kitchen table and exhaled. Right now, his life seemed like a dream, but he couldn't help wondering when the other shoe was going to drop.

"All right, it's time for dinner." Dana came inside with a tray of barbeque chicken, Chris took the tray from her hands. The lustful look in his eyes told her that dinner was going to have to wait. Chris pressed Dana against the bar. He slowly ran his tongue across her lips and she wrapped her legs around his waist as he hoisted her up on the bar. Dana plunged her tongue into his mouth, savoring his sweetness. Chris pulled Dana's tee shirt over her head and his hands roamed her satin smooth skin. He hadn't realized just how much he'd missed the feel of her against him, the taste of her kisses, the firmness of her breasts. His fingers danced to the waist of her jeans. As he unbuttoned them slowly, he laid her back on the counter. A bowl of peaches crashed to the floor, but neither of them noticed or cared. A searing heat raced though Dana's body when she felt Chris's lips on her erect nipple. His kisses were hot and wet, much like her body. Dana clutched his neck, pushing his head deeper into her bosom. She didn't have to say she wanted him; Chris could feel her body melting against him as he scooped her up into his arms.

Chris carried Dana into her bedroom, his gaze never leaving her face. He thought she looked like an angel in his arms. She stroked his cheek as he walked up the stairs. Gently he laid her on the bed and stood back to admire her chocolate brown body. She was a vision he couldn't wait to wake up to every morning.

With love and lust in her eyes, Dana beckoned Chris to join

her in the bed. He climbed in bed on top of her and kissed her lips gently. "I need you," Dana moaned. Chris traveled down Dana's body with his tongue, tasting every tantalizing crevice and curve. She arched her back, pushing herself deeper into his kisses. She dug her nails into his shoulders, begging an end to his sensual torture. Dana wanted to feel his throbbing manhood buried deep inside her warm valley. She wrapped her legs around his waist, urging him to come inside. Chris obliged her silent request, plunging into her, basking in her warmth. Dana rolled her body against his as she roamed her hands up and down his sculpted back. Chris pressed deeper, harder, faster. Dana matched his intensity. Her mouth was open, but the sound stayed buried in her throat. Chris pulled her closer to him as he began to climax and his breath tickled her neck as they rocked back and forth. Dana could feel her love juices coming down, but she didn't want to break away from Chris. She needed this closeness. She squeezed her legs tighter around him, pulling him into her even deeper. Chris groaned in delight, then collapsed on top of her, whispering "I love you" in her ear. Dana closed her eyes and kissed Chris on the cheek. They both drifted off to sleep, forgetting about the dinner downstairs.

Chris and Dana awoke in each other's arms. She looked into his eyes and fought back the tears. She wasn't sad; she was happier than she had been in months.

"What's wrong?" he asked when he saw the tears.

She shook her head. "It's what's right."

Chris gently kissed her lips. "I missed you so much," he whispered.

"Can we just stay like this forever? Lock the world out and just be together."

"I wish." Dana wrapped her arms around Chris's waist and held on tightly. "Is this about your parents and our dinner date tomorrow?" he inquired.

Dana nodded. Chris twirled a strand of her hair around his finger. "We don't have to think about it tonight," he whispered. "Just let me hold you."

She buried her head in his chest. "You won't hear any objections from me."

⊷⟞⟜⊶

Morning seemed to come quickly. Dana had finally decided to take Josh's suggestion and took some much-needed time off from work. She looked over at Chris as sunlight poured down on his sleeping frame. She tilted her head to the side and watched his chest rise and fall. As she gently stroked his cheek, Chris stirred underneath her touch. She didn't want to wake him, but she couldn't stop touching him. When his eyes fluttered open, he grabbed Dana's hand and kissed it.

"Good morning," he said groggily.

"Morning."

Chris stretched his lanky body and pulled Dana on top of him. "Why aren't you getting ready for work?"

"I'm taking a few days off."

Chris smiled. "You're locking me up in here for a few days?"

She shook her head. "Would you like me to?"

Chris gently bit Dana's bottom lip. "You can do whatever you want to do."

Dana wormed out of his embrace. "I'm going to cook breakfast," she said. "Any requests?"

Chris shrugged his shoulders. "I'm easy to please."

Dana winked at him as she headed downstairs to the kitchen. When she saw the dinner from the night before sitting on the stove, she smiled. The chicken might have been good, but spending the night with Chris was so much better. Dana hummed as she wrapped the food in foil and slid it into the refrigerator.

Just as Dana was about to pull out a few eggs for omelets, Chris walked into the kitchen. "Hey, I have to dash out," he announced.

"Why?"

"I'm supposed to meet Tito to tell him about the contracts and to ask him to be my partner."

Dana masked her disappointment. She was hoping to spend a quiet morning with Chris, eating breakfast, making love and basking in the afterglow. "Okay."

"I'll try to be back for lunch," he said as he kissed her on the cheek. She waved him out the door. Now she was going to be alone with her dread about tonight's dinner. *I should have gone to work,* she thought as she cracked the eggs into a bowl.

# CHAPTER THIRTY-ONE

Chris and Dana pulled up to the Ellison house and looked at each other. She grabbed his hand and squeezed it.

"We can't just sit in the car," he said.

Dana nodded and grabbed the handle. She started to open it, then turned to Chris. "Promise me that no matter what happens in there, we're still getting married."

"I'm not going to risk losing you again," he said before kissing her on the cheek.

Dana got out and Chris followed her up the steps. When she pressed the doorbell, she held her breath as she waited for the door to open. Frank peered out the window before opening the door.

"Why didn't you use your key?"

"Hello to you too, Daddy." She gave him a quick hug. Frank looked at Chris, but didn't extend his hand. Chris shook it off. He hadn't been expecting to be welcomed with open arms. Frank led then down the hall to the dining room, where Denise was setting a platter of roast beef in the center of the table.

"Hello," she said. Dana walked over to her mother and hugged her. Denise smiled and squeezed her daughter's shoulder. "Chris, it's good to, uh, see you again."

"Thank you, ma'am," he replied.

"Let's sit down and eat," Frank said. Dana bit her bottom lip. Things weren't going as well as she'd hoped they would. She'd thought her talk with her parents would soften them up. She'd been wrong. Frank still seemed against this marriage. *It doesn't matter, because this is the man I love,* she thought. She and Chris sat down beside each other. He grabbed Dana's hand and stroked it reassuringly, his touch saying that everything was going to be fine.

"So," Denise said, trying to break the ice, "Dana says you're working for the city now."

"Actually," Chris began, "I have my own company and we've been contracted to build the memorial garden."

Denise nodded her head slowly. She was impressed. So he wasn't just a gardener. Frank wasn't as impressed. He didn't care if Chris was going to build gardens all over the state of South Carolina. This wasn't the man for his little girl. Dana looked at her father, seemingly reading his thoughts, and narrowed her eyes at him. Frank cleared his throat.

"I'm not one for small talk," he began. "My daughter says you make her happy and I should get to know you."

Chris looked at Dana, then turned to Frank. "I love your daughter and we're going to be married."

Frank rolled his eyes and turned to Dana. "I won't fight you two on this."

Dana dropped her head. "This isn't about fighting. I want you to walk me down the aisle." She turned to her mother. "I want you sitting on the front row in a blue dress."

Denise fingered her silver necklace and exhaled slowly. "You know I'm going to be there," she said in a voice barely above a whisper.

Dana looked hopefully at her father. He frowned, causing his forehead to wrinkle like that of a pug puppy. "Pass me the roast," he said.

Dana picked up the tray of meat and held it in her hand. "Is this what you call acting like an adult?"

Frank reached over the table and took the platter from his daughter's hands. "Dana, why don't you and your mother leave me and Chris in here to talk, man-to-man, for awhile."

Dana looked at Chris and he nodded. Denise stood up and motioned for Dana to follow her into the kitchen. Dana's stomach was tied up in knots as she and her mother walked out of the dining room. What was going to happen? Her father could be a cruel man when he wanted to be. How was Chris going to handle it?

"Dana," Denise said.

"What?"

"Sit down, honey. Your father has to come to grips with this on his own terms."

"Like you have?"

Denise smiled pensively. "I wouldn't say that. All of your life I've just wanted the best for you. I forgot to think about what you wanted for yourself. I know I may have pushed too hard, but I did it because I love you."

Dana looked at her mother and willed herself not to cry. She knew her mother loved her and she loved her mother as well. She chewed on her bottom lip and stared at the dining room door. "It's quiet in there."

"That's a good sign."

Dana stood up and paced back and forth as if she were an expectant father.

"Dana, sit down."

"I can't. I love Chris so much and if you and Dad would give him half a chance you would love—at least like—him too."

"I hope you're right," Denise said. "I just want the best for you."

Dana nodded and smiled. "He is the best."

Denise walked over to the stove and opened the pots. She started piling collard greens, rice and beef on a plate.

"You want something?"

The only thing Dana wanted was to rush into the dining

room and find out what Chris and her father were talking about.

⁓⁐⁓

Frank cut into his roast, slowly putting the piece of meat in his mouth. Chris watched his future father-in-law with bated breath. "Something wrong with the food?" Frank asked.

Chris shook his head. "I thought we were going to talk."

"I can't do this on an empty stomach."

Chris looked down at his food. What was Frank trying to do? "Look, Mr. Ellison, I don't know what we're doing here, but I want us to come to some kind of understanding."

Frank dropped his fork. "An understanding? Chris, I'm not impressed with you and I think Dana can do a lot better."

"This isn't your decision to make. Dana's mind is made up and we're getting married. I know she wants you to be a part of our wedding."

Frank picked up his fork and dipped it into his mashed potatoes, then dropped it again. "Young man, Dana doesn't know what she wants. Today, she wants to be your wife, tomorrow, it will be something else."

"I don't think so. Dana and I love each other. Mr. Ellison, do you really know your daughter at all?"

Frank rolled his eyes. "I guess you think you do."

Chris looked at Frank and fought back a sarcastic comment. "I don't want to come between you and your daughter, but we're getting married."

"I wouldn't bet on it."

Chris shook his head from side to side. "You don't get it do you? Dana has made her decision."

Frank narrowed his eyes at him, curving his lips into a grin. "If you say so, son."

Chris cut into his food, then looked at Frank. "You're never going to approve of my relationship with Dana, are you?"

"My daughter can do better."

Chris stood up. "Then why fill her with false hope? Dana wants you to walk her down the aisle. Are you going to break her heart?"

Frank jumped up and faced Chris. "I love my daughter and I would do anything for her."

"All she wants is for you to accept her decision. Look, you don't have to like me but think about Dana and her feelings."

Frank stroked his forehead. "I guess we'd better sit down and get through this dinner. Denise," he called out.

Chris hid his smile. Nothing was going to stop him from marrying Dana now. The dining room door opened and Dana and Denise walked in slowly, feeling as if they had entered a battle zone. "Is everything okay in here?" Denise asked.

"Fine," Frank replied.

Dana looked to Chris for confirmation. He nodded and winked at her. She released a sigh of relief. "So when is this wedding?" Frank asked as he picked up his glass of iced tea.

"Um, we haven't set a date yet," Dana replied.

Frank nodded and looked at Chris as if to say *I told you so.* "We've been here before," Frank said.

"Meaning?" Dana asked.

"You and Andre never set a wedding date either."

Dana grabbed Chris's hand.

"Well, when are you going to set a wedding date?" Denise asked.

Chris and Dana looked at each other. "May 15," he said. "That's our wedding date."

Denise rubbed her hands together. "We have a lot of work to

do. That's only a few months away. We need to get a church, pick the colors. I need to call the wedding planner and—"

"Slow down," Dana said. "We're going to plan our own wedding."

Denise threw her hands up. Dana turned to her father. "Daddy, are you going to walk me down the aisle?"

Frank sucked his teeth, then saw the hopeful look in Dana's eyes. "Yes, I will." Dana leapt up and hugged her father tightly.

"Thank you, Daddy," she whispered as she kissed him on the cheek. Chris smiled as he watched Dana and Frank embrace.

After dinner was over, Dana and Chris said their goodbyes and headed to her place. On the drive over, she looked at him and smiled.

"What's that look for?" he asked.

"I'm just wondering what you said to my father."

"That's a man thing. You don't need to know. Let's just say we have a gentleman's understanding."

Dana rolled her eyes. "Thank you," she said.

"I did this for me as much as I did it for you. Dana, I know you love your parents. It wouldn't be right to get married without them being there. Even if they don't think we're going to make it down the aisle."

"You don't believe that, do you?"

"I know you love me."

Dana smiled as she put the car in park. "And I am going to be Mrs. Christopher Johnson."

Chris smiled and kissed Dana on the cheek. "You got that right." They rushed into the house to celebrate their victory at the Ellisons'.

# CHAPTER THIRTY-TWO

Dana was up to her elbows in chocolate and sugar. She had been at the bakery since six a.m. Now the sun was leaving orange footprints across the sky. The catering side of Capitol City had taken off since the holidays. Dana's cakes were constantly on the menu at state dinners in the governor's mansion and at museum openings. She baked wedding cakes, birthday cakes and many other celebratory desserts. But today, Dana was tired of cooking.

Josh walked into the kitchen. "Why are you still here?"

Dana turned around and let out a low whistle. "Don't you look dapper," she said taking note of his black Ralph Lauren tuxedo. Josh opened his jacket in runway model fashion and twirled around.

"You think I'm going to knock Zariah off her feet?"

Dana nodded as she poured the batter into a tree shaped cake pan. Josh looked at the stressed look on Dana's face as she slid the pan into the oven. "Are you and this cake going to make it to my party?"

"I'll try, but it was hectic today. I'm a little tired."

He smiled in agreement. For the first time since Dana was hired at the bakery, Josh had spent the better part of the morning in the kitchen, baking muffins and packaging Internet and party orders. He wasn't going to complain, though. The bottom line for Capitol City was looking really good.

"I'm going to get out of here. We'll be waiting to see your smiling face and eat that cake."

Dana waved him away. "Go before you get flour on yourself."

When Josh was gone, it seemed as if fatigue crept into the

kitchen and settled on Dana. She rubbed her forehead with one hand and clutched her lower back with the other one. She had been on her feet entirely too long. Dana kicked her canvas mules off and hopped up on the edge of the counter. She was about to doze off when a loud knocking jolted her back to reality. Dana's head jerked up and she dashed to the back door.

"Josh what did you—Daddy."

He walked in and looked at his daughter. "Something wrong?" she pressed.

Frank shook his head and continued to walk around the kitchen. "Dana, I'm sorry," he finally said. For a proud man like Frank Ellison, admitting he was wrong was worse than a visit to the dentist for a root canal.

"Sorry?"

Frank nodded slowly as he stole a plump date from the bowl on the counter. "Your mother and I have been talking about you and I've realized that you're always going to be my little girl. I just don't have to treat you that way. You have made me proud."

She wrapped her arms around her father's neck and squeezed him tightly. "Daddy," she whispered.

Frank stroked his daughter's back gently, much as he had when she was six years old, sitting at his knee as he explained Grimm's fairy tales to her.

"So you're going to marry this man in May? I'll be there to give you away."

Dana stepped back and eyed her father as if he were an alien. "Are you going to accept Chris?"

Frank sighed. "I'm working on that."

Dana smiled. "That's all I've ever wanted."

Frank watched Dana as she walked over to the oven. She gently removed the pan from the oven and set it on a wire cooling rack. Turning around, she caught her father's gaze. "What?"

"You remind me of my mother. She loved to cook too. But

you already know that. Right now, at that stove, you looked just like her."

Dana stirred her frosting. "Nana taught me everything I know."

Frank smiled warmly. His mother would have made a great chef and Dana was shaping up to be one as well. "I'm proud of you," he said.

Dana couldn't believe her ears. The last time she'd heard those words from her father had been in her teen years when she'd aced a test.

"Daddy."

"I don't say it enough. You need to know that I am proud of what you have done with your life and what you are going to do in the future. Now I have to go. Your mother and I are having drinks with some old school board friends."

Dana hugged her father tightly. "I love you, Daddy."

Frank smiled and walked out the door. Dana tossed her head back and sighed with relief.

# EPILOGUE

Dana linked arms with Frank at the entrance of the church. The sun was just about to set, wrapping the church in a golden glow. But Frank's smile outshone the sun. He glanced at Dana as they stood at the door underneath the ivy archway. She looked divine in her strapless white Vera Wang gown. Sparkling beads wove an intricate design across the bodice and the skirt bloomed out like a bell with the hem skimming the floor.

Chris had fashioned the archway into the shape of a heart with different kinds of ivy and white roses. He'd used his company's reputation to get the most beautiful flowers money could buy. This was the day his dreams were going to come true; Dana was going to be his wife. This was his first wedding day gift for his soon-to-be-wife. Tonight, he'd shower her with rose petals as they made love for the first time as husband and wife. Chris smiled as he thought about peeling the designer dress from Dana's supple body and lying with her in their marital bed.

Tito touched Chris's shoulder. "All right, man, this is it," his business partner said.

"I know."

"No turning back."

Chris shook his head. As if he would want to. When, the opening chords of "The Wedding March" began to play, Chris fixed his gaze on Dana as she walked down the aisle. She looked like a life-sized doll. Her hair was pulled up in a curly bun and a small tiara sat on her head, making her look like a queen walking down the aisle. Dana met Chris's piercing gaze. Love radiated from his eyes, his smile, even his stance. Warm tears of joy sprang into her eyes. This day couldn't have been more magical, more perfect.

Denise watched her daughter march down the aisle. She had never seen Dana look more beautiful or this happy. Her daughter's smile lit up the church more than the sun. Denise was going to submit a picture of her baby to *Columbia Bride Magazine*. She was definitely a cover girl.

Frank gently patted Dana's hand as they walked. Each gentle tap said "I love you, I'm proud of you, I'm happy for you." Dana struggled to keep from crying. She'd promised herself she wouldn't be a blubbering bride. But when she saw the moistness forming in the corner of Chris's eyes, the waterworks began.

Dana and Frank made it to the altar. Frank looked at his future son-in-law. If he made his daughter happy, how could he not accept him? Frank reached out and shook Chris's hand, silently giving him approval and acceptance. Chris looked deep into Frank's eyes, thanking him and reassuring him with a smile.

*I'm going to love her for the rest of my life,* he said with his warm brown eyes.

Seemingly reading Chris's thoughts, Frank mouthed, "I know."

Dana's heart swelled with joy and happiness. The two men she loved most in life had made their peace. Dana glanced back at her mother. She was dabbing the corner of her eyes with an antique lace powder blue handkerchief which matched her ankle length blue dress. Dana had the matching handkerchief stuffed in her bra, the same thing Denise had done when she married Frank.

"Who gives this woman away?" the reverend asked.

"My wife and I do," Frank proudly responded.

Chris clasped Dana's hand. "I love you," he whispered before bringing her hand to his lips.

As the reverend pronounced them husband and wife, a thunderous round of applause erupted from the church.

Chris pulled Dana into his arms, kissing her as if they were in an old Hollywood movie. He scooped his wife up in his arms, lifting her from the floor. Dana wrapped her arms around Chris's neck, losing herself in the excitement and joy of her husband. Finally, she had found a love of her own.

# AUTHOR BIOGRAPHY

**Cheris F. Hodges,** a native of Bennettsville, South Carolina, knew she'd be a writer one day. She attended Johnson C. Smith University in Charlotte and received a degree in journalism. Since graduating in 1999, she has worked for four newspapers in Georgia and North Carolina. Currently, she is the features editor of the Charlotte Post, an African American weekly. She lives in Charlotte where she is trying to cultivate a green thumb.

Other titles by Cheris F. Hodges:
*Cautious Heart* ISBN 1-58571-106-3

*Excerpt from*

# ECHOES OF YESTERDAY

## BY

# BEVERLY CLARK

**Publication Date February 2005**

# PROLOGUE

"I'll bet you anything your mystery man is here tonight just like clockwork." Mikki Howard spoke matter-of-factly to her boss, Tammy Gibson, as they waited in her dressing room at the Café Moonlight for Tammy's turn to perform.

Tammy knew exactly to whom her companion was referring. She didn't know the man's name or anything else about him. But as Mikki had said, he appeared like clockwork to hear her sing, occupying a seat at the shadowed end of the bar. He hadn't missed a single one of her performances since she started singing in the San Francisco Bay area six months ago. No matter where she sang, he was there.

Although she couldn't see him, Tammy could feel his presence. Who was this man? She'd commanded Mikki to find out, but he'd managed to deftly elude her. Harry Houdini himself could not have topped this man's disappearing expertise. Mikki had questioned the bartenders. All any of them could tell her was the man seemed spellbound by Tammy's singing. And, they added, the only time he ever spoke to them was to order his drinks.

The fact that he remained so aloof irked Tammy. What was it about her that fascinated him so much? It wasn't as though she was an R & B superstar. She'd recorded several albums, but none had made it to the charts. But since she had a pleasing voice, she'd had no problem getting singing engagements in night clubs. And although she enjoyed performing in them, she yearned for more, much more. Her goal was to solidly establish herself in the music business. What she needed was a songwriter of some worth, one she could share a rapport with, one who really understood her singing style and would be willing to work with her. So far that hadn't happened, and lately she had begun to think it never would.

After graduating from Julliard, Tammy had gone on to take private coaching lessons in voice control. A few music critics likened her voice to a cross between Lauryn Hill, Toni Braxton and Mariah Carey. Her singing range and sensuality astounded and entranced many; obviously and irrevocably her mystery man.

Her mystery man!

Now where had that come from? He wasn't her anything. No man was her anything, not since David.

Why was he being so enigmatic? Why was he so interested in her? Surely he wasn't one of those obsessed fans who ended up hurting the object of their adoration, or maybe even killing them. She remembered what had happened to Selena a few years back. No, she didn't think he was like that. At least she hoped he wasn't.

Tammy banished the thought of him, closing her mind to

everything, focusing on her coming performance, letting the excitement build inside her as it always did just before she was introduced.

Mikki guided Tammy over to a cleverly constructed pedestal that allowed a blind performer more freedom of movement without calling attention to their handicap. Tammy insisted on minimizing that aspect from all of her performances. She wanted people to focus on her singing talent, not pity her because she was blind.

Tammy heard the noise level in the club gradually die down as the band started its intro. She felt the familiar flutter of butterflies in her stomach. Then the bars from an old favorite, Jeffrey Osborne's 'On the Wings of Love,' started to play. From that point on she lost herself completely in the song and her music.

He sat as usual in the shadows at the end of the bar. Tammy Gibson totally captivated him with her earthy voice which not only touched his heart, but encompassed his very soul. He felt a special connection to her.

Ever since he'd heard her sing in a club in San Jose six months before, he'd been consumed by an overpowering need to see her face, to hear her voice over and over again. He recognized that the feelings he had for her went beyond admiration, passing into obsession.

If the media ever discovered his identity, he knew they would hound him once again. Although it had been years since he'd been the focus of their attention, they wouldn't hesitate to splatter his name and picture across the front pages of the tabloids. And that he definitely wouldn't let happen. Despite his concern over that very real possibility, however, he still sought her out every weekend.

As Tammy began to sing 'Without You I'm Nothing,' old memories threatened to overwhelm her and tears stung her eyelids. When she heard a low, pained groan, she knew instinctively it had come from her mystery man. She also knew instinctively that he would leave, and moments later, she felt the aura of his presence fade into the dark silence. She wondered why that particular song had affected him so profoundly. Had he lost someone close to him? Had the experience left him bruised and feeling empty? She knew only too well how that felt.

## 2005 Publication Schedule

### January

A Heart's Awakening
Veronica Parker
$9.95
1-58571-143-9

Falling
Natalie Dunbar
$9.95
1-58571-121-7

### February

Echoes of Yesterday
Beverly Clark
$9.95
1-58571-131-4

A Love of Her Own
Cheris F. Hodges
$9.95
1-58571-136-5

Higher Ground
Leah Latimer
$19.95
1-58571-157-8

### March

Misconceptions
Pamela Leigh Starr
$9.95
1-58571-117-9

I'll Paint a Sun
Al Garotto
$9.95
1-58571-165-9

Peace Be Still
Colette Haywood
$12.95
1-58571-129-2

### April

Intentional Mistakes
Michele Sudler
$9.95
1-58571-152-7

Conquering Dr. Wexler's Heart
Kimberley White
$9.95
1-58571-126-8

Song in the Park
Martin Brant
$15.95
1-58571-125-X

### May

The Color Line
Lizette Carter
$9.95
1-58571-163-2

Unconditional
A.C. Arthur
$9.95
1-58571-142-X

Last Train to Memphis
Elsa Cook
$12.95
1-58571-146-2

### June

Angel's Paradise
Janice Angelique
$9.95
1-58571-107-1

Suddenly You
Crystal Hubbard
$9.95
1-58571-158-6

Matters of Life and
Death
Lesego Malepe, Ph.D.
$15.95
1-58571-124-1

## 2005 Publication Schedule (continued)

### July

Pleasures All Mine
Belinda O. Steward
$9.95
1-58571-112-8

Wild Ravens
Altonya Washington
$9.95
1-58571-164-0

Class Reunion
Irma Jenkins/John
Brown
$12.95
1-58571-123-3

### August

Path of Thorns
Annetta P. Lee
$9.95
1-58571-145-4

Timeless Devotion
Bella McFarland
$9.95
1-58571-148-9

Life Is Never As It Seems
June Michael
$12.95
1-58571-153-5

### September

Beyond the Rapture
Beverly Clark
$9.95
1-58571-131-4

Blood Lust
J. M. Jeffries
$9.95
1-58571-138-1

Rough on Rats and
Tough on Cats
Chris Parker
$12.95
1-58571-154-3

### October

A Will to Love
Angie Daniels
$9.95
1-58571-141-1

Taken by You
Dorothy Elizabeth Love
$9.95
1-58571-162-4

Soul Eyes
Wayne L. Wilson
$12.95
1-58571-147-0

### November

A Drummer's Beat to
Mend
Kay Swanson
$9.95

Sweet Reprecussions
Kimberley White
$9.95
1-58571-159-4

Red Polka Dot in a
Worldof Plaid
Varian Johnson
$12.95
1-58571-140-3

### December

Hand in Glove
Andrea Jackson
$9.95
1-58571-166-7

Blaze
Barbara Keaton
$9.95

Across
Carol Payne
$12.95
1-58571-149-7

Other Genesis Press, Inc. Titles

| | | |
|---|---|---|
| Acquisitions | Kimberley White | $8.95 |
| A Dangerous Deception | J.M. Jeffries | $8.95 |
| A Dangerous Love | J.M. Jeffries | $8.95 |
| A Dangerous Obsession | J.M. Jeffries | $8.95 |
| After the Vows | Leslie Esdaile | $10.95 |
| (Summer Anthology) | T.T. Henderson | |
| | Jacqueline Thomas | |
| Again My Love | Kayla Perrin | $10.95 |
| Against the Wind | Gwynne Forster | $8.95 |
| A Lark on the Wing | Phyliss Hamilton | $8.95 |
| A Lighter Shade of Brown | Vicki Andrews | $8.95 |
| All I Ask | Barbara Keaton | $8.95 |
| A Love to Cherish | Beverly Clark | $8.95 |
| Ambrosia | T.T. Henderson | $8.95 |
| And Then Came You | Dorothy Elizabeth Love | $8.95 |
| Angel's Paradise | Janice Angelique | $8.95 |
| A Risk of Rain | Dar Tomlinson | $8.95 |
| At Last | Lisa G. Riley | $8.95 |
| Best of Friends | Natalie Dunbar | $8.95 |
| Bound by Love | Beverly Clark | $8.95 |
| Breeze | Robin Hampton Allen | $10.95 |
| Brown Sugar Diaries & | Delores Bundy & | $10.95 |
| Other Sexy Tales | Cole Riley | |
| By Design | Barbara Keaton | $8.95 |
| Cajun Heat | Charlene Berry | $8.95 |
| Careless Whispers | Rochelle Alers | $8.95 |
| Caught in a Trap | Andre Michelle | $8.95 |
| Chances | Pamela Leigh Starr | $8.95 |
| Dark Embrace | Crystal Wilson Harris | $8.95 |
| Dark Storm Rising | Chinelu Moore | $10.95 |
| Designer Passion | Dar Tomlinson | $8.95 |
| Ebony Butterfly II | Delilah Dawson | $14.95 |

| | | |
|---|---|---|
| Erotic Anthology | Assorted | $8.95 |
| Eve's Prescription | Edwina Martin Arnold | $8.95 |
| Everlastin' Love | Gay G. Gunn | $8.95 |
| Fate | Pamela Leigh Starr | $8.95 |
| Forbidden Quest | Dar Tomlinson | $10.95 |
| Fragment in the Sand | Annetta P. Lee | $8.95 |
| From the Ashes | Kathleen Suzanne | $8.95 |
| | Jeanne Sumerix | |
| Gentle Yearning | Rochelle Alers | $10.95 |
| Glory of Love | Sinclair LeBeau | $10.95 |
| Hart & Soul | Angie Daniels | $8.95 |
| Heartbeat | Stephanie Bedwell-Grime | $8.95 |
| I'll Be Your Shelter | Giselle Carmichael | $8.95 |
| Illusions | Pamela Leigh Starr | $8.95 |
| Indiscretions | Donna Hill | $8.95 |
| Interlude | Donna Hill | $8.95 |
| Intimate Intentions | Angie Daniels | $8.95 |
| Just an Affair | Eugenia O'Neal | $8.95 |
| Kiss or Keep | Debra Phillips | $8.95 |
| Love Always | Mildred E. Riley | $10.95 |
| Love Unveiled | Gloria Greene | $10.95 |
| Love's Deception | Charlene Berry | $10.95 |
| Mae's Promise | Melody Walcott | $8.95 |
| Meant to Be | Jeanne Sumerix | $8.95 |
| Midnight Clear | Leslie Esdaile | $10.95 |
| (Anthology) | Gwynne Forster | |
| | Carmen Green | |
| | Monica Jackson | |
| Midnight Magic | Gwynne Forster | $8.95 |
| Midnight Peril | Vicki Andrews | $10.95 |
| My Buffalo Soldier | Barbara B. K. Reeves | $8.95 |
| Naked Soul | Gwynne Forster | $8.95 |
| No Regrets | Mildred E. Riley | $8.95 |
| Nowhere to Run | Gay G. Gunn | $10.95 |

| | | |
|---|---|---|
| Object of His Desire | A. C. Arthur | $8.95 |
| One Day at a Time | Bella McFarland | $8.95 |
| Passion | T.T. Henderson | $10.95 |
| Past Promises | Jahmel West | $8.95 |
| Path of Fire | T.T. Henderson | $8.95 |
| Picture Perfect | Reon Carter | $8.95 |
| Pride & Joi | Gay G. Gunn | $8.95 |
| Quiet Storm | Donna Hill | $8.95 |
| Reckless Surrender | Rochelle Alers | $8.95 |
| Rendezvous with Fate | Jeanne Sumerix | $8.95 |
| Revelations | Cheris F. Hodges | $8.95 |
| Rivers of the Soul | Leslie Esdaile | $8.95 |
| Rooms of the Heart | Donna Hill | $8.95 |
| Shades of Brown | Denise Becker | $8.95 |
| Shades of Desire | Monica White | $8.95 |
| Sin | Crystal Rhodes | $8.95 |
| So Amazing | Sinclair LeBeau | $8.95 |
| Somebody's Someone | Sinclair LeBeau | $8.95 |
| Someone to Love | Alicia Wiggins | $8.95 |
| Soul to Soul | Donna Hill | $8.95 |
| Still Waters Run Deep | Leslie Esdaile | $8.95 |
| Subtle Secrets | Wanda Y. Thomas | $8.95 |
| Sweet Tomorrows | Kimberly White | $8.95 |
| The Color of Trouble | Dyanne Davis | $8.95 |
| The Price of Love | Sinclair LeBeau | $8.95 |
| The Reluctant Captive | Joyce Jackson | $8.95 |
| The Missing Link | Charlyne Dickerson | $8.95 |
| Three Wishes | Seressia Glass | $8.95 |
| Tomorrow's Promise | Leslie Esdaile | $8.95 |
| Truly Inseperable | Wanda Y. Thomas | $8.95 |
| Twist of Fate | Beverly Clark | $8.95 |
| Unbreak My Heart | Dar Tomlinson | $8.95 |
| Unconditional Love | Alicia Wiggins | $8.95 |
| When Dreams A Float | Dorothy Elizabeth Love | $8.95 |

*ESCAPE WITH INDIGO !!!!*

Join Indigo Book Club©
It's simple, easy and secure.

Sign up and receive the new releases
every month + Free shipping and
20% off the cover price.

Go online to www.genesis-press.com and
click on Bookclub or
call 1-888-INDIGO-1

# Order Form

## Mail to: Genesis Press, Inc.

**P.O. Box 101**
**Columbus, MS 39703**

Name _____
Address _____
City/State _____ Zip _____
Telephone _____

*Ship to (if different from above)*
Name _____
Address _____
City/State _____ Zip _____
Telephone _____

*Credit Card Information*
Credit Card # _____ ☐ Visa  ☐ Mastercard
Expiration Date (mm/yy) _____ ☐ AmEx  ☐ Discover

| Qty. | Author | Title | Price | Total |
|------|--------|-------|-------|-------|
|      |        |       |       |       |
|      |        |       |       |       |
|      |        |       |       |       |
|      |        |       |       |       |
|      |        |       |       |       |
|      |        |       |       |       |
|      |        |       |       |       |
|      |        |       |       |       |
|      |        |       |       |       |
|      |        |       |       |       |
|      |        |       |       |       |

Use this order

form, or call

1-888-INDIGO-1

**Total for books** _____
**Shipping and handling:**
 $5 first two books,
 $1 each additional book _____
**Total S & H**
**Total amount enclosed** _____

*Mississippi residents add 7% sales tax*

Visit www.genesis-press.com for latest releases and excerpts.

# Order Form

### Mail to: Genesis Press, Inc.

**P.O. Box 101**
**Columbus, MS 39703**

Name _____
Address _____
City/State _____ Zip _____
Telephone _____

*Ship to (if different from above)*
Name _____
Address _____
City/State _____ Zip _____
Telephone _____

*Credit Card Information*
Credit Card # _____  ☐ Visa      ☐ Mastercard
Expiration Date (mm/yy) _____  ☐ AmEx      ☐ Discover

| Qty. | Author | Title | Price | Total |
|------|--------|-------|-------|-------|
|      |        |       |       |       |
|      |        |       |       |       |
|      |        |       |       |       |
|      |        |       |       |       |
|      |        |       |       |       |
|      |        |       |       |       |
|      |        |       |       |       |
|      |        |       |       |       |
|      |        |       |       |       |
|      |        |       |       |       |
|      |        |       |       |       |

Use this order

form, or call

1-888-INDIGO-1

| | |
|---|---|
| Total for books | _____ |
| Shipping and handling: $5 first two books, $1 each additional book | _____ |
| Total S & H | _____ |
| Total amount enclosed | _____ |

*Mississippi residents add 7% sales tax*

# Order Form

**Mail to: Genesis Press, Inc.**

P.O. Box 101
Columbus, MS 39703

Name _____
Address _____
City/State _____ Zip _____
Telephone _____

*Ship to (if different from above)*
Name _____
Address _____
City/State _____ Zip _____
Telephone _____

*Credit Card Information*

Credit Card # _____ ☐ Visa ☐ Mastercard

Expiration Date (mm/yy) _____ ☐ AmEx ☐ Discover

| Qty. | Author | Title | Price | Total |
|------|--------|-------|-------|-------|
|      |        |       |       |       |
|      |        |       |       |       |
|      |        |       |       |       |
|      |        |       |       |       |
|      |        |       |       |       |
|      |        |       |       |       |
|      |        |       |       |       |
|      |        |       |       |       |
|      |        |       |       |       |
|      |        |       |       |       |
|      |        |       |       |       |

Use this order form, or call
1-888-INDIGO-1

Total for books _____
Shipping and handling:
  $5 first two books,
  $1 each additional book _____
Total S & H _____
Total amount enclosed _____
*Mississippi residents add 7% sales tax*

Visit www.genesis-press.com for latest releases and excerpts.